PIXIE

A BALLSY BOYS PRODUCTION BOOK 5

K.M. NEUHOLD
NORA PHOENIX

Pixie (Ballsy Boys Book Five) by K.M. Neuhold and Nora Phoenix

Copyright ©2019 K.M. Neuhold and Nora Phoenix

Cover design: K.M. Neuhold

Editing: Jamie Anderson

All rights reserved. No part of this story may be used, reproduced, or transmitted in any form by any means without the written permission of the copyright holder, except in case of brief quotations and embodied within critical reviews and articles.

This is a work of fiction. Names, characters, places, and incidents either are the products of the author's imagination or are used fictitiously. Any resemblance to actual persons, living or dead, businesses, companies, events, or locales is entirely coincidental. The use of any real company and/or product names is for literary effect only. All other trademarks and copyrights are the property of their respective owners.

This book contains sexually explicit material which is suitable only for mature readers.

1

BEAR

It took him two weeks to contact me, that adorable little twink we met at P!NK. Usually, the boys go out without me, especially in places like that. I'm too old for that shit, and I'm their boss. I don't need to see them hooking up and everything. They deserve some level of privacy, considering how much of them I already see anyway.

But since Heart was new, I decided to join them that night. And when I spotted him, this perfect creature that radiated sparkles and sunshine, I knew he'd be perfect for me. Not for *me* me, but for my studio, of course. I don't date guys that young. I may hook up with them, but they're not what I'd want for a relationship. Not that I'm even looking for something serious, but that's beside the point.

God, I always feel like a total perv when I talk to boys like him about doing porn, but he was too cute to let that prevent me from trying to snag him for my studio. And *boy* is the right term, because he's twenty-one, young enough to be my son. As if I didn't feel old already at forty-four.

But I couldn't let him go. Something about the combination of innocence and sultry sexiness totally drew me in, and I knew it would do the same for viewers. I've been in this business long enough to know what viewers want and appreciate.

It's one of the reasons why my gay porn studio, Ballsy Boys, is so popular. We deliver high-quality gay porn, and we have the best boys in the business. It takes a lot to be hired by me. You need a love for sex, a good chemistry with your partners, and most importantly, a great connection with the camera. In this case, I only needed to imagine his lithe body with that plump little ass bending over for a man like our main star Rebel with his award-winning cock to see the possibilities.

I sit in my office and study his online application form again, even though I practically know it by heart now. When he contacted me through email, I sent him the link to the form. It's the necessary first step so I can weed out the worst weirdos. Not that I figured he'd be in that category, but you never know.

Eli Ritters. For some reason, the name doesn't fit him. It's too formal, too official for how cute he is. He was like a little imp, all bubbly and indignant about me calling him a kid. I can't help it, how protective I get about my boys. And he may not yet be one of them, but it's how I'm wired.

His answers are surprisingly open. Sweet, if a little naive. Definitely not an LA native, and I didn't need to see the copy of his Illinois driver's license to determine that. Anyone who's been in this town longer than a few months gets a crash course in real life. He hasn't reached that point yet, and something inside me cringes at the idea that he will.

Nothing in his form raised any flags, so I asked him to send in some pictures and a video. It's what I ask of everyone who applies, because there's a big gap between saying you wanna do porn and actually doing it. If you can't bring yourself to jerk off on camera or play out any of the suggestions we do in the instructions, you're never gonna make it. Simple as that.

No one else sees these but me, and sometimes, I don't even need to see more than two, three minutes to know if it's a yes or no. Usually, I stop as soon as I know, because trust me, I don't watch these for personal gratification. Hell, I make porn for a living. A shaky amateur video of some random guy shoving a dildo up his ass doesn't really do it for me, you know?

But Eli's video, I've watched entirely. *Twice.* And even as I tell myself there's no earthly reason why I should watch it a third time, my hand moves to the mouse and clicks on it again. For an amateur, he did well. He used his phone to film himself, which is fine, but he was smart enough to read our tips and get himself a tripod of some kind. He got the angle right and the soft lighting as well, which illuminates his smooth skin and makes it glow.

The little makeup he put on doesn't hurt either, as it highlights his highly kissable lips. You see them and can't help but wonder how they'd look around your cock. Pretty damn good, would be my guess.

"Hello," he starts shyly, looking directly into the camera. "My name is Eli, but I guess I'll have to come up with some kind of alias if I'm gonna do this."

He's right about that. You should never do porn under your real name. Not because it's something to be ashamed of, but you can't predict the future, and there may be circumstances where it'll be advantageous to distinguish between your porn identity and your real one.

Not that I ever managed to separate the two. It's been a long time since I did porn myself, but I still go by the nickname Bear. It's been such a crucial part of me that I hardly respond to my legal name anymore. The only one who still calls me Maxwell is my mother, god bless her, and the people at my volunteer job. Even my two brothers have started to call me Bear.

I wonder what the little twink's porn name should be. Something flirty, I think. Something playful and slightly seductive that plays up his image. Most of my boys choose their own name, though I have given some suggestions here and there. I know their legal names, of course, since I'm their employer, but I guard those like state secrets.

Eli turns around on camera, showing off his body. He's naturally lean, all graceful moves and elegance. Almost like a ballet dancer, except those would be more muscled, I think. But there's an easiness to his moves, a familiarity with his own body that makes him captivating to watch.

"So, I guess I should talk a little about myself and my sexual experience," he continues.

It's one of the prompts we provide for the video. We need to hear if they can string a coherent sentence together. Porn may not be high-level acting, but there's still some skill involved and our boys need to have chemistry, both with each other and with the camera. You have to flirt with viewers a little, make them feel engaged.

"Well, what can I say? I really love sex." He lets out a little giggle. "I was a late bloomer, didn't discover sex until my senior year of high school. I had a fumbling experience that left me wanting, but then ran into this big, furry papa bear who showed me the stars and the entire universe."

He smacks his lips, and something coils inside me, making my muscles tense up.

"I've had my fair share of hookups and a serious relationship, and I love sex. Well, bottoming that is." He scrunches his nose. "I tried topping, but that's not me. I'm happy to be on the receiving end, and I haven't met a dick that was too big for me."

That camera chemistry? He *has* it. He owns the camera, owns me. My god, the combination of shyness and sexiness that radiates off him in intoxicating waves is irresistible. My boys are gonna be lining up to fuck him into next week, that's for certain. And viewers will pay good money to watch it.

On the video, Eli chats away, while showing his body and playing with himself a little. Then he gets down to business, and smart as he is, he chooses to focus on his best feature—that gorgeous bubble butt. Even now, the third time I'm watching it, I get hard again as I see his ass swallow that dildo whole, moans falling from his lips like summer rain. I should stop watching, I really should, but I can't. I'm mesmerized all over again as he brings himself to climax. And when he does, I push down hard on my own erection, my underwear damp.

It's unnerving, this effect he has on me. It feels wrong on so many levels, not in the least because he's too young. Way too young. And did I mention that he'll be working for me? I don't fuck around with my own boys. That's a hard and fast rule. I can't. I'm their boss, and bringing sex into that relationship would not only muddy the waters considerably, but it would also lower me to the sewer level of so many of my less reputable colleagues.

I've heard too many stories of men—and women—who thought they were auditioning for porn, only to find out the owner or director or whoever persuaded them to do a free scene and then put it online. This can be a shady industry for sure, and that's not how I run Ballsy Boys. Everything I do is ethical, and that means my boys are hands off to me.

I click on Eli's video to close it, telling myself that was the last time I watched it. I don't need to watch it again to know that I want him. For Ballsy Boys, of course. For one second, it crosses my mind that if I reject his application, it would make it possible for me to pursue him, but I suppress that notion immediately. It wouldn't be fair to him. I'm definitely not opposed to a relationship, don't get me wrong, but not with a kid like him. If I ever look for something serious, I'd need someone my own age. With an age gap, there's the risk of me putting someone through what I had to endure, and I will never do that.

No, the best thing for Eli is to get a job with Ballsy Boys. We'll take good care of the little imp. He reminds me of a little elf, all happiness and glitter.

Pixie. That's what we should call him. It fits him to a T. My decision made, I reach for the phone to call him and set up a meeting to sign the official paperwork for a three-month trial.

2

PIXIE

My hands are shaking so badly I'm sure everyone on set can see it. I work hard to pull in full, deep breaths so I don't start hyperventilating again. It was one thing to have a full-on panic attack back at my apartment, but if I do it on set—my first day on set, to be exact—I may actually die of embarrassment.

I cross my arms over my skinny chest and dart my eyes around the currently dark set. Men are everywhere—setting up lights and cameras, laughing and talking like this is any normal day at a normal job. I suppose it is to them, and hopefully one day it will be for me too. But right now, it's my first day in porn, and I'm hoping like hell I don't make a fool out of myself. What if I'm too nervous to get hard? What if I come too fast? What if I make a really awkward noise or facial expression? What if Rebel goes to rim me and I fart? The thought alone has my entire face heating up, no doubt turning a bright shade of cherry red.

I chew my bottom lip until the coppery taste of blood fills my mouth and I gag a little. Out of the corner of my eye, I see Rebel walk in, looking all kinds of confident and calm.

He smiles and greets everyone as he moves through the maze of people and equipment like he could do it with his eyes closed. My heart flaps wildly against my ribcage, lodging itself in my throat.

I can't believe I'm doing this. In a few minutes, I'm going to be completely naked, getting fucked by one of my favorite porn stars. Neither of those things is an issue; it's all the people watching that has my stomach twisting itself in knots.

When Rebel reaches me, my knees start to buckle, and I do my best to look casual as I lean against the set wall. Unfortunately, it doesn't seem to have been made for leaning, because it shifts under my negligible weight, sending me toppling backward as the flimsy wall falls with a loud *thud*.

"Oh shit," Rebel curses, scooping me up quickly and setting me back on my feet while a few of the set guys hurry over to right the wall.

"Sorry," I mutter to them all awkwardly.

"Our fault, this should've been sturdier," one of them assures me.

"You okay?" Rebel checks, brushing me off and looking me over to make sure I appear unharmed.

"Fantastic, just wishing I'd made a better first impression on you," I admit, looking up at him shyly through my eyelashes.

"I'm Rebel.," He introduces himself, and I nearly laugh.

"I know. I mean, I've seen your videos. You're... I know who you are."

"Damn, Bear was right, you're fucking adorable." He licks his lips, his eyes gobbling me up.

I can feel myself blushing again, but this time a pleased

smile tugs at my lips. The mention of Bear has my heart going wild again.

I had only been in LA one week when I first met Bear. I was sitting in a gay bar, the first gay bar I'd ever been to, when the gorgeous older man approached me. I thought he was picking me up at first, and I was *more* than amenable to that plan. Instead, he told me he owned a gay porn studio and that I had exactly the look he'd been searching for in a new model.

Doing porn was the last thing I had in mind when I moved from my podunk Midwest town to LA, but the paycheck was hard to say no to. Plus...if I'm being completely honest with myself, it sounds exciting.

Rebel makes small talk for a few minutes, asking about my favorite Ballsy Boys scenes I've watched, helping me to feel more relaxed.

"Are we about ready on set?" A deep rumble of a voice rolls through the chaos and prickles warmly at my skin. My breath catches as I whip my head around to set my eyes on the man I'd just been thinking about.

He stands in the crowd with so much authority and confidence that it should be intimidating, but it's hot as fuck. My cock starts to plump. *I guess I don't have to worry about being too nervous to get it up.*

His dark hair is brushed back stylishly, gray hairs peppering his temples and his short beard. Muscles strain his black T-shirt, more gray and dark brown hair peeking out of the collar of the shirt. My cock grows harder, wondering what he looks like without his shirt on.

I'm not ashamed to admit that after I learned about Bear owning Ballsy Boys, I did an internet search and came up with some old videos from his porn days as well. His dick was *huge*, thickly veined and uncircumcised, a slight curve to the right. Yes, I studied it *thoroughly*. I'm not sure how many hours I've spent in the past week watching those videos, mesmerized by the loud slap of skin on skin, his growly moans as he fucked into those other men I barely spared a look at, his large, heavy balls bouncing with each thrust.

"You think you're ready to strip down to your underwear, Pixie?" Rebel asks kindly. It takes me a second to realize he's talking to me. It's going to be weird getting used to people calling me by my brand-new stage name. But maybe it'll be nice, like a fresh start here in LA. No one knows the shy kid I left back in Illinois. Here I can be whoever I want to be.

"Yeah," I answer with a nervous smile.

The lights come up, illuminating the set—a comfortable-looking couch and general living room set up.

"We'll start with the interview. Try to relax. I'll take the lead, so keep your eyes on me and simply have a conversation with me, okay?"

I bite my lip again and nod.

"They can edit anything out, so don't worry too much about saying something stupid. Follow my lead, and you'll be fine."

"Okay," I agree, forcing another slow breath.

Rebel strips his shirt over his head, and I follow suit, my hands trembling as I slip out of my clothes and fold them gingerly. I chose a pair of red boxer briefs to wear today, knowing they make my butt look really cute. Rebel runs his hands through his long mane of hair, getting it back into place with one well-practiced move.

"Ready to do this, kid?" he checks again.

"Ready," I agree with more confidence than I feel.

Bear pulls a chair over, right in front of the couch but out of the frame of the camera, and my breath catches. I didn't realize *he* was doing the interview. Is he going to sit that close the entire time? Heat licks at my skin and my cock starts to tingle again. How hands on of a director *is* Bear exactly? Is he going to tell us exactly what to do? Come over and position us?

"Mmmm, looks like you're getting into the spirit of things," Rebel whispers playfully near my ear before turning to Bear and smirking.

"Look at that adorable blush. Can you imagine how he'll look when he's well-fucked? His cheeks all rosy and heated, those lips puffy and swollen from kissing and sucking, his gorgeous hair all messy."

Bear laughs. "You like him, huh?"

Rebel's eyes travel over my body again, and I squirm a little under the scrutiny. "Damn right I do. Can't wait to get started."

Bear asks Rebel what he wants to do to me, and I can hear Rebel answering in a sultry tone, but all I can truly focus on is the heated look in Bear's eyes while Rebel talks, like Bear's imagining doing *exactly* what he's describing.

I shiver, licking my lips and trying hard to look into the camera instead of directly at Bear.

"But maybe Pixie has some ideas of what he wants to do as well?" Rebel concludes, forcing my attention away from Bear. I pull in a deep breath. It's time to focus and get my head in the game if I want to keep this job. Fantasizing over my ridiculously hot boss can wait until I'm at home alone. Right now, I need to make the viewers fall in love with Pixie.

"I prepared well for this, you know," I say in a breathy voice, looking up at Rebel from under my eyelashes.

He smiles and leans closer "You did?"

"I watched every video of you at least twice. All in the name of research, of course," I flirt, putting on a wide-eyed expression that I've been told makes me look innocent and fuckable.

"Mmm, I can appreciate that. What did you learn about me?"

I reach over and put my hand on his bicep, still channeling my inner sweetness that I know makes me irresistible. If the viewers are going to fall in love with me as a porn star, then I'm going to seduce them the way I would any other lover.

"Everyone always raves about your cock," I muse, trailing my finger up and down the bulge of Rebel's arm muscle.

"I've been told it's one of my best assets."

I curve my lips into a smile, biting my lip in a sexy gesture. "Oh, it's damn near perfect, don't get me wrong. But personally, I'm partial to your hands."

"My hands?" His surprise is obvious, and a small giggle bubbles past my lips as I drag my touch from his bicep down his forearm, finally reaching his hands.

"You have beautiful hands. Long fingers. Graceful. I can't wait to feel them on me, to watch you touch me."

The words are barely past my lips when he pulls me onto his lap, the hard ridge of his cock nestling against my ass as he runs his hands along my stomach and up my chest to tweak my nipples. I arch into his touch, gasping and moaning as he teases my sensitive peaks.

His mouth joins the fun next, his hot, wet tongue gliding over my skin like I'm the most delicious treat he's ever had. I let my head fall back, and out of the corner of my eye, I see Bear again, watching us intently from his chair. There's a slight bulge in the front of his pants that sends a jolt of lust through my body.

"Where exactly did you picture my hands when you imagined us playing?" Rebel asks in a gravelly voice.

"Everywhere. God, I want you to touch me everywhere," I beg, my cock now painfully hard, pressing against his stomach through the soft fabric of my underwear.

"Now that I've got you exactly where I wanted—though we're both still a little overdressed for the occasion—I'm dying to know what makes a cute thing like you tick. What are you into, Pixie-boy?"

I grind myself against the hard steel of Rebel's cock again, my hole quivering to be filled now that my fears are melting away. The camera crew is a distant memory. Right now, I'm putting on a show just for Bear.

"I love sex. I swear to god, I love everything about it. My parents honestly couldn't care less about me, so I've been on my own for a long time. I was a virgin, had never even kissed a boy till my senior year of high school. That changed after my first hookup. This big, furry papa bear fucked me, and I was hooked. Figured if I liked being fucked so much, I might as well make a career out of it," I confess.

Rebel seems speechless, and Bear reaches into his jeans to rearrange his erection, making my mouth water for it.

"So, you like to be bred by a big ol' daddy, pretty boy?" Rebel concludes.

"God, yes," I moan, nodding my head so fast my teeth rattle. "I love getting fucked, having my hole stretched so wide I can hardly breathe, running my fingers through thick chest hair."

"Fuck, you're a dirty boy, aren't you, Pixie?" Rebel teases, nipping at my earlobe, his hands still moving over my body from my nipples to my thighs, occasionally cupping my balls.

Before I can answer, his mouth is on mine, his hot, deep

kisses making it hard to think. Damn, Rebel can fucking kiss.

His hands slip inside my underwear, tracing my crack in a teasing way for several seconds before brushing over the plug I inserted at home before coming to work. He gives the base of the plug a light tap, and it shifts against my prostate, making my cock jerk and a loud moan erupt.

"Cut," Bear calls.

Rebel breaks the kiss and pulls his hands out of my underwear, giving me a playful smack on the ass that makes my cock throb even harder. Damn, I'm *way* too close to the edge already. I wonder if I'm allowed to come more than once or if that would be frowned upon?

Rebel moves me off his lap, standing to stretch, his impressive erection tenting his boxers proudly without a care in the world. I awkwardly climb to my feet as well.

"How are you holding up, Pixie?" Bear asks with genuine concern in his eyes.

"I'm good. Rebel's...nice."

Rebel and Bear start to joke and tease each other, and a wave of longing swells inside me. I want to belong here. I want to be part of the comfortable family they've so obviously formed.

Rebel turns back to me and explains that we're going to move things along to me blowing him. He gives me some tips on deep throating and making it look good for the camera, but this time I just smirk. If there's one thing I know how to do, it's suck a dick and put on a good show while doing it.

"Time to lose the plug."

My face flames again as I realize just how real this is. My eyes dart to everyone standing around casually. Am I just supposed to get on my hands and knees and pull the plug out while they all watch?

"Lie down, I'll help," Rebel offers with a gentle smile.

I splay myself out on the couch and close my eyes, relaxing so he'll be able to pull it out. As embarrassing as it is, I find my cock getting impossibly harder as Rebel spreads my cheeks and starts to work the plug free. Precum drips from my slit, pooling on my stomach.

He pulls it free, tossing it to the side and wiping his hands on a towel. We pull our underwear back on for scene continuity and get back into our original position.

"Action," Bear calls, and I can see the exact moment the switch flips in Rebel's eyes from play to work.

He kisses me again, sloppy tongue-heavy kisses that probably look incredible on camera. It's a strange feeling, having sex but focusing on the aesthetics of it rather than on how it feels. Not necessarily *bad* strange, just...different. I always wondered how porn stars kept their work life separate from their personal sex life, and now I think I understand. This *feels* completely different than regular sex.

Rebel tugs at the waist of my briefs, and I take his cue to wiggle out of them, pulling his down as well as our tongues play and our hands wander. His heavy cock gets hooked by his underwear, slapping back against his stomach as I free it.

One of the things I was most nervous about when I sent in my audition video was the fact I don't exactly have what most would consider a porn star cock. I mean, it's a nice-looking dick, don't get me wrong, but I'm five foot five and about a hundred pounds soaking wet, and my cock is proportional to the rest of my body. It's a cute little dick, and I've never been self-conscious about it until I started considering applying to Ballsy Boys. When Bear called to offer me the job after reviewing my audition tape, he didn't mention the size of my dick, so I figured it wasn't something I should worry about. Rebel doesn't seem put off by it either, so I'm guessing it won't be a problem for the viewers.

His cock is even more impressive in person than it was in his videos, long and thick. It's going to feel amazing when he fucks me. He slips his fingers into my crack and teases my already slicked and stretched hole, sending an excited shiver through me, my cock jerking between us. A few low moans and eager whimpers fall from my lips, and the feeling of Rebel's smile forming as we continue to kiss tells me this is going to play great on camera. When Bear had initially been giving me instructions and tips, he'd said not to fake moan because viewers can tell and they don't like it, but if a moan is genuine, don't hold back. So, when Rebel slips the tip of his finger into my entrance, I don't bother to bite back my gasp.

After a few more minutes of kissing, Rebel pulls his finger out, and I take that as a hint to move things along. Dropping down onto my knees between his spread legs, I lick my lips when I'm eye level with his erection.

"Can I please suck you off? I've been dreaming about having your cock in my mouth..." I ask in my most innocent voice.

"Mmm, polite and eager. I like it," he quips, wrapping his hand around the base of his cock and placing the head against my lips.

I look up at him with wide, hungry eyes and part my lips slowly. Letting my tongue slip out, I can taste his salty precum on my lips. Lapping at his slit, I greedily gather more, and Rebel moans. I don't waste any more time before taking it into my mouth and easily down my throat. What can I say? I love huge cocks, so I've had a bit of practice handling them. Rebel gasps loudly, threading his fingers through my hair as I suck him, making noisy, sloppy sounds as I throat his cock over and over again.

I don't hold back, pulling out all my best moves as I suck him, not stopping at his cock but also licking his balls and taking the liberty of rimming him as well. Even though I wasn't expressly told to lick his ass, I don't get any admonishment, so I figure it's all good. He's clearly had a lot of practice holding off his orgasm because no matter how much he pants, groans, and squirms, he doesn't tap out. I happily give him everything I have until Bear calls for us to cut again.

I release his cock from my mouth with a resounding, wet pop and wipe the back of my hand over my lips. I'm pleased to see him flushed and sweaty, affirming that I'm doing a good job. Not that I've ever doubted my blowjob skills.

"Holy shit, Bear, I think I might have to take the kid home and keep him for myself," Rebel jokes breathlessly, and I preen under the praise. Unable to help myself, I peek over my shoulder at Bear. The slight bulge from earlier is far more noticeable now, and he's not even bothering to pretend it's not there.

"Am I doing okay, Bear?" I check, unsure why he called cut, or if this is standard to take breaks throughout the scene like this.

"You're doing amazing. The viewers are going to go wild for you," he assures me, his praise warming me all over. "I could just tell Rebel was about to blow if he didn't get a break."

"If you felt Pixie's mouth, you'd understand why," Rebel defends.

Bear squints a half scowl at Rebel before his features return to normal, and he cuts his gaze in my direction. "It's important to read the body language of the person you're doing a scene with so you can back off when they get too close. Rebel can give you tips when the scene ends if you need them."

I nod and fidget a little, not liking the feeling of being admonished, no matter how lightly.

"I'll do better, I promise."

"You're doing fine. It's your first scene. I don't expect you to know everything on day one," he assures me and then pulls a condom out of his pocket and tosses it to Rebel. "Suit up and let's keep things moving."

Once Rebel is ready, Bear tells me to kneel on the couch, facing the back. Rebel positions himself behind me and the cameras start rolling again. The thick head of Rebel's cock nudges at my hole, and my entire body throbs in response, desperate for that perfect, full feeling that will make me come.

"Ready for this, Pixie baby?" Rebel whispers into my ear, and I nod eagerly.

He sinks into me, and I moan as he fills me in a few careful strokes. His cock is the perfect combination of long and thick that leaves me gasping for air and trying not to finish too fast. I know we're supposed to make this last as long as possible. Bear explained that the longer we can go, the easier it makes editing. In the end, it'll only be about an hour-long video from start to finish, but if we can get through multiple positions and go for a while without finishing, they can edit it down to just the best parts.

I think of as many unsexy things as I can manage while Rebel fucks me like his life depends on it. I manage to last about fifteen minutes, and I'm extremely proud of myself. Then Bear steps into my line of sight, and the pit of my stomach tightens, heat rushing through my body as I feel his eyes on me.

"Oh fuck," I gasp in warning. "I can't."

Before Rebel has a chance to pull out or give me a second to compose myself, my orgasm washes over me, my cum painting the couch as I tremble and moan through it.

Luckily, they assure me they can edit it out if I'm up to keep going. I nod eagerly, my cock still hard, even though it's now sticky and wet with cum. Rebel pulls out and flips me onto my back, using his tongue to clean the remnants of my release off my overly sensitive erection before he pushes inside me again in our new position.

With one orgasm out of the way, I'm able to hold off until Rebel pulls out, whips off the condom, and unloads on my stomach thirty minutes later. Using his cum as lube, I wrap my hand around my length and jerk myself to my second completion.

My muscles are still spasming with aftershocks when Rebel starts to lick up our combined seed off my skin, giving me a filthy kiss, our cum dripping from my lips and chin.

"Welcome to the Ballsy Boys," he says with a smile, giving me one last cum-sticky kiss before Bear yells *cut*.

3

BEAR

Fuck me sideways.

I am in *so* much trouble with this kid, though maybe I should stop calling him that after the scene I just watched because it brings up connotations that are ten kinds of wrong. God, the way he responded to Rebel's every little prompt and touch. *Hot* doesn't even begin to describe it. So fucking eager, so needy.

And the sounds he makes, all these little sighs and moans and pleas. I'm amazed Rebel lasted as long as he did. Me, I would've blown my load in under ten minutes.

I swallow as I make a beeline for my office, closing the door firmly behind me. My cock is throbbing, and I can damn well guarantee you that's not my normal reaction on set. Sure, I get aroused from time to time watching my boys. I'd have to be a robot not to.

But not like this. Not this fiery, demanding need inside me. This is a whole new level, my body physically aching with want. I can't even remember the last time I felt like this, so turned on.

A shaky breath leaves my lungs as I let myself fall into

my desk chair. What the fuck is wrong with me? You'd think I was some horny teenager, the way I'm responding. I'm not used to having such fierce reactions on set. I mean, I've been doing this for years now, first as a porn star myself and then with Ballsy Boys, which I started eight years ago. All this is to say that sex has been my life for a long time, and I don't get *excited* like this very often.

It must be too long since I last got laid. Come to think of it, when *was* the last time I had sex? I frown as I try to remember, and my cheeks heat up as I realize it's been more than a few weeks. Hell, it's closer to a few months. I'm really getting old, aren't I, if I don't even notice a dry spell like this? Damn, this is sad. Especially considering I work in porn.

To be fair, I've been super busy with the studio, to the point where I'm considering hiring someone to help me. Ballsy Boys is doing really well, better than I could've ever dreamed. I need a right-hand man, someone I can delegate tasks to. It's become too much to do it all by myself, but I've been reluctant to bring someone on.

It's a tight ship I'm running here, and an ethical one at that. I don't want to allow just anyone access to my boys. I need someone I can trust, someone who shares my philosophy and work ethics. Someone who understands what Ballsy Boys is about and who can help me further realize that vision. And with a list of requirements that long, it's not gonna be easy finding anyone.

But maybe the short-term solution is to score myself a hookup. Reluctantly, I pick up my phone and open Grindr. I prefer to score in person, but I can't be bothered to go out tonight purely to find a guy willing to let me fuck him, so this will have to do.

I'm proud to say I've never had issues finding a willing partner, online or in person. Sure, over the years I've slowly but surely transitioned from the hot bear category into the silver fox one, but I'm willing to embrace that if it means finding me a sweet thing willing to bottom for me. And if they wanna call me *Daddy* and have me boss them around a little or even engage in a little spanking, I'm all for it. That shit gets me hard, no problem.

To be fair, it's not just in the bedroom that I find the daddy dynamic fascinating. I could see myself live that out in real life as well, if not for the almost required age gap that comes with it. I'd love to take care of someone that way, but I can't do it with the cute twinks that are usually attracted to me. If I could find someone close in age to me who'd see me as daddy it could work, but not with a twenty-year age difference. Hell to the no am I getting involved in a relationship with them. Not gonna happen.

Not even with an adorable, cock-hungry little imp like Pixie. God, the way he said he loved to be fucked... *Having my hole stretched so wide I can hardly breathe*, he said, and my cock hardens all over again.

I *would* stretch him wide open, I can't help but think. Sink so deep inside him he'd be writhing on my dick, begging for more. Those luscious cheeks would jiggle perfectly when I fuck him hard, maybe even reddened by a little spanking first. Fuck knows a dirty boy like him could use a good spanking.

My phone drops from my hand to my desk, jolting me from my erotic daydream. I shake my head. No, I can't do this. I can't allow myself to jerk off to him. It's *wrong*. I just need to get laid, that's all.

I pick up my phone again, the app still open, and swipe until I find a cute-looking guy with a tight ass and a pair of gorgeous brown eyes. Modern technology does its work, and within a few minutes, we've set up a date. Not a *date* date, but a fuck date. Luck is with me, as he lives only ten minutes from the studio. After the scene we just filmed, I can be missed for a bit.

"I'll be back in an hour or so," I tell the crew, who are breaking down the set.

"Sure thing, boss," Joey, the head cameraman, says, and I ignore his curious look.

The shower is still running in the dressing room, so I leave Rebel and Pixie be and head out the door. I make my destination in nine minutes exactly, eight of which I spent thinking about that scene I witnessed, and when Jared—if that's even his real name—opens the door, my cock is still iron hard.

He's as cute in real life as his picture—always a relief. He's also young, probably not much older than Pixie, and I groan inwardly as my thoughts land once again on my newest boy. Oh for fuck's sake, I really need to get him out of my system. That's where Jared comes in, hopefully. His big smile as he lets his eyes wander down my body is a promising indication.

"We good?" I check with him for consent.

"Hell yes," he says, and he's on me before he's even closed the door behind me, dragging my jeans down and taking my underwear with it in the same move. "Hot damn," he says, his voice thick with admiration as he sinks to his knees.

I kick off my pants, then slowly circle my hand around my cock and fist it once. "You like?" I say.

My voice is full of embarrassing pride, but then again, I've never been able to resist it when someone admires my cock. It's this deep, primitive urge I can't explain. God knows it's stupid, because it's not like I *chose* my dick or made it myself, but it must be some weird male thing, I don't know. And apparently, it's not something you grow out of either.

"I love it," Jared says, smacking his lips. "Can I suck you off?"

"Like I'm gonna say no to a pretty boy like you," I tell him.

He bats his eyelashes at me. "You think I'm pretty?"

"Boy, you're delicious, and you damn well know it."

His smile spreads across his face. "Can I call you Daddy?"

I put my hands on his head, subtly directing it toward my dick. "You can call me whatever the hell you want as long as you get those sweet lips around me."

Jared smiles, then leans in for a quick lick, letting out an appreciative growl when he tastes me. He gently sucks my crown for a bit, making delicious sloppy sounds that make me even harder. Just when I think he's content with mere teasing, his right hand grabs my base, and he takes me in deep, hollowing his cheeks. His brown eyes peer up at me as if asking for approval, and I feel myself mellow in a soft smile.

"You're even prettier like this, with your mouth all full of cock," I say and watch his eyes light up.

He's hungry for praise, this one. I let out a low moan as he takes me in even deeper, and I make a careful thrust in his mouth, testing how far he can take me. He gags a little, but recovers quickly, giving me a little wink to indicate he's good.

"Aren't you a sweet boy, sucking your Daddy's cock so well," I praise him, and I swear, he's about to start floating, judging by the look on his face.

He opens his throat for me, and I slide my cock with slow, deep moves. His eyes water as he gags a little. "You can do this for Daddy, can't you?" I ask him, keeping a close eye on him to make sure I don't push him past his limits.

I pull out and he gasps for breath, smiling at me proudly. "More, Daddy," he says, his voice a little hoarse, and I discover I really like that word.

"Good boy," I tell him and slide back in again. His technique could use some improvement, but his eagerness to please me is a damn turn on. Considering I was already hard when I came in, it won't take much for me to come. But do I wanna come in his mouth or in his ass?

I could do both, what with how on edge I am. My recovery time isn't what it used to be—oh, the joys of growing older—but I have another round in me today. "Pretty boy, are you up for two rounds?" I check with Jared.

He slowly releases my dick, his lips red and swollen, his cheeks painted with an adorable blush. The sound my dick makes when it slips out of his mouth is wonderfully sexy, and I caress his hair in appreciation. He rubs against my hand, practically purring.

"I'm game for whatever you want, Daddy," he says, his voice a little rough.

Two minutes later, I come all over his face, and I have to admit, that's a damn satisfying sight. We move things into the bedroom, where I fuck him into an explosive orgasm, then come again with a force that leaves me shaking.

But when I walk out the door after having exchanged phone numbers with Jared—who would be all too happy with a repeat performance, he tells me—my thoughts still wander back to Pixie. And when I dream that night of hot sex with a gorgeous boy, it's not Jared my mind pictures in vivid detail.

Dammit.

Pixie

I'm flying high as I exit Ballsy Boys studios, my insides fizzing with the thrill of what I just did. I got fucked, on camera, while a dozen other people stood around watching...and it was *incredible*.

A little giggle bursts from my lips, and then, because there seems to be no other place for all these crazy feelings to go, more follow until I'm nearly doubled over with laughter in the parking lot.

I'm a porn star.

Oh my god, if everyone back home could see me now... they probably wouldn't be all that shocked, actually. I *know* my parents wouldn't be surprised, considering their dire predictions of me having to turn tricks to pay the rent out here in big, bad LA. They made it sound so dirty and shameful when they said it, but nothing about what I just did felt wrong. Not the way I expected it to anyway. Sure, it was a little strange being covered in cum, the high of great sex wearing off, and realizing how many people were actually standing all around casually watching us, but it didn't feel gross, just a little different.

I wish there was someone I could call and tell about this. It feels like the kind of thing to share with a friend...if I had any. I had a couple of friends in high school, but after we graduated, they went off to college, and I wasn't sure what I wanted to do with my life. Then, I met Daddy Luke while I was working at a crappy job at Dairy Queen, and I guess I got so wrapped up in him it was hard to relate to other people my age.

I manage to get over my giggle fit and pull out my phone to get an Uber home. But once the car pulls up, the thought of going back to my empty apartment right now when I'm still feeling the rush of filming my first porn sounds terrible.

"Hey, sorry, but little change of plans," I tell the driver. "I'm going to need a different drop-off location."

"No problem, where do you want to go?"

"Do you know of any gay bars around here?"

He snorts and looks at me in the mirror. "Honey, you're in LA, you can throw a stone and hit a dozen. What kind of a vibe are you looking for? Chill, slutty, dance...?"

"Dance," I decide, and the driver pulls away from the curb to take me to wherever he has in mind.

I pull out my phone and thumb through Instagram while we drive, liking a few pictures from friends back home, a longing starting in my chest. Honestly, *friends* is a strong word for them, but at least I was less alone than I am out here in California. I've been here a month, and so far the only real interaction I've had with anyone, aside from today at Ballsy, has been a couple of Grindr hookups.

On the bright side, there is *incredible* shopping in LA, so that's been a small consolation. But it hasn't done much for the lonely ache in my chest. Being at the studio today is the first time since I got here that I felt like *maybe* I could find a place to belong. I know it's going to take some time to get to know Rebel and the rest of the guys, but I *really* hope we become friends. I could use some friends. In the meantime, there's always dancing.

"Here we are," the driver declares, pulling up in front of a club.

It's early still, so I'm sure it won't be busy inside, but I'm more than okay with that.

"Thank you." I pull up my Uber app and add a big tip plus a five-star review before climbing out and heading inside.

The doorman asks to see my ID, which isn't a surprise considering I look sixteen, even though I'm twenty-one. He squints at my picture and back at me for several seconds, no doubt trying to figure out if it might be a fake, before finally handing it back to me and waving me inside.

I'm blasted by music as I step through the door. It's dark and loud inside, the main source of light coming from colored strobe lights. I look around until I spot the bar in the back corner. It's a little busier than I expected, but not much compared to some of the clubs I've been to since getting to LA. I easily move through the sparse crowd on the dance floor to reach the bar.

"Can I get a hurricane, please?" I order from the cute bartender. He's not my type at all, but he has a nice smile and pretty eyes. Five out of ten, would bang.

"Coming right up, cutie," he says with a wink.

While I wait, I let my gaze wander around the club, scoping out the talent tonight. Not that I'm particularly horny after getting fucked so good by Rebel, but it never hurts to check out the options. Plus, going to the club horny is worse than shopping hungry—god knows what you'll end up taking home, but you're almost guaranteed to regret it.

The bartender returns, setting my drink in front of me. "That'll be fifteen dollars."

Damn, that's pricey. Everything in LA seems to cost three times as much as stuff did back in Illinois. Until now, I haven't had a job to get me by either. Thank god for credit cards. I pull out my shiny Mastercard and hand it over to him.

"Start me a tab?"

"No problem."

Drink in hand, I make my way out onto the dance floor to work off some of this excess energy.

I shake my ass to the beat of the music, feeling random hands on me, unknown bodies pressing against me, but none of them long enough for me to really register or pay attention to. I'm not looking for a hookup tonight, and that's strangely liberating. Although, I wouldn't *hate* the idea of taking someone home just to help keep my bed warm.

I don't much like casual sex, much preferring the feeling of being someone's one and only, the love and care given by someone who thinks I'm special. But a boy's gotta do what he's gotta do, and if it's the choice between one-night stands or nothing, I'll take the randos any day of the week.

As I dance, I look around at the men surrounding me, smiling at me, touching me, and I imagine them logging onto BallsyBoys.com to see my debut scene. The thought of hundreds of men—and I'm sure women too—watching me suck Rebel, get fucked by him, has my cock growing hard.

Eventually, I return to the bar to get a second drink, repeating the process of drink, dance, drink, dance, until I lose track of the time or how many drinks I've had. The loneliness hasn't eased much, and as I stumble out onto the sidewalk and into a cab, I pull out my phone and type out a text.

Pixie: You'll never guess what I did today
   Luke: What's that baby boy?
   Pixie: I filmed a porn lol

My phone starts to vibrate with a phone call, and I giggle. I'm not surprised that got me a call rather than a text back.

"Hi, Da-Luke," I answer. "I'm in a cab, can I call you back when I get home in a few minutes?"

"Of course. You've got me curious now."

I laugh again and then promise to call soon before hanging up. I'm not sure if it's the alcohol or hearing Daddy Luke's voice for the first time since moving to LA that has my insides all warm and gooey. It felt weird to call him Luke when I answered, but it wouldn't have been right to call him daddy either. He's not *my* daddy anymore.

It feels like ages before the cab pulls up in front of my apartment. I whip out my credit card again and pay the fare, then head up to my apartment on the fifth floor. I kick my shoes off and wander into the tidy kitchen with all its brand-new, gleaming appliances and fancy light fixtures and pour myself a glass of water. Then I go into the living room and plop down on the couch before pulling out my phone again to call Luke.

He answers on the second ring, his voice warm and rich when he says hello.

"Now, what's all this about porn?" he asks with a hint of amusement.

"Well, I went through the money you put in my account before I moved really fast because everything is *so* expensive. So, I've been looking for a job pretty much since I got here. Then, I was at a bar and met this guy, Bear, who owns Ballsy Boys. He offered me an interview, and today I filmed my first scene."

"That's wild. Did you have fun?"

"Yeah, it was weird but really cool."

"What about school? Are you enrolled?" Luke asks, and my stomach clenches.

"Um...not yet," I confess, feeling the shame of disappointing him before he can say anything.

I started dating Luke when I was eighteen. It raised a lot of eyebrows because he's...a *bit* older than me. But I liked him, and I *really* liked all the things he introduced me to, like how it feels to have a Daddy Dom love and take care of you. He loved me so much that when he realized I had dreams that were too big for the little town we lived in, he put as much as he could into my bank account and bought me a plane ticket to LA so I could follow my dreams. I make it sound like it was easy for him, but I don't think it was. We talked about it for a *long* time, and he told me he hated the idea of sending me out here with no support system. I think if he didn't have his business in Illinois, he would've come with me. But honestly, coming out here on my own was for the best. I loved Daddy Luke, but it wasn't a forever kind of love.

"*Eli.*" He says my name sternly. "You moved out there to pursue a career in fashion. I expected you to get enrolled in school right away."

"I know, and I'm going to. It's just been a little harder to settle in than I expected." *And tuition costs a* lot *more than I thought it would*. "I promise I'll get enrolled soon."

"You may not be *my* boy anymore, but don't think I won't get on the first flight out there to spank your ass if you don't do as you should," he threatens, and my stomach quivers again, this time with want. It's not that I still want Daddy Luke in particular. But it's been so hard without the structure and care I got so used to back home with him.

"I will, I promise," I say in a small voice. "Thank you."

"Don't thank me, just do what you're out there to do. You're going to do amazing things, Eli. I believe that."

I pull my knees up to my chest and press the phone harder to my ear, wishing I could feel a pair of big, strong arms around me right now, or have a broad, furry chest to rest my cheek against.

"I should go to sleep," I say after a few seconds, because

I'm not sure what else to say if I'm not supposed to thank him again.

"Sleep well, and call me again sometime."

"Yes, D—" I clear my throat. "Yes, I will. Good night."

I hang up and shuffle to my room, stripping out of my clothes and leaving them in a big pile on the floor near my bed before crawling under the covers, cuddling my pillow until I fall asleep.

4

PIXIE

My arms are nearly weighed down with bags full of clothes from one of my favorite stores when my phone starts to ring from my pocket.

"Fuck me," I mutter, trying to juggle everything into one hand so I have the other one free to get my phone.

"Is that an invitation?" a man in a baggy shirt that does *nothing* for him asks as he walks by, shooting me a bawdy wink.

"Not dressed like that," I quip back, giving up on holding everything and setting some of my bags down instead so I can pick up the call before I miss it. I can't imagine who would be calling me, especially when I see it's a local number. Bear is literally the only person in LA who has my number, but I have his saved to my phone, so it can't be him.

"Hello?"

"Hey, Pix, it's Rebel."

I'm sure I look comical to anyone walking by because I'm startled enough to drop my remaining bags at my feet, my eyes going wide and my mouth forming into a surprised O. I *know* he fucked me last week, but I'm still completely starstruck. He's a freaking porn star, and he's calling *me*.

"Oh hey, hi, um, are you calling to let me know when my next scene is or...?"

"Oh no, this is a social call," he assures me with a laugh. "I hope you don't mind. I snaked your phone number from Bear's Rolodex. Can you believe the man still has an honest to god Rolodex?"

I giggle at the image. Actually, I can totally believe it. I can see him being a bit set in his ways. I wonder how old he is. Not that it matters...

"Pixie?" Rebel asks, making me realize I haven't responded to his question.

"I don't mind," I assure him. "So, you want to, like, hang out?"

I try not to sound as giddy as I feel. It's not just because he's a porn star either. For the first time since I can remember, I feel like this is a chance to make a real friend. I've imagined the kind of closeness shared by all the guys who work at Ballsy, and it was one of the reasons I even considered Bear's offer for a job in the first place. When I saw them that night at P!NK, laughing and enjoying hanging out, I was jealous. I've always wanted friends like that.

"Yeah, if you want. I know you haven't had a chance to meet the rest of the guys yet, so I thought we could all get together for dinner?"

"Yeah, that sounds great." My stomach flutters excitedly at the prospect of meeting everyone else and hopefully making some new friends.

"Awesome. How about the taco place around the corner from Ballsy studios in an hour?"

"I've been out shopping, so I need to get an Uber home

first to drop my stuff off and then another Uber to the restaurant, but an hour might be doable."

"I can pick you up from your place if you want to text me the address?"

"Sounds good, I'll see you there soon."

We hang up and I shoot him a quick text with my address, then save his number and request an Uber.

By the time the Uber drops me in front of my apartment, I spot Rebel leaning against the building, thumbing through his phone.

"Hey," I greet him much less awkwardly than I had on the phone.

"Hey," he says, nodding in greeting and smiling. His eyes drop to the bags in my hands and he crooks an eyebrow. "Couldn't wait to spend that first paycheck, huh?"

"I love clothes," I confess, setting down some of the bags to fish my key out. Rebel picks them up and carries them the rest of the way, following behind me up the steps to my apartment. "Do you mind waiting one second for me to change? I'd like to look a little nicer meeting everyone for the first time."

"Go right ahead. But honestly, don't stress too much about impressing anyone. They're the most laid-back group of guys you'll ever meet."

"A fresh shirt, at least," I reason before hurrying to my bedroom, leaving Rebel in my living room.

"This is a really nice place," he says loudly enough for me to hear while I hurry to look through my closet, trying to pick the perfect shirt for the occasion. "It must be expensive. Do you have a roommate?"

"Isn't everything in LA expensive?" I reply, ignoring the roommate comment, and his laugh booms down the hall. I considered a roommate when I first moved, but what if I ended up with one who borrowed my clothes without asking or missed the toilet when he peed or something? Best not to risk it.

I settle on a Prada polo, changing quickly and then fixing my hair in the mirror before heading back out to the living room.

"Ready," I declare.

He looks me up and down with an appreciative look in his eyes. "I hope you know, the other guys are going to be fighting over who gets to do a scene with you next. I can't wait to see how ours turned out. I have a feeling it's going to be a new viewer favorite."

My cheeks heat and I smile. "It was fun. I wasn't sure if it would feel weird or not, but I really liked it."

"You did great, especially for your first time. I was so nervous during my first scene I kept losing my erection. I was sure Bear was going to fire me after that. Instead, he took me aside afterward and gave me a few pointers on how to relax and have more fun with it."

"That's nice of him."

"Bear's a great guy," Rebel says. "I can't imagine working at any other studio. Ballsy has such a great group of guys, and Bear is the best boss anyone could ask for."

"I'm excited to meet everyone else."

"Yeah, they should all be there waiting. Bear texted me a couple of minutes ago to let me know they got a big table."

"Bear's there?" I ask, my mouth going dry and my heart fluttering. Maybe I should've picked something nicer to wear. I could stand a quick shower actually, after getting a bit sweaty while shopping. I didn't even re-apply any deodorant.

"Come on," Rebel grabs my hand and pulls me out of

the apartment before I can turn back to my bedroom to make myself more presentable before seeing Bear.

Rebel and I chat in the car, and I'm happy to discover he's easy to talk to. He tells me a bit about how he got into porn and about his family, who seem extremely awesome and totally make me jealous, and he tells me about the other Ballsy Boys.

I'm still nervous when we get to the restaurant, but less than I was before talking to Rebel for a little while. I notice a certain confidence in Rebel's stride as he leads me inside, and I wonder if that's inherent or if it's something he's built over time. I'd love to feel as confident as he seems to be.

I recognize all the men around the table, even if I haven't met them in person until now. Before I decided to apply at Ballsy Boys, I spent a *lot* of time watching their videos. It wasn't that I was getting off watching them—well, okay, maybe just a little—it was more that I was studying them to figure out if I really might have what it would take to be a porn star. I stalked their Twitter and Instagram, read tweets from and about them, and took pictures of myself in my bathroom mirror similar to the ones they shared on their promo shots. I thought about it and thought about it until I nearly talked myself into just flipping a coin to decide so I could stop obsessing about it.

Then, I stumbled on Bear's old videos. I don't know what it was about them, but as I'd sat on my bed, mesmerized by the large, furry body of the man twenty years earlier, I knew in an instant that my answer had to be yes. When the video had ended, I'd picked up the business card he'd given me weeks before at the club and sent him an email asking about the application process.

All the guys around the large table greet us happily when we reach them, shouting hellos and playfully catcalling Rebel. Once they settle down, Bear offers a more subdued head nod in welcome, and my stomach flutters.

"Hey new guy," Brewer says, pushing the empty chair beside him out a little.

"Pixie," I offer my stage name, proud of myself for the sexy lilt that overtakes the nervous quiver.

"You're cute as fuck. I'm super mad at myself right now that I wasn't able to make the shoot when Bear called and Rebel got to break you in instead." Brewer flirts, patting the chair since pushing it out clearly wasn't enough of a hint for me. I'm not surprised at the way Brewer's eyes roam over me or the suggestive smile he throws as I come around the table to sit down next to him. He comes off as very playful and flirtatious in his videos, and it's nice to see that translates into real life as well.

A growling noise at the other end of the table draws my attention, and I notice the *very* large man, who goes by Tank on screen, grumbling and shooting a glare at Brewer. I swear I read the word *slut* on his lips, and I'm taken aback. But before I have a chance to linger on whatever the beef is between Tank and Brewer, the next person draws my attention.

"You're going to be a fan favorite, I can tell," Heart says, smirking at me from my other side. Heart was one of my favorites when I was watching the videos. Hell, they're all fantastic, so it's really difficult to nail down *one* favorite, but I will say, Heart's face when he finishes is something to aspire to.

I blush and wave off the compliment. "You guys are a bunch of flatterers."

"He's right. The viewers love fresh meat, and add to that the fact you look like a sweet little virgin they'll all want to fantasize about defiling? You're going to break the internet,"

Campy agrees. He was the hardest to get a read on from his videos. He always seems enthusiastic and engaged, but he doesn't connect the way the other guys do. He's holding part of himself back on camera and it shows.

"Well, I'm far from a virgin, but if it'll sell subscriptions to the site, I'm happy to be whatever people want me to be," I say diplomatically, and I notice an approving look from Bear out of the corner of my eye.

∼

BEAR

I LOVE HANGING out with the boys, though I don't always join when they meet each other outside of work. They gotta have their fun without their *boss* being present as well. These informal get-togethers are important.

I'm not one of those cheesy corporate guys who claims their company is like a family, because that always makes me cringe. Mixing family and business is rarely a good idea, because lines become blurred and it makes it hard to make decisions that are in the best interest of the business. Or of the family, whichever you prioritize more.

But I do want us to be more than just coworkers. You kinda have to be, if you want the kind of movies I'm striving for. Look, plain porn to jerk off to, you can get that everywhere. That's not hard to shoot—pun intended. But scenes that go a little deeper—and god, look at me with all the double entendres, yuck—and that show genuine connection, that's not so easy. In order to achieve that, you need a familiarity between your actors, a friendship.

That's why I encourage my boys to hang out outside of

work. Plus, it's fun. If Tank and Brewer don't end up killing each other, that is. Tank is aptly named, a big bear of a guy who growls more than he speaks but fucks like it's nobody's business. And Brewer is the mother of all flirts, always joking and rarely without some man candy on his arm.

The two of them together are like gasoline and fire: a highly combustible combination that's bound to explode at some point. I love all my boys, but those two exasperate me. They behave like kindergartners half the time, what with the *he looked at me angry* and the *he stole my pencil* type of shit.

I swear, those two are gonna end up either fighting or fucking one day, and maybe both at the same time. If they do, I hope to catch it on video because I can't be the only one who would pay good money to see that.

I watch as Pixie chats with the boys, happy to see him gel well with the others. I frown. A little too well with Brewer, maybe, whose hands are even more touchy-feely than usual. He's not a bad kid, Brewer, not at all, but I've never seen him do anything but flirt.

There are times when I can totally understand Tank's frustration with him. Though Brewer does seem to have a more serious side, as I've spotted him talking to Campy from time to time about those weird-ass documentaries they both seem to like. *Man survives flesh eating worm that crawls up his dick*, that kind of shit. That would be a hell to the fucking no from me. I've got enough nightmares as it is, no need to add shit to that.

"So how did your first scene go, Pixie-boy?" Brewer asks in that flirty tone of his.

Pixie looks at Rebel. "You'd have to ask him. I have nothing to compare it to."

Rebel sends him a warm smile. "He did awesome. One of the best first scenes I've ever seen, right Bear?"

Heart, another relatively new addition to the Ballsy Boys family, looks insulted. "Really?" he says, but I hear the humor in his voice. "I lost to a fucking elf?"

I'm curious to see how Pixie deals with ribbing like this. He'll have to get used to it, 'cause it's how these boys roll. Honestly, there are few places I can take them like this because they're not exactly fit for public consumption. But this Mexican place loves us, and the owner is always happy to see us.

Pixie looks at Heart, then bats his eyelashes. "I'm not a *fucking* elf," he says, his face all innocence. "I'm a bottoming elf."

Oh, he'll do just fine, I think with relief as around me, everyone bursts out in laughter.

"So boss man, when do we get a shot at him?" Brewer asks.

"I assume that's a royal *we* and you actually mean *you*?" Rebel asks.

Brewer shrugs. "Of course. I wanna have a go at that sweet ass."

Rebel's usual friendliness gets a sharp edge. "You maybe wanna tone it down a little? Show some respect? You know this is not how we roll," he says, and Brewer flinches just a little.

"Sorry," he mumbles. "I meant it as a compliment."

Tank lets out one of his standard-issue growls that seem to be his go-to response whenever Brewer opens his mouth.

"It's a thin line between a compliment and a sexual harassment suit, Brew," Rebel says, and I shoot him a look of approval.

We may work in porn, but that doesn't mean there are

no boundaries. Consent is everything, maybe even more in our industry. Pixie signed up to shoot porn, not to get treated like a piece of ass outside work.

I'm glad Rebel said something. He's a good guy, that one. Steady as can be, super reliable, and his on-camera chemistry is unrivaled. That, plus he has a dick to drool over, and if that sounds weird, just remember how many I've seen. His is legendary for a reason.

He's been doing this for a while now, the Ballsy Boy I've had the longest, and I've wondered recently if he's still happy. He hasn't said anything, and his work ethics are exemplary as always, but it's just a gut feeling. Something tells me he's getting ready to move on, and as much as I would miss him, I would never want him to be held back. Maybe I should bring it up with him.

I shake myself out of my thoughts when I hear Heart say *HIV*. Even after all this time, it's a trigger for me.

"I'm saying that if you use PrEP, you don't have to worry about HIV anymore," Heart says.

"And I'm saying that I think PrEP is awesome and all that, but if someone's viral load is undetectable, they can't transmit it," Brewer says, and I have to hold myself in check to not let my mouth drop open.

That's gotta be about the most adult thing I have ever heard come out of his mouth. That, too, is Brewer, but it's a side he shows us so rarely. He's complicated, that one, but then again, aren't we all?

"I call BS," Heart says. "There's a reason so many people died of AIDS. That shit is seriously contagious."

Heart's casual remark about calling HIV *shit* doesn't sit well with me, but I know that's me being sensitive. He doesn't mean anything by it. Even though he's aware how many people died of it, he doesn't know their stories, their names. Not like I do.

They're too young, all of them. For them, dying of AIDS is history, something that happened to celebrities like Freddie Mercury. They don't know about the unknown Freddies, about *my* Freddie, or about the thousands of men dying. Plus, even from the little I know about his complicated background, Heart doesn't exactly have a healthy attitude toward sex. That's one damaged kid, and all I can do is hope he'll find his way back while working for us.

I clear my throat. "Actually, Brewer is right. If someone has HIV but their viral load is so low it's undetectable, they can't transmit the disease. They can still transmit other STDs, so you should still wear a condom, but not HIV."

"See," Brewer says, shooting a triumphant look in Heart's direction. "I fucking told you so."

"And he's so magnanimous about it too," Tank mumbles, scoring some guffaws from the rest and earning a glare from Brewer.

"And even if you get HIV, it's not a death sentence anymore," Brewer says, focusing his attention back on Heart. "Viral cocktails and other meds have gotten so good that it's unlikely you'd die of it."

"Don't underestimate it," I say, fighting to keep the emotions out of my voice. All these years later, and I still get emotional about it. It's been twenty-six years, and I don't think I'll ever forget. "Doctors have come far in treating HIV and prevent it from becoming AIDS, but the body adapts and fights in ways no one fully grasps. Just like some infections have become resistant to all but the strongest forms of antibiotics, that can happen to HIV as well. Just...just be careful, is all I'm saying."

Brewer cocks his head and looks at me, his eyes narrowing, and for a few seconds, there's little left of the fuckboy I know. It's as if he sees more in me as well, and I squirm a little in my seat. Then his face breaks open in one of those infamous smiles, and I know some kind of lewd joke is coming even before he winks at me.

"Enough with that serious talk about death and disease," he says. "Let's talk about our favorite D-word instead. *Dicks*."

Ah, that sounds more like the Brewer I know.

5

PIXIE

In the few weeks since I started at Ballsy Boys, I've discovered that Friday nights at the club Bottoms Up is a tradition for the guys, and I'm thrilled to be included. The music is loud, the drinks are strong, and the guys are hot, which all adds up to a great Friday night in my book.

We stand around talking about work and generally gossiping while I sip my drink. Bear never comes out with us to Bottoms Up, or rather, he hasn't since I've been coming. Strangely, Heart doesn't come either. I wonder what that's all about.

I can't keep myself from wondering about Bear, thinking about him more than I probably should, wanting to get to know more about him. He's been on set for all of my scenes, directing, observing, making me feel hot all over with his intense gaze and ever-present erection pressing against the front of his pants. But he never sticks around to chat once the scene wraps, and he never seeks me out for conversation like I see him do with the other guys on occasion. I wonder if it's because I'm new and we just haven't gotten to know each other yet, or maybe he doesn't like me. Then again, it could be that I'm reading too much into things, paying too much attention to him and making myself paranoid. The man is trying to run an entire production company, and I'm sure a new employee is one of the last things on his mind.

"What are you thinking about so hard, Pix?" Rebel asks, bumping his shoulder against mine in a friendly gesture. I glance over at him. His shirt has been bugging me all night. The color is all wrong for his complexion, and when I touched him earlier, I noticed the material is rough and scratchy, and don't even get me *started* on the stitching—poor stitching is the hallmark of cheaply made clothes. And I realize that obsessing about his cheap shirt right now is an avoidance tactic on my part.

"Oh, nothing much." I take another sip of my sweet, pink drink that I already forgot the name of. "Just wondering if Bear ever comes out to the club with you guys."

"Bear at Bottoms Up? I honestly can't picture that," Brewer chimes in with a laugh.

"Oh, is the club scene not his thing?" I ask as casually as I can manage.

"Nah, as far as I know, he spends all of his time in his office or at home like a hermit. He makes it out for lunches with us on occasion, but that's about it."

"Does he date or anything?"

All the guys share a look like the thought had never occurred to them before. Great, I'm totally giving away my stupid little crush.

Rebel puts an arm over my shoulder and kisses the top of my head.

"If he dates, it's not something he discusses with us," he says. "But, from everything I've learned about Bear in the years I've worked for him, it's that he prides himself on being professional. I'm sure it's not an accident that we don't know about his personal life, because he keeps his personal life and professional life separate."

Disappointment sweeps over me as I read between the lines of what Rebel is saying. Bear would never date an employee because that would be unprofessional. I didn't realize how deep my crush was already going until this moment filled with a longing I know will have to be left unfulfilled. In this industry, it's rare to find someone with as much professionalism and integrity as Bear, and I need to respect that. I'm sure eventually I'll get over this stupid crush, and we'll be able to have a normal employee-boss relationship. And until then, I'm just going to have to focus on doing my job well and getting closer to the rest of the guys.

Something catches Rebel's eye, and a huge smile breaks over his face. His arm drops from around my shoulder.

"Hey, it's banana boy!" he shouts.

I look over to see a man standing a few feet away looking mortified. His eyes dart around to all of us, and I have no doubt he's blushing, even though it's impossible to know for sure in the dim lights of the club.

"Banana boy?" Brewer asks with a chuckle.

"I can't believe I didn't tell you guys. This dude showed up at my place in a banana suit the other day," Rebel explains.

I watch with interest as Rebel angles his body toward his *banana boy* and they start to whisper and smile at each other. My heart aches a little as I watch them flirt. I've been getting my sexual needs easily met with all the scenes I've been filming, but it hasn't done much for my longing for a deeper connection.

I let my eyes wander around the club a little as the rest

of the guys keep talking and Rebel and his friend head out onto the dance floor. Most everyone here seems to be in their twenties from what I can see, which is a bit of a disappointment. I wonder where all the hot daddies hang out in this city. Is that something I can Google?

It's not that I *never* sleep with guys who are closer to my age and totally not daddies, but when I'm feeling lonely like this, I know any random guy won't do. I down the rest of my drink and make my way up to the bar to get another one. I get appreciative looks from a number of guys who either recognize me from Ballsy Boys or just want to get to know me better because, let's face it, I'm cute as fuck.

I consider a few of them, throwing them flirty smiles and winks, but ultimately return alone to the rest of the Ballsy Boys with a fresh drink in hand. I wonder if it would be weird if I asked one of them to come home with me tonight just to cuddle? Do I really want to be that needy? I'm sure after a few more drinks, I won't have a choice.

"You okay, Pixie-boy?" Brewer asks, sidling up close to me, taking the spot Rebel had previously occupied.

"Do you ever just feel lonely in this business? Like, all the sex is great, but sometimes you don't want to go home all alone to an empty bed?"

Brewer takes a sip of his drink, considering my question. "I think we all do, kiddo. Tell you what. Finish up your drink, and I'll come home with you tonight so you won't have to be alone."

"Really? You'd do that?"

"Of course. It's not exactly a hardship to cuddle up with a cute little imp all night," he teases with a wink.

"Thank you." My heart fills, and it's all I can do not to cry at how sweet Brewer is being. I haven't been with Ballsy Boys long, but I've never felt like I belonged anywhere more.

Bear

It's cute how the boys think they can get one past me. I mean, come on, did they really think I wouldn't know they're planning a surprise party for my birthday? Most of them can't lie worth shit, with the exception of Heart, and I don't mean that as an insult. He's had to learn the hard way, so I don't blame him one bit. But seriously, Pixie trying to pretend he doesn't know what's going on is fucking hilarious.

I first got wind of what they were up to a week or three ago when Rebel asked me just a little too casually what I had planned for today. It seemed too much of a coincidence, considering my birthday is tomorrow, but I pretended it didn't arouse my suspicion and played along. I appreciate them trying to do something for me, so pretending to be surprised is the least I can do. I can only hope my acting skills will be sufficient to pull it off.

I show up at the studio at the expected time, parking my car in my usual spot. As soon as I open the door, confetti rains down on me amid shouts of "Surprise!" and "Happy birthday!" I don't have to even feign shock because the sheer volume is enough to make me startle.

"Happy birthday, boss man," Rebel says, the first in line to hug me.

There are hugs from everyone, accompanied by gentle ribbing about me turning forty-five and the amount of gray hairs both on my head and the rest of my body. The boys also bought me presents, ranging from a book I casually mentioned to Rebel to a series of documentaries Joey and I talked about.

They've arranged for cake and drinks, and they've set up the studio with some chairs and tables so we can all hang out for a bit. That explains why Rebel didn't want to book a scene for today.

Everyone is animatedly chatting with each other when Pixie slips onto the chair next to me. He looks cute as a button in a soft pink shirt, sinfully tight hot pants, and a little hint of lip gloss on those kissable lips.

"Happy birthday, Bear," he says, making my name sound like a caress.

"Thank you. I'm getting old," I add, not even sure if I'm saying it for his benefit or for my own.

He lets out melodious giggle. "You're not old. You're mature. Experienced."

He's flirting with me again, and I find myself responding to him. "You like your men experienced, little imp?"

He bats his eyes at me. "Experienced and mature. Perfect combination. I like a man who knows what he's doing."

Even flirting with him like this is already crossing a line I never imagined myself disregarding, but he's so hard to resist. I really shouldn't engage him, let alone encourage this line of conversation, but I can't help it. "I'm sure you'd have no trouble finding a man to take good care of you, like you deserve."

He pushes his bottom lip out in a little pout. "It's harder than you would expect. My standards are pretty high, you know?"

"What are your standards, Pixie-boy?"

He shrugs with one shoulder, but his eyes find mine, and the fire I see there negates the feigned nonchalance in his posture. "I want a BMW."

I frown, completely confused as to what he means. "Not sure I'm following."

He leans forward, his eyes never leaving mine. "Some men are like Hondas. They're super reliable, but boring as fuck. That's not for me. Others are like a Lamborghini or a McLaren, these flashy, expensive supercars. We all love spotting them on Rodeo Drive, but at some point, they'll inevitably crash. I don't need that either, some dude who sweeps me off my feet and then crashes."

I'm starting to see where he's going with this, and it makes a surprising amount of sense.

"What I want is a BMW. They're sleek, sexy, and they last. They're dependable, and they'll take care of you while still giving you the ride and experience of a lifetime."

I don't know which is more astonishing: the fact that Pixie is using a car analogy or the fact that I totally get what he's saying and it's hot as fuck. My pulse has sped up, my body reacting to both his words and the way he looks at me—as if I'm that BMW he can't wait to climb into.

My throat is too parched to speak, so I have to swallow before I answer him. "I hope you'll find your BMW man," I say, ignoring the flash of red jealousy that courses through me at even the thought of Pixie with another man.

That's ridiculous, of course. He and I are nothing to each other, except boss and employee.

"Oh, I think I have found him," Pixie says, his tone sweet as honey. "Now it's just a matter of making him see he'd be perfect for me."

I shake my head, about to say something to him to make sure he understands this can never go past flirting, when he breaks eye contact to reach for a little bag he's had under his chair the entire time. "I made you something," he says.

He hands me the black gift bag, which, I swear, sparkles

in some way. "Thank you," I say, still adjusting to the sudden shift in topic. "Do you want me to open it now?"

He laughs as he shakes his head. "Open it at home. I think you'll love it."

Conversation flows easily, and at some point, everyone starts talking about how they ended up in porn. That's a tricky subject, considering some reasons are private, but I can sense there's enough respect among the boys to accept when not everyone is open about it.

"What about you, Bear?" Rebel asks. "You've been doing this for a long time now."

Inwardly, I cringe at the not-so-subtle reminder of how much older I am. But he doesn't do it on purpose, so I let it slide. Besides, I will be forty-five tomorrow, so there's no sense in denying it.

"I started out as a model," I say. "My older brother is a photographer, and he needed to build up a portfolio back in the day, so he asked me to model for him. Turns out, I was good at it, and when he showed the photos to a modeling agency he wanted to work with, they not only hired him but asked to meet with me as well. I signed with them a day later. It helped me pay for college."

"You were a model?" Pixie asks, his eyes big.

I nod, smiling. "If you look up old Coca-Cola ads, you may spot me. I shot a few TV commercials as well for various products. Body wash, some clothing brands. It was fun."

"But how did you get from that to porn?" Campy asks.

I shrug. "It's not that original, not in those days. I tried out for some TV work and got some minor parts in series and in movies. But then they found out I was openly gay, and that was it."

There are some audible gasps, and their faces all reflect

shock.

"As liberal as Hollywood may seem, at the core, they do care about family values, at least on the surface. They don't care what you do privately, as long as you keep it out of the limelight. And I've always been out and proud, a flag-carrying participant in every pride parade. When they saw an interview with me in a national magazine about the stigma of being gay after the AIDS crisis, nobody wanted to work with me anymore."

"Ugh," Brewer says. "That's just wrong. Not surprising, but wrong."

I shrug. "It is, but I wasn't surprised. I worked some odd jobs, but then a friend of mine had done a porn and asked me if I was interested. I was leery because it was a shady business back then, but when the guy assured me he was only shooting with condoms, I gave it a try. Turns out, I loved it, and it was good money, so I was in."

The conversation has turned much more serious than I had anticipated. Surely they can't be interested in me rehashing the past, especially considering it wasn't the brightest of times for us back then. But they're all listening with rapt attention, including Pixie, who looks at me with stars in his eyes.

Instead of changing the subject, Brewer asks, "They were shooting bareback back then? That's crazy stupid, considering the risks for STDs and especially HIV then."

"Yeah, I know. There was a lot of resistance, for the same reasons we hear it today—because condoms aren't sexy," I say, barely able to keep the fury out of my voice.

"They had nowhere near the knowledge we have about HIV today," Brewer said. "And hardly any effective meds to keep it from developing into full-blown AIDS. So, *not sexy* is a pretty stupid reason to risk your life."

Once again, I'm blown away by the glimpses of the serious, adult Brewer he treats us with every now and then. The contrast with his usual playboy image couldn't be bigger.

"I've always insisted on using condoms," I say. "I lost out on some profitable deals because of that, but I never wavered. And when I started Ballsy Boys, that was my primary goal: to make it safe for everyone. Of course, the risks have lessened significantly, but that goal stands."

"And we respect you for it," Rebel says. "It's one of the reasons why Ballsy Boys has such an excellent reputation."

He couldn't have paid me a bigger compliment. It almost makes up for making me feel old.

We hang out for another hour, the conversation turning to lighter topics. All that time, I can feel Pixie's eyes on me, following me as I chat with everyone. I'm not sure how he felt about that conversation. It seems too heavy for him, too depressing. Almost like tainting something pure and pristine with something dark and stained. My past isn't exactly rainbows and unicorns, and I feel the strange urge to protect him from it.

I thank the boys extensively for the party when it's winding down, and when I want to help clean up, I'm sent to my office. Seconds after I've closed the door, I'm opening Pixie's gift bag.

I pull out a black V-neck T-shirt, the material soft under my fingers. When I see the words on the front, my face breaks open in a smile. That cheeky little elf. *Silver Bear*, it says. I brush the letters with my fingers, noticing they're not printed on. A quick check on the inside shows me they're sewed on, and I realize Pixie must've made this for me.

He made me a perfect T-shirt. By *hand*. How the hell am I supposed to say no to him now?

6

PIXIE

I hop out of the shower, steam billowing around me and the scent of my vanilla body wash strong in the air. Most of the guys shower at Ballsy after their scenes, but whether they shower beforehand at home too, I don't know. But since I always bottom, I like to make sure I'm squeaky clean before heading in to work.

After a few months at Ballsy, I can't believe how quickly I'm settling in. I figured I wouldn't mind doing porn, but it turns out I *love* it. Not just getting fucked, although that is pretty fantastic, but the guys were right: the fans love me. There's a thrill in reading all the comments on videos and on Pixie's social media that I hadn't expected. It makes filming each scene all the more exciting, to know people are eagerly waiting for it.

I reach for my towel and bring it up to pat my face dry first before running it over the rest of my body and quickly tossing it aside. My hand finds its way to my only slightly hard cock, cupping it and giving it a little squeeze to start the blood flowing to it.

I think this is the weirdest thing about doing porn, actually. It's always been that when I'm horny, I go out and find someone to have sex with, or got my daddy to play with me. But now, when a scene is scheduled, if I'm not particularly horny, I have to *get* horny. I mean, I'm twenty-one—it's not like that's exactly a difficult task. It's just something to get used to.

I step over in front of my mirror, using one hand to wipe the fog off, the other still casually playing with my slowly growing dick. Looking at my face, I try a few different expressions that I thought might look sexy on camera. Most of them make me look constipated, so I stop trying and turn away from my reflection, heading into my bedroom to finish getting myself ready to go to work.

Flopping down on my bed, I reach over and grab the lube and butt plug off the top of my nightstand, my cock tingling with more enthusiasm as soon as I hear the snick of the lube bottle opening. *God, I'm such a bottom.* I set the plug down on the bed beside me and squirt lube onto my fingers, putting my feet on the bed and spreading my knees so I'll have plenty of access to get my hole nice and stretched for my scene with Brewer.

Bringing my slicked fingers between my cheeks, I tease them around the rough pucker of my entrance. I have it on good authority that I have an adorable asshole, and I *should,* considering I get it waxed and bleached regularly. Even before I started doing porn, Daddy Luke loved it when my hole was pretty for him. I always got special kisses and cuddles for it.

Remembering the way it felt to be held in such strong arms has my cock fully hard and leaking now, my pucker fluttering under the teasing pads of my fingers, begging to be filled and stretched. I slip one finger inside, and it only makes me more desperate to be *truly* stretched, taken, and used for daddy's pleasure.

I shiver and moan, my hips twitching and my cock bobbing in the air. I shove a second finger in, and my eyes fall closed. Images of Bear fill my mind as I work my hole open and I whine in frustration. I know I promised myself I would get over this crush, but no matter how hard I try, he always seems to dominate my thoughts when I'm touching myself or getting off. I've slipped and flirted with him a few times, like at his birthday a few weeks ago, and every time, I see a spark of interest before he quickly shuts me down. He wants me, but he doesn't *want* to want me, and that makes it that much harder to squash this crush.

A trickle of precum drips from my slit onto my hairless belly, and I know I need to slow my roll, or I'm going to bust, and then I'll be in trouble when I get to work.

A whimper falls from my lips as I pull my fingers out of my hole, my body trembling for release, my chest heaving and my balls aching. Drinking in deep breaths, I try to think of unsexy things to calm myself down—*puppies, baseball, a sandwich...okay, that's better.*

Blowing out an unsteady breath, I reach for the plug on the bed beside me. I squirt some lube onto the tip and use my already sticky hand to smear it around before positioning the rounded tip against my hole. It slides in easily because it's not the biggest plug in the world. I do have various sizes stashed in the top drawer of my dresser. Little did I know when I started my butt plug collection how handy they would become in my porn career. Brewer isn't the biggest of the guys, so I'm able to go with one of my medium plugs.

I wonder if Bear is as big in real life as he looked in his videos. If he is, I'd need my biggest plug to be ready for him.

My cock jerks again against my stomach as I imagine how full Bear's thick cock would make me feel. I squirm against the plug, biting my lip and fisting my sheets to resist the urge to touch myself again. I need to wash my hands, style my hair, and get dressed. I need to get to work. *I need to get wildly fucked by Brewer while Bear watches from behind the cameras.*

With Herculean efforts, I drag myself out of bed and back into my bathroom so I can finish getting ready. Sometimes we have specific outfits we have to wear for a scene, but today I was told to make sure I wear a cute pair of underwear, and that was it. I pick out a pair of pink and black Andrew Christian briefs and then set about styling my hair. Even though it doesn't matter what I wear to set today, I still take a good half hour to decide on an outfit, settling on a pink Ralph Lauren polo and a pair of Saint Laurent distressed jeans that cost nearly a month's rent.

On my way out the door, I grab my mail, and my stomach twists a little at the sight of an envelope from Mastercard. Maybe I'll wait until later to open that.

The bustle inside the studio has already started to become comfortable and familiar. I still feel weird once a scene ends and I'm sitting there with cum all over me, my cock shrinking, and a million eyes on me. But I'm not sure that particular aspect will ever feel less awkward.

Several cameramen and other crew greet me as I head toward the locker room to get out of my clothes. I make quick work of stripping down to my briefs and checking my hair in the mirror again before heading out onto the set. This is my second scene with Brewer, and I'm looking forward to it. Honestly, I like working with all the guys, so I wouldn't complain about any of them.

I *have* noticed the one person I have yet to film a scene

with is Tank, and I'm starting to wonder about that. I know he's rougher than the other guys when he fucks, and I know I'm all small and dainty looking, but I know I could take whatever Tank could dish out and walk away with a smile on my face.

I spot Bear hovering near the set, chatting with Joey, our head cameraman, but no Brewer yet, so I make my way over to my boss to say hello. My skin prickles with awareness as I near him and his attention flicks to me. I'm not sure why it took me until I'm standing directly in front of Bear, looking up at him, to realize I'm in nothing but a pair of tight underwear with a butt plug in my ass. *Awkward*.

Bear's eyes wander over me slowly like a warm caress, and a smile spreads over my lips. Okay, maybe not so awkward after all.

"Hi, Bear," I say with a breathless edge to my voice, looking up at him through my eyelashes. I *know* he's my boss and I shouldn't flirt, but god he's just so...*ungh*.

"Pixie," Bear acknowledges me with a nod, his hands twitching before he shoves them into his pockets.

Joey coughs, which sounds suspiciously like he's covering up a laugh, and Bear shoots him a glare.

"I was just thinking, and I wanted to ask: when do I get to film with Tank?"

Bear frowns. "I'm not sure if you two are the best pairing."

"Oh." I frown now. "Does he not want to film with me?"

"That's not it," he assures me. "I just think he's too rough for you. He likes to throw guys around a bit, and you're so small..."

I narrow my eyes and put my hands on my hips.

"You don't think I can handle him? You think I need to be coddled?" Don't get me wrong, I *love* to be coddled, but only by my daddy, and Bear isn't my daddy. "I may be young, and I may not have all the worldly experience of some, but if there's one thing I know, it's what I can and can't handle sexually."

"I understand that," he says. "But you're not filming with him."

I stick my lip out in a pout, crossing my arms over my chest. The air conditioner chooses that moment to kick on, and I'm suddenly very aware of how little I'm wearing as goosebumps pebble on my skin and a shiver runs through me. I wrap my arms around myself and look over at the bed we'll be using to film today, considering climbing under the covers while I wait for Brewer to get here.

"Are you cold?" Bear asks, concern filling his voice and making it somehow deeper and more appealing. Resisting the urge to press myself against him and ask him to warm me up is the hardest thing I've done all day, and yes, I'm counting the effort it took not to get off thinking about him at home.

"Just a little."

My mouth falls open as he whips his shirt over his head and hands it to me like it's not the sexiest thing I've ever seen. I stare for a few seconds at the spattering of gray in his chest hair, my eyes gobbling up the sight of his still hard physique. He looks just as good as he did when he was *in* porn. Actually, he looks *better*. Granted, that may be my preference, but *damn*. Ten out of ten, would absolutely bang.

"Pixie?" he says, still holding his shirt extended in his hand.

"Thanks," I murmur in a stupor, taking it from him and pulling it over my head. It's the softest T-shirt I've ever felt, and that's really saying something. I want to peek at the label to see who the designer is, but I resist. "I was more right about the *Silver Bear* thing than I realized. You're so hot, Daddy Bear."

The name falls from my lips without thinking. And, even though I know I shouldn't, I reach out to touch him. The smell of his deodorant and cologne from his shirt tickle my nose, and my cock starts to harden. There's no hiding my reaction in these tight briefs. Luckily, the shirt falls to midthigh, so my erection is fully covered.

Bear makes a deep rumbling noise in his chest and then clears his throat as my fingers run through the gray hair on his chest.

"I need to go to my office," he says stepping away from my touch, turning on his heal, and walking away.

∼

Bear

This weird obsession I have with Pixie needs to stop. He's been working here for months now, and I can't stop focusing on him. What the fuck is wrong with me? Every time I see him, it's like I'm magically transported back in time and turn into a horny sixteen-year-old with a one-track mind. Hell, I think I was way more mature at sixteen than I'm capable of when I'm around Pixie. It's like he takes away my capacity for rational thought.

I keep telling myself I shouldn't flirt with him, yet every time we hang out socially with the boys, I'm drawn to him like a damn magnet. What is it about him that pulls me in so much?

Plus, I have this deep urge to take care of him that makes no sense at all. He's an adult, and even though he's young, he's old enough to stand on his own two feet. Why do I keep trying to be his daddy?

Taking off my shirt because he's cold—it's insane. Well, he *was* shivering, I'll admit that. I didn't imagine that part, because I could see the goosebumps on his skin popping up everywhere except for what was covered by that cute little pair of underwear that looked like it was painted on him. It's not fair that he's exactly my type, down to his cute cock that I just wanna swallow whole and suck on until he...

Dammit, here we go again with the inappropriate thoughts. He's my employee. A kid. Over twenty years my junior.

This. Can't. Happen.

How the hell do I get this message across to my cock though? To be fair, it's not just my dick that wants him. If it were just that, it would be easier to shrug off. I've been attracted to guys I couldn't have before. It goes away as soon as you find another body to meet your needs.

But this is different. I don't just wanna fuck him until he's thoroughly claimed and my smell is all over him—I wanna *take care* of him. Pamper him. Spoil him a little and then spank him when he gets too sassy, which he will. I've never been a daddy before, not outside of the bedroom, but with him, I want to. He's triggering all these protective instincts in me, and it scares me. That's the part that's dangerous because that's not so easy to find with somebody else.

I thought hooking up with Jared a few times would get it out of my system, but it hasn't helped at all. We met up twice more, but then Jared admitted to developing feelings for me, and I was out. The kid's only twenty-three, way too young for me. Besides, it wouldn't be fair to him, not when my mind is fixated on someone else. Even if I can never, ever *have* that someone else. Whoever said that wisdom comes with age was clearly delusional.

From a professional viewpoint, hiring Pixie was a stellar decision though. Damn, the kid is popular. Our website is flooded with comments from viewers who want to see more shoots with him. There's quite a few suggestions of pairing him with Tank.

I lean back in my chair, considering it once again. It's not like I can't see why this would appeal to viewers, and yet I haven't scheduled them together. It's just that Tank is so big and he can be quite rough, and Pixie is...*delicate* is a word that's gonna get me in trouble, but I'm just not sure he'd be able to take it.

Rebel warns me when the shoot starts, and I watch as Brewer and Pixie do their thing. From the get-go, it's a great scene, the two of them having great chemistry and both clearly having a good time. Brewer may not be as good an actor as Campy is, but he doesn't need it here, and Pixie is just genuinely happy to take whatever Brewer is dishing out. This will be another winner, and I couldn't be more proud.

I've already gotten word that one of our videos, *Extortion*, is nominated for Best Gay Porn Production in the yearly Porn awards. When I got the phone call, I did a little victory dance, and then called Rebel to tell him the great news. I'm so, so proud of where the company is going, and shoots like this prove to me we're on the right track. The boys are coming with me to New York, I decide. They should celebrate our success.

Joey and I share a satisfied look after the shoot is done. He knows we've got gold as well as I do. He's a funny one, Joey—a straight man who excels at shooting gay porn. He's been with me from the start, and his eye for detail in the camera work is unrivaled. I bet he could get a job with any production company or studio if he wanted to, but he keeps telling me he's happy right where he is.

I can't deny it raises questions, but I'm not asking them. People will come out when they're ready. Or not. I was never big on that whole pressure to use labels. Joey is a good guy and one hell of a cameraman. That's all I need to know.

"Good job, you two," I say to Brewer and Pixie.

"Thanks, Boss," Brewer says, wiping his sweaty face off with a towel. "Sign me up for this anytime."

He hugs Pixie and slaps him playfully on his ass, eliciting a little giggle from him. "You were great, Pixie-boy."

When he stalks off toward the dressing room, Pixie just stands there, staring at me from between his lashes until he all but runs toward the locker room as well. I jam my hands into my pockets. Pixie can be a total flirt with me at times, and then other times, he can't get away from me fast enough. I'm not sure what's causing the hot-and-cold behavior.

Maybe it's the difference between being on set and off camera? It seems he's more nervous when he's doing a scene, giving me monosyllabic answers when I try to make small talk. He flirts with me like crazy when we hang out with the boys—and god, how embarrassing to admit that I look forward to that to the point where I've started to hang out with the boys more.

Of course, when we do hang out, I try and keep my distance from him, because I don't want to give him the wrong idea. Guess he's not the only one doing a hot-and-cold routine.

"Something wrong?" Rebel asks. He'd asked if we could talk after the shoot. God, I hope this isn't bad news. I know he's been seeing a lot of his boyfriend, Troy, lately, and it seems things are getting more serious.

With great reluctance, I turn my head to face him. "Do you think Pixie likes it?"

"Working for us? For Ballsy Boys, I mean. I think so. He loves to be fucked, that much is clear."

Us. That one word speaks volumes about how he feels about his job here, and it makes me proud. I love how Rebel has grown in his role at the studio. He's been helping out more and more lately, and his suggestions are excellent. I've been thinking about asking him to come on as my assistant, but it's never been the right time for that conversation.

"Every time I try to make small talk, he clams up," I say, not quite ready to let the topic of Pixie go just yet.

"He's shy," Rebel says. "And I don't think he's fully used to being naked around us yet."

That makes sense. He's free on camera, but as soon as the shooting is done, he seems a bit embarrassed. That's something that takes a while, I know from experience. It's a strange job to have.

I focus on Rebel, whose face is tight. *Uh oh.* I don't like the look of this at all. Please, don't tell me he's gonna quit. I've seen it too many times to count, one of my boys getting a boyfriend who wants them to quit porn. It makes sense, and I never tell them to stay, but it does suck for me. "Anyway, you said you wanted to talk to me. What's up, kiddo?"

Rebel gestures toward my office. "Can we talk in private?"

"I wanna quit," Rebel says once we sit, and my stomach drops. Dammit. "Wait, no, that's not what I meant. I love working for you, for Ballsy Boys. I'm proud of what we do here. At the same time, I think it's time for me to move on. I was hoping you would be interested in taking me on as an assistant. Full time. Or at least, enough hours so I could stop doing shoots."

I swear, it feels like someone just stepped off my chest, and I shoot him a big smile. "That's it? Fucking hell, Rebel, I thought you were gonna tell me you were moving on to another studio or that you were gonna quit completely. That would've broken my fucking heart."

"I would never do that. This is my... I love working here, Bear. You know that. These guys, they're my friends. Family, more like. I don't wanna leave, but I..." He sighs. "I met someone. He's... He's special to me, and I need to put that first."

He's in love. It's obvious to me, the way his eyes soften when he talks about his man, the way he smiles a little even when just thinking about him. He loves him. But when I ask him, he tells me it's complicated. Yeah, no shit. Love is always complicated.

"Have you ever been in love?" he asks me.

God, my Freddie, my bigger-than-life Freddie who withered away right before my very eyes. I loved him so much, and he loved me, and we thought we had forever...when we only had a few moments. Life can be cruel...and love even harsher.

"Once. He..." God, why does it still hurt so fucking much? You'd think that after twenty-six years, I'd be able to talk about him without tearing up. "He got sick and passed away. But that was years ago."

"Would you do it again, knowing what you know now?"

The question triggers me, but I don't know why. Maybe because it's something I've never asked myself before. Freddie has always been a crucial part of my life, and the thought of not having experienced all that, it's like an ice-cold splash of water to my face.

I give Rebel some answer about the horrors of watching someone die, unable to come up with something better, but even after he's left my office, I keep thinking about it. If I had known Freddie was gonna die when I met him, would I still have loved him? Would I have made the same choice to be with him?

On impulse, I call my mom. Yes, I'm a mama's boy, so sue me. The woman is a force of nature, and her love is of the fierce, unconditional kind. I wouldn't be who I am today without her love and support.

"Hey, Mom," I say when she picks up.

"Maxwell, how good to hear your voice. How have you been, my sweet boy?"

And just like that, I'm a small kid again who crawls on his mom's lap because that will make everything okay. "I'm good, Mom. How's your hip?"

We talk for a bit about the hip surgery she had recently and that she's still recovering from. She broke her hip after falling off her bike, and I'm talking about her Harley, not some wimpy-ass bicycle.

"You sound a little sad. Are you okay?" she then asks, and I smile. You can't get anything past her.

"Mom, if you had known Dad would die so young, would you still have married him?" I ask.

My dad died of a heart attack that came out of nowhere when he was only in his forties. Turns out, he had an undiagnosed heart condition that never was a problem until it killed him. My mom never remarried, though she did have some boyfriends throughout the years. None of them lasted longer than maybe a year though, which is about the same length of my longest relationship after Freddie.

Granted, I was in porn first, which made it hard to find a boyfriend willing to put up with that, and after, I was focused on building my own studio. I had some flings, you could call it, a few that had the potential for more, but they always fizzled out. The last few years, I've only hooked up. It's easier that way.

"Good lord, Maxwell, what brings on a question like that?"

I let out a soft sigh. "Thinking about Freddie, you know."

"Did something happen?"

"Just...could you tell me, Mom? I'm curious."

She clicks her tongue, then blows out a breath. "Of course I would, darling. How could I want to erase you? But even if that was not a consequence, I still would've chosen him. He was my big love, the one who stole my heart from day one. The twenty-five years we had together were worth it, even if they were so much shorter than I had hoped. We packed a *lot* into those years."

I wince, knowing all too well how much *living* those two did. They were classic flower power children, my parents, completely in tune with the sex, drugs, and rock and roll vibe of those times. That's probably why they didn't even blink an eye when I came out at age eleven, nor when I found myself befriending a group of gay men twenty years my senior as a teen. They trusted me, supported me. They loved me. And when Freddie died, they held my hands when we buried him, even when his own family never even showed.

"It hurt so much, when Dad died, when Freddie died. How could you be willing to put yourself through that again?"

She's quiet for a few beats. "But we're not talking about me, are we? Darling, you were eighteen when Freddie died. You can't stay alone for the rest of your life."

I have to swallow before I can answer. "I'm not talking about me staying alone, Mom. I'm... How could I put someone else through that willingly?"

"Maxwell, are you telling me you're sick? Is there something wrong with you?"

My sigh is so hard it blows papers off my desk. "No, Mom. I'm fine. Just...thinking about stuff. I gotta go."

"One last thing, Maxwell. Don't forget that the joy of being loved outweighs the sadness and grief over losing that love. That's why I'd do it all over again, because your father's love for me was the single best feeling in the world, and I'd have my heart broken a thousand times to feel like that again."

I hang up and stay in my office for a long time, thinking about Rebel's question and about her answer. Would I do it again? The correct answer would be yes, of course, but the truth is that I'm not so sure. I only had Freddie for such a short time, and losing him was... It damn near broke me. It changed me forever, and honestly, if I had known that was the price I would pay for being with him? I'm not sure I would do it again.

That thought alone makes guilt wash over me like a flood. I was the light of Freddie's life, so how horrible is it to feel this way? Maybe it's not so much that our love wasn't great, because I think it was. Granted, I was just eighteen, but still. I loved him with everything I had. It's just that his death was so much bigger, so horrible that it doesn't feel like the love we had balanced it out.

No, I have to disagree with my mom on this one. I would do anything not to get hurt like that again, for myself and for others. Love can't be worth *that*.

7

PIXIE

I'd be lying if I said I'm not a little nervous about my performance review. All the guys assured me it's standard after ninety days working at Ballsy and is mostly Bear making sure his employees are happy and that they aren't having any negative experiences from the get-go. But from the instant I woke up this morning, I've been running over every second of the last three months in my mind—every one of my shy moments on set, each flirtatious comment made to Bear that seemed to have an equal chance of either eliciting him flirting back or sending him running for his office to escape me.

I *know* I need to stop flirting with him, but it's *so* hard—pun intended.

Stopping outside Bear's office, I knock, and to my surprise, Rebel is the one who calls out for me to come in. I enter to find Rebel and Bear both seated behind Bear's desk.

"Hey, Pixie, come on in," Rebel greets me happily, waving me inside.

"Um, hi. I'm here for my ninety-day review?"

"Yeah, Bear asked me to sit in on it, if that's okay?"

"Oh." I dart a quick glance in Bear's direction to find him looking relaxed and casual with a friendly smile on his lips. My heart skips a little when I notice he's wearing the *Silver Bear* T-shirt I made him. It clings sinfully tight to his biceps and chest.

"Rebel found the shirt you made me and thought it was hilarious. He sort of blackmailed me into wearing it today."

"Right." I cover my disappointment with a small laugh. "And, of course you can sit in," I assure Rebel, finally managing to close the door and make my way over to sit down in the chair on the opposite side of the desk from the two of them.

"Thank you. I like to have a second person present for reviews so it's a little more professional. And Rebel and I have recently had a discussion about him stepping away from filming to essentially learn my side of things and assist in a more managerial and creative aspect, so I thought your review would be a good place for him to start learning the ropes."

"You're not filming anymore?"

"I've been at this for a long time," he says wryly. "I love this business and I don't want to leave it completely, but it's time I move to this side of the camera. I'm doing an official announcement for the fans next week, so if you could keep this between us for now, it would be appreciated."

"Of course."

"Great, so let's get started on your review." Rebel clicks his pen and poises it over a piece of paper.

For the most part, Bear sits quietly, only interjecting a few times, while Rebel and I have a back-and-forth about how I've been doing and what I like and dislike at Ballsy Boys Studios. I glance at Bear frequently, wondering if it really is standard for him to have someone here when he does reviews or if he didn't want to be alone with me. Wanting Rebel to get his feet wet with managerial tasks like this makes sense, but there's something about the tense set of Bear's shoulders and the detached smile that hasn't left his lips that makes me wonder if there's more to it than that.

"Thanks, Pixie," Rebel says as he finishes jotting down notes on my response to his final question. "I think it goes without saying that you're doing fantastic here. The fans love you, the other guys all want to kidnap you and take you home with them, and you always come across as comfortable and natural on set."

He goes on to detail some of his plans on how to grow Ballsy Boys even bigger—new types of scenes, more social media presence, more appearances. I start to tune him out, smiling and nodding in all the appropriate places while I imagine climbing into Bear's lap and slowly pulling his shirt up to get another look at his strong, furry chest. I want to press my face between his pecs while he wraps his arms around me and holds me tight. I want him to want me as desperately as I want him. I want so fucking much.

"Oh shoot, I've gotta take this," Rebel says when his phone starts to ring. "I'll be right back." He gets up, answering his phone as he steps out of the office and closes the door behind him, leaving Bear and me all alone.

"So...you think I'm doing a good job?" I ask Bear.

"You're doing fantastic," he assures me, his smile even more tight now that we're alone, confirming my theory that he didn't want to be alone with me.

"I want to do a DP scene," I tell him, mostly to see his reaction. Bear's eyes go wide and then he frowns.

"I don't think that's a good idea."

"Why not? Didn't Heart's DP scene just get nominated for an award?"

"That's beside the point."

"I've never been DP'd before," I continue. "But I *love* being stretched so full I feel like I can't breathe for a second. I love the feeling of being split in two by a huge cock. Two cocks must be even better, right?"

He shifts in his seat and clears his throat. "I know you're pushing my buttons on purpose, and it's not going to work." He levels me with a look that makes me hot all over, full of authority and confidence.

"Why does it push your buttons?" I know I should quit while I'm ahead, but for some reason I'm feeling daring and bratty today. I'm getting sick of the back and forth between us, the hot looks that come right before he pushes me away, the flirting that always ends in him shutting down and then avoiding me for days. "I'm your employee, discussing a potential scene with you. How is it any different than Brewer walking in here and talking about setting up a three-way scene with Heart and Campy?"

"Pixie, I—"

"Sorry about that," Rebel says, bursting back into the room and making both Bear and me jump. "Anyway, do you have anything else you want to discuss, Pixie?"

"Nope, I'm good," I fake a smile, standing up quickly from my chair, my heart pounding. What was Bear going to say? I can only guess, because his expression is closed off again. "I can go?"

"Yeah, thanks for coming in to chat. We're working on a scene for you next week, so I'll text you the details later," Rebel says, waving as I hurry out of the room like my ass is on fire.

∽

Bear

I'VE BARELY HUNG up my leather jacket in the closet next to the entrance when Susan, the coordinator of Almost Home, the hospice where I volunteer at least twice a week, calls out to me. And if you've ever heard of a worse name for a hospice than Almost Home, I'd love to know, because I think it's horrific. Apparently, some woman who donated a shitload of money to the place years ago stipulated it should be called that for at least ten years, so they can't change it, but it's *bad*.

I stick my head around the door of Susan's office. "You called?"

"Yeah, so glad you're here. We have a new guest that I think could use your company."

It's clear there's more she wants to tell me, so I step into her office and close the door behind me. "Anything special I need to know?"

She gestures at the chair across from her desk, and I sit down, the old wood croaking under my weight. "His name is Travis, he's fifty-eight, single, and he's gay."

Okay, the last part somewhat explains why she thinks I would be a good fit for him, but something tells me there's more so I merely nod.

"He's HIV positive," Susan then says softly, and it all makes sense.

"Ah," I say. "I see."

"He's got lung cancer, inoperable. From what little I've learned, his family situation is complicated. He could use a friend, Maxwell."

I always mentally wince at hearing my legal name, but I can hardly go by Bear here, now can I? Not that Susan doesn't know what I do. I've been completely honest with her predecessors from the start, and I've volunteered here for close to ten years now. They know, but that doesn't mean I have to scream it from the rooftops.

"Okay, let me go see him. I wanna stop by Mrs. Gromley's room first, if that's okay."

Susan sends me a sad smile. "She passed away last night, very peacefully."

A soft wave of sadness rolls over me. After ten years, I've grown accustomed to death, but it's rarely a welcome visitor. "I'm glad to hear she went in peace," I say. "She was so scared of having a struggle at the end."

"She was, but she fell asleep and her heart simply stopped."

"Okay, let me check in with Travis."

Her smile is all gratitude. "He's in the garden room."

The garden room is my favorite room. If you see the view from the French doors in that room that open into the garden, you wouldn't believe we're in LA. It's colorful and pretty, even to an absolute ignoramus about gardens like me. I couldn't tell you what flowers it boasts if my life depended on it, but I do know that looking at it makes me happy, and I imagine it's the same for the people waiting to die. Nick, one of the volunteers, works in that garden every week to keep it looking pretty, and some days I swear he matters more than any of us.

I knock on the door of the garden room, which already has Travis's nameplate. A soft voice calls out, "Come on in," and I step inside.

Travis's face lights up when he sees me, and he pushes himself up in bed. "Well, that's a nice bonus I wasn't expecting. They sent in the gay brigade."

I grin. "I'm Maxwell."

I deliberately extend my hand, knowing how important that physical contact is. You'd think that people would know better by now about HIV not being contagious through skin-to-skin contact, but ignorance runs deep. So does prejudice.

Travis sends me a cheeky smile as he shakes my hand, his grip frail in my strong hand. "A handshake is a good place to start."

He's flirty and I love it. Everyone reacts differently to facing their mortality, but I respect the hell out of people who can keep a sense of humor.

"I never kiss on a first date," I say and watch his face light up with a big smile.

"That sounds promising," Travis says. "Apparently, there will be a second date."

"Only if you behave like a gentleman," I warn him.

His grin is infectious. "Somehow, I doubt I'm your type."

"What, you don't think I want a gentleman?" I play along.

"Nah, you like naughty boys. And my guess is you like them a lot younger than me."

I'm a little amazed at his remark. "Why do you figure that?"

He gestures at me. "You have *silver daddy* written all over you. Twinks must go crazy for you."

He's not far off the mark, and yet it frustrates me. I want to be attracted to someone my own age, or at least close. Why does my heart insist on latching onto boys I can't ever have? It's annoying as fuck, the way I can't move past my obsession for Pixie when he's all kinds of wrong for me. But this is not something I'm willing to discuss with a complete stranger, of course, and so I simply shrug.

His eyes narrow a little. "You know," he says, "this sounds like a horrible cliche, but you look familiar."

A gay man in his fifties. It doesn't take a genius to figure out what he knows me from. "Don't take this as an offense, but have you ever watched gay porn? What we would now call vintage?"

His eyes narrow farther, and he cocks his head, his gaze roaming my body as if looking for clues. Then I see the recognition dawn in his eyes. "You're Bear. The porn star, that's you. Man, you were something else back in the day. I think I still have some of your stuff on tape. Don't you own the Ballsy Boys now?"

I nod. "Former porn star, but yes, that's me."

"It's my favorite site," Travis says without any shame, and I love him for it. "I've had a subscription since you went live. That's some high-quality porn you produce. I love your boys, if you don't mind me saying so."

"I'm always happy to hear that," I say. "Mind if I grab a seat?"

Travis frowns. "No, but what are you even doing here?"

I pull the chair up close enough so I can sit right next to his bed and he doesn't have to strain to see me. "I'm a volunteer here. Been here for many years."

Travis blinks a few times. "I don't get it. You're alive, you must have a fantastic life. What the hell are you doing spending time with the dying?"

I gently take his hand and squeeze it. "Reminding myself how lucky I am. Making sure that on my watch, no one dies alone."

The tears in his eyes are not a surprise, not even after his seemingly carefree flirting. "You're not alone, Travis," I say softly. "If you'll permit me, I'll be with you till the end."

He keeps blinking until he gets the tears and his

breathing under control. "Yeah, I'd like that," he says, his voice rough. "Talk to me about your boys. Is Rebel's cock as impressive from up close as it looks on camera?"

I never talk about my boys outside of work, because I want to treat them with respect, both to their profession and to their privacy. But I can make an exception for a dying man, and I know Rebel won't mind.

"It's a thing of beauty," I tell him, my voice barely above a whisper. "Did you see his scene with Pixie, our new boy? We released it a few weeks ago. The way those two responded to each other, it was almost magical."

Travis grimaces. "I must've missed that one. I spent a lot of time in the hospital, not many opportunities to watch. And the Wi-Fi rules in here don't allow porn. That would've been a nice thing to watch before I die."

I grin. "I'm sure I can arrange a private viewing next time."

Travis squeezes my hand. "I like you already, Bear, sneaking in porn. You're my kind of man."

He sounds tired, and I watch his eyes flutter, recognizing his fight to stay awake. "Any man who recognizes quality gay porn is a friend of mine. Go to sleep, Travis. I'll stay for a bit."

He's asleep in seconds, and I stay for another hour, holding his hand even in his sleep, browsing on my phone with my other hand and catching up on news and gossip. He's not alone, and he won't be when he dies either.

And when I leave, I think of my Freddie and how I see him in every patient I meet here. It's not always easy, this work I do here, and it breaks my heart into a million pieces every time, but I'm keeping a promise I made to the man I loved twenty-six years ago, and how could I ever regret that?

8

PIXIE

I was shocked when Rebel told me I was invited to the Gay Porn Awards in New York City. I wasn't part of the scene that was nominated, but Rebel said I was part of the Ballsy team and they wanted me there to share the excitement.

It took me over a week to pack. There were just too many variables to narrow down my outfit choices, and expecting it all to fit into *one* checked bag is just plain cruel. I tried convincing the other guys to leave a little room in their suitcases for my hair care products, but they wouldn't go for it. Big meanies.

It's only the second time I've been on an airplane, the first being when I flew out to LA. I wiggle excitedly in my seat, leaning forward a little to make sure I'll be able to peek around Tank's large body to see out the window once we're in the air.

"Do you want the window seat?" Tank offers and I shake my head quickly.

"No, it's too scary, I like to see out but also have the

chance to *not* look out, if that makes sense?" I explain, and Tank snorts a laugh.

"All for the best, since I'd rather not be bumping elbows with Bear the whole flight."

I suck in a sharp breath. How did I not know Bear would be in the seat on my other side? Sure enough, once Rebel and the other guys are seated a few rows in front of us, Bear keeps moving past them and eases into the aisle seat beside me. In the confined space, our arms brush, and heat races through me. No matter how much I've tried to get over it, I still can't stop thinking about Bear as more than my boss. The hot and cold between us doesn't help. If anything, I think it keeps me even more interested. Maybe if we had the chance to fuck I could get it out of my system?

I look at Bear out of the corner of my eye and find an easy, relaxed smile on his lips. My heart beats faster and my stomach warms. *God, I want him so bad.*

A sigh escapes past my lips, and Bear turns his head to look at me with concern.

"Are you okay? Are you a nervous flier?"

The worry in his eyes makes my cock start to harden. I shift in my seat and nod my head in answer to his question.

"Yes you're okay, or yes you're a nervous flier?"

"I'm okay," I say, although I'm half tempted to pretend I'm terrified of flying just to see if he'll offer to hold my hand.

Once the plane starts moving, I consider changing my answer because I kind of forgot I *am* a tiny bit afraid of flying. I close my eyes and grip the arm rests as the plane takes off, the statistic popping into my mind that planes are most likely to crash during takeoff or landing. *Thanks, brain.*

I feel a warm touch on my arm and ease my eyes open to

see Bear's hand resting there, offering comfort. The simple touch makes my heart beat faster. In the months I've known Bear, I can tell he's the type who always takes care of people, especially his employees. Is that all this is?

"Thank you," I say quietly, putting a hand over his before closing my eyes again and focusing on thinking about *not* crashing.

Bear's hand stays in mine, warm and comforting, for nearly an hour until my fingers start to cramp from clutching him so tightly and I have to stretch them out. He gives me a small smile when I ease my hand out of his, and as soon as we break contact, I regret it. With his typical hot and cold routine with me, the chance to touch him seems like a fleeting thing that I doubt I'll get back anytime soon. Can I pretend to be scared again before the flight is over, or will that be too transparent?

It feels good to stretch my legs when we get off the plane, and I can only imagine how Bear and Tank are feeling after having their huge bodies crammed into such tiny seats for so long. Everyone's excited, talking loudly and joking around as we make our way to baggage claim. I spot my Gucci suitcase coming down the conveyor belt and pull it off, stumbling a little under the weight of it. I know we're only here for two days, but I needed to make sure I had plenty of outfits to choose from for the awards ceremony, not to mention my hair care products...

Bear snatches the heavy suitcase out of my hand without a word and then reaches for his own small bag as it passes by. He doesn't make a big deal out of the gesture, but to me it feels like a bomb just went off between us. The casual way he's taking care of me—holding my hand on the plane, carrying my bag—is doing nothing to curb my feelings for him. He would be such a good daddy, and it's making me ache all over with longing.

In the car on the way to the hotel, I look out the windows, craning my neck to see all the tall buildings. Rebel and the rest of the guys are talking about Rebel's man problems, and I'd love to give my two cents, but I'm too engrossed in the scenery to pay much attention to what they're saying.

I gasp when we pull up in front of a fancy hotel. It's *way* nicer than any hotel I've ever set foot in before, not that that's saying much. The floor is all shiny marble, and everyone inside looks like they probably don't have a credit card bill pinned backward on their refrigerator because they can't bear to look at it.

Once we're checked in, the guys start making plans for sightseeing and things tonight while I eagerly nod, happy to go along with what they decide to do.

"No excessive drinking tonight. It's a work day tomorrow, and I need you looking bright and sharp," Bear says, his firm tone sending a thrill through me.

We all nod, no one seeming shocked by the instruction. I'm sure this is old news for most of the guys. Aside from Campy and me, they've all been doing this for ages. I wonder about all the cool places they've gone and the places I might get the chance to go. I know it's not like a vacation since we're here to work, but it's still really cool.

"Who's rooming with who?" Campy asks, and I quickly dart a glance at Bear. Surely he'll room with Rebel since the two of them are so close? And they're both sort of the bosses now, so that would make sense.

"I'm not rooming with him," Tank and Brewer declare at the same time, pointing at each other.

Bear sighs and pinches the bridge of his nose. "The two of you need to grow the fuck up. This is getting really old."

"I'll room with Tank," Rebel offers quickly.

"I'll take Brewer," Campy says next.

My eyes go wide when I realize that just leaves me and Bear. My heart hammers, and I can feel my face heating, not with embarrassment but with excitement. This could be my chance to make something happen with Bear. I've seen the way he looks at me. He wants me too, I'm sure of it. It's not like I think he'll be my forever daddy or anything, but if we don't get this out of our systems, I'm worried we're both going to combust. A night of insanely hot sex might be exactly what we both need.

Bear shifts on his feet, an uncomfortable grimace crossing his face. Is it because he doesn't want to room with me, or because he wants it as badly as I do and he feels guilty about it?

"I can..." Rebel starts, and I have no doubt he's about to try and change the arrangements.

"It's fine. I don't mind," I cut him off before he can finish. This is my one shot to either get over my crush on my boss once and for all, or see if there might be something to it.

∼

Bear

I can't believe I ended up rooming with Pixie. After all the trouble I've gone through to distance myself from him, I end up sharing a damn hotel room with him. God, I've wanted to bash Tank and Brewer's heads together at least a hundred times before today, but right now, they're lucky I don't want to commit a felony while out of state, because I could fucking kill them for being such a pain in my ass. If not for that ridiculous feud between them, I could've roomed with Rebel and everything would've been fine.

"Is it really that horrific, rooming with me?" Pixie asks when we get into the elevator to our floor, his voice timid, and I realize I must've looked like I was about to blow a gasket. The others are on a different floor and took a different elevator. It's just him and me now, and my palms get a little sweaty at the thought.

"Of course not," I say quickly, my heart squeezing painfully when I spot the crestfallen look in his eyes. "It's...complicated."

Pixie's eyes narrow slightly. "Maybe you should try explaining it to me, because I'm getting a little tired of you not knowing whether to flirt with me or ignore me."

His words hurt, like an icicle stabbing my heart. Is that how he perceives it? *Well, isn't that what you're doing?* my conscience asks me. *How else could he interpret it when you've never taken the time to explain it to him?*

I wince. "I'm sorry," I tell him, meaning it. "I didn't mean to make you feel like I didn't want to share a room with you."

"But you don't," he says, studying me closely.

How do I talk myself out of this one? "It's—"

"Don't you dare tell me it's complicated," Pixie says with sudden fire. "Choosing the right skinny jeans that don't make you look like a midget when you're my size is complicated. Finding high-quality skin care without breaking the bank is complicated. Hell, leaving a hookup in the morning without entanglements is complicated. But telling someone you like them or not really isn't."

"God, Pixie, I *do* like you. How the hell could I not? You're... You're perfect," I blurt out, immediately feeling like a teenager trying to express interest to a crush.

I like you? What are we, back in high school?

The elevator dings to announce our floor, and Pixie stares at me with big eyes. Our eyes lock, and I have a hard time breathing. He's just so goddamn beautiful. Doesn't he understand that if I'm this close to him, there's no way I'll be able to restrain myself? Not when he looks at me with those big eyes, all needy and admiring. Just holding his hand on the plane was enough to make my insides roar with want.

Just before the doors close again, I block them with my hand. "This is our floor."

"Right," Pixie says and he walks out, looking over his shoulder twice.

We don't say another word until we've reached our room. I grind my teeth when I open the door and take in the size, or rather, the lack thereof. It's literally one queen bed with enough space on either side for a night table and that's it. We have one chair and a desk that would barely hold a laptop, and the bathroom is the size of a fucking bath towel. I know this is New York City, but would it fucking kill them to make rooms where you're not on top of each other?

I quickly dump my suitcase in the tiny closet and hold out a keycard to the room to Pixie. "Here. Don't lose it."

He looks at me questioningly. "Are you going somewhere?"

"Yes. I have...things I need to do. For the awards. I need to talk to some people," I say, almost cringing at how much I suck at lying. I'm pretty sure he can see right through my pathetic attempts, but he merely looks at me with a bit of sadness.

"Oh, okay."

"Don't venture out alone," I tell him, shooting him a look that I mean it. "The others wanted to go sightseeing, so go with them."

"Yes, Daddy."

We both freeze, and then our eyes meet, his as shocked as mine. It wasn't a joke, not something he said to tease me about sounding like his dad. This was out of reflex, something he's done before. Those words fell off his lips so easily because he's said them before...because it's habit.

"Pixie," I say, and my body moves toward him all on its own.

"Yes, Daddy?" he asks, his voice a mere breath, and everything inside me is screaming with how right this feels that he calls me that. It's the word I never realized how much I needed from him until he uttered it just now, and it floors me.

I stagger back as if drunk. Drunk on him, on his smell, his body, the innocence in his eyes. Drunk on the roaring need inside me to have him...and hold him. And I can't. I fucking can't.

"I gotta go," I manage, and then I'm out the door before he can say another word, which is good because I swear, if he'd asked me to stay, I wouldn't have been able to say no.

I walk around the hotel in a daze, not really seeing anything, until my phone starts ringing with a Facetime call from Travis. I'm missing my visit with him today because of this trip, so I told him to call me when he was awake.

"Hey, handsome," I tell him when I see his face appear, every time a little paler and more sunken than before.

He laughs. "You need glasses."

One of the things I've learned is that asking how someone is doing is senseless when they're in the final stages. They'll tell you if they want to talk about it, but Travis is someone who wants to focus on life, not talk about his decline.

"Actually, I do," I confess. "Reading has been getting harder and harder, man. I need me a pair of those glasses for old people."

That gets a chuckle out of him. "It's the beginning of the end, I'm telling you."

"Tell me about it. I'm hanging around all these young men and I feel like their fucking daddy at times."

Travis cocks his head. "Are you sure you weren't supposed to say *dad* there and not *daddy*?"

Oops.

"I…"

I close my mouth again, unable to come up with a single excuse or explanation.

"Bear, it's okay," Travis says, his voice understanding. "We don't have to talk about it if you don't want to."

I lower myself to the carpet in some empty hallway, leaning with my back against the wall. "Have you ever been attracted to someone you couldn't have?"

"Oh, Bear," he sighs, and his eyes grow sad. "It's the story of my life, man. My best friend, Ryan, he's straight as an arrow. Happily married, gorgeous wife, two wonderful kids who I am godparent to."

I don't know why, but my eyes well up. There's this longing in his voice that hits me deep. "You're in love with him," I say softly.

"All my life. I've had boyfriends and hookups and even one long-term relationship, but he's it for me. There's nothing I can do, you know?"

"Does he know?"

Travis shakes his head. "No. I'll never tell him, because I'm too scared of losing his friendship. Maybe if I'd had even the slightest bit of hope, but he's so in love with his wife, and Deanna is lovely and I would never hurt her like that. I've never even told anyone else," he says. "You're the first."

We share a sigh that sounds an awful lot like pining. "There's this boy," I say, and Travis merely listens. "I want to be his daddy something awful, even though I've never been in a relationship like that. But he makes me want to take care of him and protect him. He draws me in like a magnet, and he pushes all my buttons, but I can't do anything about it. He's cute and sweet and sexy and he makes me want to do things to him and with him...but I can't."

"He's not gay?" Travis asks.

I have to laugh at that question, because I'm not sure if I have the words to express just how gay Pixie is. "He is. Very much so."

It makes Travis laugh. "I didn't know you could be very much gay."

"Oh, trust me, there's gay and then there's Pixie."

Oops again.

"Pixie, huh?" Travis says. "Things are starting to make sense now."

"Why?" I ask, feeling myself get a little defensive.

"You wanting to be a daddy to that boy. From what you told me about him, he needs it, needs a daddy to keep him safe."

"It can't be me," I tell Travis.

He looks puzzled. "Because he works for you?"

"Yes, and because I'm old enough to be his father."

"But isn't that what you both want? The second part, I mean. The not messing around with an employee, I totally get. That shit can get dicey. But the age gap, who the fuck cares? He's old enough to make his own decisions, and if this is what he wants, why not?"

I shake my head. "It's complicated," I say, almost cringing at hearing myself use the same words I told Pixie.

"Maybe," Travis says. "But maybe you're making it far more complicated than it is."

9

PIXIE

Sightseeing with the guys is amazing. I feel a little bit like an over-the-top tourist, snapping pictures of everything, but I'm hardly the only one, so it's not so bad. Bear begged off coming with us, telling us all to go have fun and be back at a reasonable hour.

I can't stop going over our moment in the room when I accidentally called him Daddy. I had said it once before to him, but that had been in a more joking/flirting way. This was completely unintentional. After the way he'd held my hand and carried my bag and then gave me a stern talk about not going out alone and getting back to the hotel at a reasonable hour... It just slipped out, and fuck if it didn't feel right. The heat in his eyes when the word tumbled from my lips is what I can't get out of my head. He *liked* it.

We stop into a small pizzeria for dinner and order a pitcher of beer—gross—and a huge pizza to share.

"Having fun?" Rebel asks.

"Yes. I never thought I'd get to come to New York. This is so cool."

"The travel is definitely a cool perk of working for Ballsy," Campy agrees, pouring himself a glass of beer from the pitcher.

"Do you feel okay about rooming with Bear?" Rebel asks in a low voice once the other guys become engrossed in their own conversation. "Because if not, we can switch."

"Why would I feel uncomfortable?"

"He's your boss," Rebel points out. "And you're so new to Ballsy. I know a lot of porn studios have certain reputations, and I wouldn't want you to feel nervous or weird about being alone in a bedroom with the man who signs your paychecks," he explains, carefully choosing each word.

I huff out a little laugh. "I know Bear would never pressure me or expect me to do anything I don't want to do."

"Good," he says, giving me a relieved smile.

I dig into the pizza once the server delivers it, my mind back at the hotel with Bear. I'm sure Rebel's reassurance that Bear would never be inappropriate with an employee should discourage me from my plan, but if anything, it makes me want Bear more. It does make me wonder if I'll be wasting my time trying though.

The last thing I want is to make things awkward if he rejects me, but I can't not try. Now that the idea of trying to seduce him has come into my mind, I can't ignore it. I've never wanted anyone the way I want Bear.

By the time we decide to call it a night, it feels like we've walked everywhere in the entire city. I've also lost track of how many times Rebel has checked his phone, presumably hoping for a text from his boyfriend. But it seems one hasn't come. Poor guy.

"It must be difficult to have a relationship while doing porn," I say as we all get into the elevator back at the hotel.

Rebel gives a humorless laugh, shoving his phone roughly into his pocket. "It can be. But believe it or not, it was telling Troy that I'm moving *away* from acting and into behind-the-scenes work that freaked him out."

He tries to play it off casually, but it's obvious he's hurting over it.

"I'm sure he'll come around," I offer.

"Hopefully," he agrees.

The elevator dings, the doors opening on our floor. We all step off the elevator and head for our respective rooms. It's not until I'm standing in front of the door to my own room that it actually hits me that I'm sharing a room with Bear tonight.

Excited butterflies swarm in my stomach. Something tells me this is my one shot to see where the chemistry between Bear and I might lead. He's too professional to give in to the sparks between us at home, but in a different city, we can pretend it doesn't count afterward. It's now or never.

I take a deep breath and stick my key card into the slot, pushing the door open and stepping inside.

The sound of the shower running greets me, and excitement bubbles up in my chest. Starting out with him wet and naked should help. I'm going to take it as a good omen. I slip off my shoes and take a second to consider the best way to go about this. With some men, the direct approach would be best, but I get the feeling with Bear he'll like a little bit of flirtatious foreplay before he's going to be willing to give in to what we both want.

I've seen the way he watches me during scenes, how possessive he can get when he thinks the other guys are flirting too much off set or that someone might hurt me. He wants me—he just needs to know it's okay to want me.

I grab my suitcase and rummage through it until I find the baby blue Andrew Christian jock I packed...you know, just in case. It's one of my cardinal rules: never be caught in an emergency without a sexy pair of underwear.

Stripping out of my clothes, I slip on the jock just as the sound of the shower shuts off. Grabbing my phone, I climb onto the bed and position myself casually on my stomach with my irresistible ass on full display, and I open a game on my phone so I can pretend I just so happen to be lying here like this.

The bathroom door clicks open, steam and the scent of generic body wash trickling into the main room. I can hear Bear's heavy footfalls as they near and then stop, followed by a low, whispered curse.

I turn my head to see him with a towel around his waist, his hand clutching the knot as if he's afraid it's going to spontaneously slip open, or maybe battling the urge to drop it himself. Water droplets cling to his skin, his salt-and-pepper hair dark and slicked back. My cock hardens underneath me, and it's all I can do not to scramble over to him and lick each drop of water off his body one by one.

"I didn't know you'd gotten back," he says apologetically, his voice huskier than usual, his eyes glued to my ass.

"I don't mind," I assure him sweetly.

He tears his gaze away from my ass, meeting my eyes apologetically. "Sorry, I didn't mean—"

"Look all you want," I say somewhat breathlessly, heat thrumming in the pit of my stomach. I want to roll over and pull my cock out, stroke it in front of him until he covers me with his large body and makes me feel like his special boy like we both know he wants to. But I don't want to move too fast and spook him. I don't know how I know it, but I can tell gently coaxing him out is the best approach to get what we both want.

"I shouldn't."

"Says who?" I challenge. "If I like it, and you like it, then what's the harm?"

Bear frowns and then fixes me with a stern look that only makes me hotter. His fist tightens around the towel and his teeth bite into his bottom lip.

"The harm? Pixie, you're my employee, and you're half my age."

"Neither of those things sound like a problem to me." I roll over, stretching my arms over my head in a would-be casual way, putting my whole body on display for Bear, not bothering to hide my erection tenting the front of my jock. "I think about you during every scene I film, and I see the way you watch me. We both want this, so why are we fighting it? I may be young, but I'm more than capable of deciding who I want to have sex with."

"Pixie," he growls my name, running his free hand over his face and tilting his head back like he's praying for the strength to resist me.

"Please, Daddy Bear?"

∼

Bear

I should walk away. I should throw on the first clothes I can find and hightail it out of this room. I should...

Maybe if I give in just once, I can get him out of my system. But even as my legs find their way over to him all by themselves, I know I'm lying to myself. Once I have him, I'll never be able to let him go. I really should walk away, but I don't.

Instead, I take a deep breath. "Are you absolutely sure, baby boy? Is this what you want?"

The smile that breaks open his face is so pure and happy it destroys my last bit of resolve. Look at him, on full display on that bed, all his graceful lines, the smooth planes of his chest, those pretty pink nipples...that gorgeous cock still hidden behind that sinful jock. I want to make him soar.

"Oh, Pixie..." I sigh and then I stretch out on the bed next to him, delighted when he immediately presses himself against me. "My beautiful, beautiful little elf."

And the words fall off my lips as if they'd been waiting there all that time, waiting for him. "Do you want Daddy to make you feel good? Stretch that pretty little hole of yours wide open with my cock?"

Pixie moans, his eyes wide open as he ruts against me. "Please, Daddy Bear... I need you."

I'm gone. Those simple words break me, and I can't resist anymore. I pull him on top of me. "Let me taste that mouth I've been dreaming about."

Pixie is still moaning as our lips meet, then our tongues, neither of us patient enough to draw this out. My need for him is so big it thunders through my body, the towel slipping off my waist as Pixie starts to move his hips against me.

His skin is so soft, so perfect, like velvet under my fingertips, and I let my hands roam freely as I explore his mouth. He tastes sweet, like vanilla ice cream, and I almost smile. It's exactly how I imagined he'd taste. He can't stay still as my fingers follow the smooth dips of his body, moving against my hands, seeking more.

That sinful jock he's wearing gives me full access to his ass, and I can't deny myself a feel anymore. God, he's so perfect, so soft and hot against me, already spreading his legs as my fingertips dance up and down his warm skin.

"Daddy," he sighs into my mouth, the word filled with longing, and my heart melts even as my cock hardens. The word sounds so perfect, falling from his lips straight onto mine. It fills my heart, my mind, my body, this heady sensation of being his protector, his strong man, his Daddy.

How I wish I had the patience to go slow, to feast on him, but I don't. My need is too big, and judging by the way he's impatiently rutting against me, he feels the same way. But I can't skip tasting him. I need to know how his pretty cock feels in my mouth.

"You wanna take off that jock, baby boy, so Daddy can see you?" I ask, his blue eyes so trusting as he nods.

I roll us both on our sides. "Hold on, I need to grab supplies," I tell him.

The towel slides off the bed with me as I grab lube and a condom from my bag. I'd be lying if I said I wasn't hoping for a hookup, though I'd never imagined it would be with Pixie.

"You're so fucking sexy, Daddy Bear," Pixie says, and when I turn around and face the bed again, he's watching me with hungry eyes. His desire is so obvious, and it's a heady feeling. "Your cock is even more beautiful and perfect than Rebel's."

Okay, I have to admit, hearing that is one hell of a compliment, because we're literally talking about being compared favorably to an award-winning cock. Granted, they didn't have awards back when I did porn, but still. I doubt he could've said anything else that would've made me feel more like a man than he did with that simple remark.

"Thank you, but I'm not half as sexy as you. Now, strip for me, baby boy. I want to see you."

I've seen him naked plenty of times, but this is different.

This is for me, a private show without cameras and pretense.

I watch as he shimmies out of his underwear, his eyes never leaving mine, as if I'm all he sees. God, how I want that, to be the only one he sees. It's a thought I need to push down, because it makes no sense and it's impossible. Instead, I focus on the slapping sound his dick makes as it springs free, bobbing against his flesh. I position myself on the bed again, and my hand curls around it instantly. Pixie lets out a sigh, pushing into my touch.

"I'm not very big," he says, peering at me from between his lashes.

"You're perfect," I assure him. "Feel how you fit in my hand, like you were made for me. And you'll feel so good in my mouth as well." I trail my other hand down his chest, flicking his nipples. "Would you like that, my mouth around you?"

"Please, Daddy..."

I grab his neck and pull him in for another kiss, wanting to taste him one more time. When we come up for air, I roll on my back and say, "Sixty-nine me, baby boy. I'm gonna make you feel so good and get you ready for me."

He obeys instantly, straddling me and pushing his cock toward my mouth, his peachy-soft and plump ass hovering over my face. Ah, is there a more perfect view than this? He's not tall enough to reach my dick with his mouth at the same time, but I don't mind. Instead, he rubs his cheek against the coarse hairs on my lower abdomen.

"I love the way you feel against me," he whispers, and the contentment in his voice is genuine.

"Feed me your cock," I tell him, and he pushes himself up, shifting his body until he's found the right angle to sink it deep into my mouth. Perfection. My hands hold on to his ass as my mouth and throat embrace his dick, the salty, creamy taste of his precum more precious than whiskey. He doesn't thrust, allowing me to set the pace—as it should be.

I have to let go of his cock for a few seconds as I tear open a packet of lube, spreading it on my fingers, then gesture at him to sink back into my mouth again. And I have to say, with my mouth around his sweet cock and my fingers breaching his little pink hole, I'm in my happy place.

He can't stay still as I open him, pushing against my fingers, then correcting himself and shoving his dick deeper into my mouth. He can't choose which he loves more, but he won't have to. It only takes minutes for me to stretch him wide, his body responding to my every touch.

Just when I want to ask him if he's ready, he lets out a plaintive whine. "Please, Daddy... I need your cock."

I let go of his dick. "Let me put on a condom."

He waits impatiently as I roll it on. "You're gonna make me feel so full, Daddy, so good," his says, his voice breathy.

The thing is that he means it. You can tell the difference between someone trying to mimic a cheesy porn line and this boy who genuinely craves my cock. There's nothing cheesy or fake about the way his eyes latch on to me, the way his pupils widen as he licks his lips.

I could ask him how he wants me, but he's already rolling on his back, pulling his legs up and giving me full access. I crawl over to him, marveling in the contact between our bodies. A big wave of softness rolls over me at seeing him lie there so vulnerable and trusting.

"I'm gonna make you fly," I promise him.

He bites his lip when I position myself and then sink in slowly, allowing him to adjust. But he's got this, opening wide for me, a throaty sigh dancing from his lips as I push in deeper. "Daddy, Daddy..." he mumbles, his eyes rolling back a bit in his head. "Oh, so good."

Good is way too tame a word. Good doesn't adequately capture the amazing sensation of being inside him, of feeling him stretch around me, hugging my cock with his slick heat. It's everything I imagined, my body covering his much smaller frame as I fill him deep until I'm bottomed out, my balls nestling against his ass.

"Are you stretched wide, baby boy? Is this what you wanted?" I whisper near his ear.

All I get in return is another moan, and then his mouth seeks mine. My moves are slow and deep at first, only my hips moving as I find a pace that will allow me to stave off my orgasm for a bit. Pixie's eyes are closed as he latches on to me, his hands digging into my arms.

It doesn't take long until I can't kiss him again because I need my breath, need to move faster, harder, deeper. Pixie throws his head back and cants his hips more. My balls meet his sweaty skin, the sound of the slaps rolling through the room, joined by his moans and pleas, by my grunts and heavy breathing.

Then I need to close my eyes as well, the sensations too overwhelming. I grind my teeth as I dig deep to last longer, because I don't want this to end. If this is the only time we'll ever have, I need to make it last.

"You feel so good, Daddy..." Pixie says, his voice barely more than a hoarse whisper.

I open my eyes again, and he's got this dreamy expression on his face, this combination of lust and desperation. My hand circles his dick and he bucks into my hand, eager for more. He's deserved it, my sweet boy, so perfect for me, so pretty and needy.

My balls clench and I speed up, Pixie whimpering under

my onslaught. My strokes are hard now, slamming into him with harsh grunts, my muscles tensing up as they sense the impending release.

"Harder, Daddy," Pixie urges me, then lets out a moan. "Ohfuckohfuckohfuck, Daddy!"

He erupts in my hand, and I follow seconds later, my body shaking and spasming as I unload in the condom. My muscles can barely hold my weight, and I have to force myself not to sag down on top of him. God, I want to stay inside him forever, but instead, I pull out and get rid of the condom, then gather him close. He snuggles against me, that lithe body pliant and warm.

"Ten out of ten," Pixie says, his voice dreamy. "Would definitely bang again."

And I know that when I tell him this can never happen again, I'm gonna break his fucking heart.

I make sure I'm up before he is the next morning, avoiding the awkward morning-after scene. And the rest of the day keeps me plenty busy, so it doesn't look like I'm avoiding him on purpose, even though I am. I don't think he notices, though, not with the excitement over the awards and the party. Then Troy shows up, making a grand gesture for Rebel, and I couldn't be happier for them.

It's late when we get back to our room, and Pixie is so tired he's asleep before I'm out of the bathroom. The next morning, we have to hurry to make our plane, leaving no room for conversation. Besides, Pixie looks a little hungover and a whole lotta tired.

I make sure I'm sitting next to Tank and Campy on the plane, leaving Pixie to sit with Brewer. Until I've figured out a way to tell him it was a mistake without hurting him, keeping my distance is all I can do.

I know. I'm a fucking coward.

10

PIXIE

A week after we get back from New York, I'm filming my first scene since Bear and I had sex. Bear's eyes are on me as always, watching my every move as I ride Campy, crying out theatrically for the camera.

"Does that feel good? Are you going to come for me?" Campy asks. He's not usually one for dirty talk outside of what's strictly in the script, and his question makes me realize that we've probably gone on long enough. I was so lost in my thoughts about Bear I hardly noticed.

"Yeah," I moan, bouncing faster, keeping Bear in my line of sight, calling up memories of his cock filling me and his sexy words in my ear as Campy wraps a hand around my cock and jerks me off until I come with an over-the-top groan.

He follows quickly behind me, pulling out, removing the condom, and finishing on my stomach.

Bear yells *cut* and, as usual, a towel appears from one of the stage assistants. I climb off Campy and wipe myself up, hurrying to pull my underwear back on under the eyes of what feels like a million people.

"Pixie, mind a quick chat with me after you get cleaned up?" Bear asks. He sounds detached and impersonal, and I wonder if he's purposefully putting on an act, or if New York meant nothing to him.

"No problem," I say.

"Great, come to my office when you're ready." A little bit of warmth seeps into his tone at the very end, and I don't miss the way his eyes flicker over my mostly naked body before he disappears down the hall.

My stomach flutters excitedly. Maybe he *has* been thinking about what happened in New York as much as I have. It's kept me up at night thinking about him, trying to decide how he would feel if I texted him.

I've written out more than one text telling him I miss his cock, miss his arms around me, can't stop thinking about what happened in New York. But I've deleted every one without sending them. He's a man who knows what he wants, and if he wants me, I have no doubt that he'll let me know.

I knock on the door to his office and step inside when he calls out for me to come in. I haven't seen much of Bear since we got back to LA, and something tells me it's been on purpose. He didn't even come to dinner with all of us yesterday like he normally would when we go out for tacos and drinks.

His eyes are on me as I close the door behind me, and it's too easy to remember the way it felt when it was his hands instead. My cock starts to get hard at the memories of the best sex I've had in my life, and believe me, that's *really* saying something.

"You wanted me?" I ask in a suggestive tone, batting my eyelashes at him.

"Yes," Bear says, clearing his throat and gesturing to the chair in front of his desk. "It's a little last-minute, but there's an underwear brand that wants to have a few of you guys model for them. They asked for you specifically."

Okay, not exactly what I was expecting.

"What brand?" I ask. I'm not about to model for some cheap pair of underwear I wouldn't be caught dead in—it's called integrity.

"Beautiful Booty. The shoot is tomorrow morning. Like I said, it *is* last-minute, but they're offering generous compensation."

"Sure, why not," I agree. I own a few pairs and I like them well enough, plus an extra paycheck never hurts, that's for sure.

"Great. You'll be going with Campy and Brewer, so I'll have Brewer pick you up in the morning." His tone is dismissive, and disappointment crashes over me. Did he really *only* ask me in here about modeling for underwear?

"Sounds good," I say, standing up. Maybe he thinks *I* only wanted New York to be a one-time thing. After all, I made the first move before, He could be waiting for that again.

Gathering my courage, I come around the desk until I'm standing right next to Bear, the slight bulge in my tight jeans still there from the erection I got as soon as I walked into his office.

"Was that all, Daddy Bear?" I ask in the sexiest, most breathless voice I can manage. I couldn't make my intentions more clear if I unzipped my pants, and honestly that option isn't off the table either.

"Eli..." He looks up at me with a conflicted expression

before pushing back in his chair to put a little space between us. "I thought it was clear that what happened in New York wasn't going to happen again. It was a mistake."

His words are like a bucket of ice water being dumped over my head. *A mistake.*

Don't cry, don't cry, don't cry, I chant as I force a smile. I push away from his desk and turn to leave. When I reach the door, I stop with my trembling hand on the handle, my throat growing thick and tears burning in my eyes.

"It wasn't a mistake to me, Daddy Bear," I say, stepping out and closing it behind me before I can hear his response.

~

When my alarm goes off at the ass crack of dawn, I consider chucking it against the wall. I can already tell that my eyes are puffy from my crying jag last night, and the memory of what brought it on has me feeling emotional all over again, but I know that I need to put it aside this morning and put on a happy face for this photo shoot.

Bear's rejection aside, it's exciting that BB Underwear wanted to have Brewer, Campy, and me in their latest ad campaign. I can't help feeling pretty good about being asked for by name. The fact that I made their list even though I haven't been with Ballsy very long is amazing.

The extra paycheck I get from doing this modeling gig certainly won't hurt my current situation either, so all in all, I need to not fuck this up.

Dragging myself out of bed, I hop into the shower, trying my hardest to think only happy thoughts this morning. I've heard that if you think positive and happy thoughts, you can trick yourself into feeling happy. It's worth a shot, right?

I'm still in the process of toweling off when my phone rings from my bedroom. I sprint down the hall to pick it up.

"Hello?"

"Hey, Pix," Brewer says from the other end. "We're about ten minutes away from your place."

"Okay, I'll be ready," I assure him. Luckily, I picked out my clothes yesterday, so I don't have to take any time going through my closet and deciding what to wear. Obviously it wouldn't be what I'd wear on camera anyway, but I still think you should look nice showing up for a photo shoot.

Once I'm dressed, I hurry back to the bathroom to style my hair as quickly as possible. My eyes are puffy, like I feared, but I'm assuming they'll put some makeup on us before taking any pictures, so I'm not going to worry about it.

Brewer's car is just pulling up in front of my building as I step outside. I climb into the backseat as Campy mumbles a hello from the passenger seat and then yawns loudly.

"It's too fucking early," he complains, and Brewer and I both agree.

We're all quiet on the drive to the photo shoot location, my nerves starting to dance in my stomach. I know it's probably silly to be nervous about a modeling gig, considering I've literally had sex on camera, but I am anyway. I don't fake much in my scenes. Sure, I may moan a little louder than usual or play up certain things, but it's more of an exaggerated reality than anything. I have no clue how to *model*. All I keep picturing is the *Zoolander* face.

Brewer seems to sense my nerves after we park and tries to reassure me everything will go smoothly as we walk inside.

We're greeted by a young woman with a clipboard who manages to look both professional and frazzled at the same time. She introduces herself as Kendra, handing out the underwear for us to wear and pointing us toward makeup and changing rooms.

We all get changed first, and I have to admit the underwear are nice. They're high-quality jockstraps that look and feel fantastic. I take a second to admire how I look, letting it ease some of my nerves, before heading over and plopping myself down into one of the chairs in the makeup area.

"Hi, I'm Tyler." A pretty twinkish guy introduces himself as I sit down. His clothes are on point, nicely fitted, all the colors perfect for his complexion.

"I love your shirt. It's a Tom Ford, right?"

"Good eye," he praises. "I did the makeup for his show in Milan last year. It was amazeballs. Models take the clothing home afterward all the time, so after they had their pick, I snagged a few for myself," he says with a wink.

"Nice," I laugh. "I'm Pixie, by the way," I say, offering my hand.

"I know," he assures me, his eyes sparkling with amusement. "Ooo, child, your face is a hot mess this morning," he says, clearly unconcerned with sparing my feelings.

"Lucky for me I have a makeup artist this morning, then. I just hope you're good," I joke.

"I'm the best," he confirms with a wink, picking up a spongy thing that totally looks like a butt plug and dabbing it into some green stuff. "Close your eyes and let Tyler work his magic," he instructs.

I'm more than happy to do as he asks, closing my eyes and relaxing as he sets to work applying all sorts of cold creams around my eyes, humming happily to himself as he works.

Before long, he declares it done, and I open my eyes to see that he wasn't underselling himself. He really is the best.

You can't tell that my eyes were red and puffy just a few minutes earlier. I look fantastic.

"God, can I hire you to make me look this fabulous every day?"

"You couldn't afford me, baby," he jokes.

His lighthearted comment makes my stomach twist, hitting way too close to home with my current predicament. I force a smile and hop out of the chair, thanking him again and then making my way over to where Brewer and Campy are waiting.

Kendra tells us we're going one at a time, and Campy is going first. Brewer frowns, looking slightly put out, but rather than argue, he simply reaches for a towel to wrap around his shoulders, and I do the same.

I shiver a little as we sit down on the wooden bench outside the studio to wait.

While we wait, we talk about the recent scene Brewer filmed with Tank that was so popular it nearly crashed the site. He complains about how hard Tank gave it to him, but there's a sparkle of something in his eyes that makes me think he didn't mind it all that much.

I harrumph a bit about Bear not letting me do a scene with Tank and how he's refused to approve a DP scene for me either, and Brewer promises to talk to him about it. Brewer gives me a knowing smile while I complain about Bear that makes me wonder if some of the guys suspect what happened between us in New York.

The air conditioning is blowing directly on us and my ass starts to go numb from the hard bench, so I take the liberty of crawling onto Brewer's lap. One of the benefits of being tiny and cute is that most guys will let you get away with shit like that.

"I'm cold," I explain when Brewer gives me a surprised look.

Brewer wraps his arms around me to warm me up further, and I cuddle close to him. "It's okay, baby boy." He nuzzles my hair. "I never mind holding you."

I rest my cheek against his shoulder and relax into him. It feels nice to be held like this, in a platonic kind of way. It's funny how I can be nearly naked in Brewer's lap and feel absolutely nothing, but when Bear so much as looks at me, it's like my entire body is a livewire.

A mistake. The words echo in my mind again, making my heart sad. How can he think something so amazing was a mistake? It felt so right. Didn't he feel it too?

"Don't you ever wish you could fall in love with someone easy? Someone like me?" I ask, absently running my fingers up and down his bicep.

"Are you calling yourself easy?" he jokes.

I slap his chest, and we both laugh. "Not like that. I mean easy as in uncomplicated. You and me, we'd be easy together, you know? We'd have fun, share some great sex, enjoy life," I explain with a sense of longing in my chest. Loving Brewer as a friend is so effortless. It would be so nice if I could love him as more and have him love me back the same way. It would be like a pair of large, comfy sweatpants —clearly the most romantic way to imagine a relationship. Daddy Luke was definitely sweatpants. I loved him, but not real, true, deep love.

"What makes you think I couldn't fall in love with you?" Brewer asks.

I snort a laugh. "Please, don't even try. We both know I'm so not your type."

Brewer joins in my laugh, but his expression turns pensive for the next few minutes. I want to ask what he's thinking about but decide against it. Eventually, he kisses the side of my head and sighs.

"I wish you were," he says.

"Me too. But you can't make your heart feel something it doesn't, right? Or stop it from feeling what it does," I tell him. Would I choose not to feel the way I do for Bear if I could? Just thinking about the stubborn older man sends a thrill through me. As nice as it would be, maybe love shouldn't be like sweatpants. Maybe it should be more like skydiving.

We sit cuddled together until Campy eventually comes back through the doors, his face tight with anger, Kendra right behind him.

"It's Pixie's turn," she says, and I unfold myself from Brewer's lap and follow her into the studio.

There are big lights everywhere and a white screen thing where I'm supposed to stand to model.

The photographer introduces himself, giving me a smile that sends a chill through me. It's predatory and unsettling, making me want to turn around and walk right back out of this room rather than be left alone with him. But this is a job, so I paste on a friendly smile and extend a hand to him.

"Mmmm, aren't you a pretty little thing," he says, taking my hand to shake and holding it long beyond the polite amount of time. I have to practically yank it out of his grip to get it back, taking a big step away from him with my phony smile still firmly in place.

"I'm so happy to be here modeling for you today. I'm new at this, so you'll have to be gentle with me," I joke, my eyes darting to the door that Kendra has already disappeared through. Knowing Brewer and Campy are sitting just on the other side makes me feel slightly better. Campy was in here all alone with this guy, and he was fine, so I'm sure there's nothing to worry about.

"You were made to wear this underwear," the photographer says, his eyes roaming over my body like a physical touch, making me want to recoil. "They aren't sitting quite right though. Let me help adjust them so they'll look best in the photographs."

"That's okay, I can—" The protest doesn't make it all the way past my lips before he's crowding me, his hands on my hips, backing me against the wall and caging me in. My eyes go wide as one of his hands moves to my dick, cupping me through the underwear.

I should scream for Brewer. I should knee this guy in the balls. I should do *something*, but all I can do is stare at him in shock.

Before I can get myself together and do anything about the creep with his hands all over me, the doors fly open and Brewer comes storming in like some kind of avenging angel —beautiful and pissed as hell.

"Hey!" Brewer shouts. "Get your hands the fuck off him."

The photographer lets go of me, spinning around to face Brewer, and I sag against the wall.

"You fucking piece of shit, what the fuck do you think you're doing?" Brewer yells.

The photographer shrugs. "I had to position his dick right. No need to create such a drama."

I can see Brewer's fists balling, and I wonder if he's going to hit the guy. "Come on, baby boy, get dressed," he says to me instead. "We're leaving."

Brewer holds his hand out to me, and I take it, hurrying behind him as we storm out of the room, the photographer shouting vaguely threatening things as we go.

We dress in a hurry, and more words are said between

Brewer and Kendra, but I don't pay much attention to any of them, just wanting to get the hell out of here.

It's not until we're on our way back to the car that it hits me. "We're not going to get paid now, are we?"

Campy's eyebrows go up, no doubt surprised *that's* my first concern.

"Probably not, Pix," Brewer says. "But don't worry, I'm going to explain what happened to Bear, and he won't be mad at us."

I cringe. *Great.* If I thought Bear was overprotective of me already, I can only imagine how he's going to be now.

11

BEAR

I can't explain why, but I wasn't happy with that photo shoot to begin with. It sounds crazy coming from a guy who owns a porn studio, but there are some shady photographers in this city. I ran into my fair share back when I was a model, and sadly, things haven't improved that much since. And this underwear brand, BB, they're not that well-known yet. They can't afford top photographers who won't risk their reputation by doing something funny.

So when Campy calls while they should still be at that shoot, my stomach drops. "What happened?" I ask, because I *know* he's not calling with good news.

"There's been an incident with the photographer," Campy says, and my blood runs cold.

"Define *incident*. Is Pixie okay?"

Campy should jump at me for only thinking about Pixie and not him and Brewer, but he doesn't. "He's shaken up but okay. The guy was a total creep. He grabbed my ass a few times, supposedly to put me in the right position. Then when it was Pixie's turn... He was alone with him for maybe two minutes when we rushed back in."

He's trying to reassure me, but he's not telling me what I need to know. "Cameron, what did he fucking *do*?"

I can hear Campy swallow. "He had his hand on Pixie's dick. I think he might've gone further if we hadn't come in."

I let out a stream of colorful curses that has Joey's head shooting up in surprise. "I'm gonna fucking kill him," I rage. "Who the fuck does he think he is, touching my boy like that?"

"Technically, he's not..." Campy starts, then stops talking again. Smart man.

"This will not stand. Just because he's in porn doesn't mean his body is available to every creep who wants him. I'm gonna beat the living crap out of him, that abusive motherfucker."

Campy sighs. "Don't do anything stupid, boss. That's all I'm saying."

"He deserves to get the shit beaten out of him," I sputter. "Someone should make it clear he can't treat people like this."

"We did," Campy says, staying remarkably cool as he bears the force of my temper. "We got him out of there and we walked out. He's okay, boss. *We're* all okay."

I wince as it hits me that I never even asked about him. My only concern was Pixie. "I'm sorry," I say, feeling so powerless. "I should've asked about you. I'm just..."

I make a helpless gesture that Campy can't see, of course, but he seems to understand what I can't even put into words. "I get it, boss. It's fine. Maybe cool off first, okay? You can't run a porn studio from prison, just saying."

When I end the call, my heart rate has dropped a little, but I'm still seething.

"What happened?" Joey asks, but I hold up my hand as I stalk to my office. I can't talk about this now because I'll get into a rage all over again. Campy was right. I need to take some time to cool off before I do something I regret. As good as it would feel to bash this fucker's head in, he has a point that I'd probably go to jail for that, considering it would be premeditated and all that by now.

I manage to close my office door with considerable restraint and then plop down on my desk chair. My Pixie, my sweet baby boy. He must've been so scared. All I want to do is call him and make sure he's okay, but I can't, not without revealing way more than I can afford to. I wouldn't be able to pretend when I hear his voice, wouldn't be able to keep the distance we both so desperately need.

I've tried so hard to forget about the amazing night we shared in New York. It was everything I had imagined and then some, and the memories of the perfect way we fit together keep playing in my mind at night.

And I know it was a mistake on some level, because he's still my employee even if the age difference wasn't an issue to me, but it was a shitty thing to say to him. That hurt him, and the way he told me it wasn't a mistake for him hit me hard. He still wants me, maybe even more than before, and I hate hurting him.

It's getting harder and harder to convince myself I'm doing the right thing, that I have his best interests at heart. Because I do. It wouldn't be fair to him if we started seeing each other, because we both know it could never be casual. We'd be all in, and I can't do that to him, because at some point, I'd have to break things off and hurt him even worse. Either that, or he'd have to go through what I went through, and I refuse to do that.

I'm still debating calling him when my phone rings again, but it's the hospice. I brace myself. "Hey Maxwell,"

Viola, one of the nurses, says. "Travis asked if you could stop by today."

I frown. He's been doing remarkably well for someone who was given less than two months to live. We're long since past that, and he's still hanging on. "Did something happen?"

"The doctor wanted to talk to him, and his friend Ryan was supposed to be here, but he can't come because of something at work, I think?"

You'd think a man could prioritize his dying friend, I think, but maybe I'm being too harsh here. "Sure, I can be there for him. Any specific time?"

"As long as you're here before five, you're good."

I check my watch and mentally run through my schedule for the day. "Would it be okay if I stopped by now? I have some stuff I need to do later today, but I'm available now. It will take me about half an hour to get there."

"That would be perfect. Thanks, Maxwell."

Yeah, spending some time with Travis is definitely a better idea than getting arrested for assault.

I make it in twenty-five minutes thanks to a surprising lack of traffic, just finishing a call Rebel to catch him up on what happened at the photo shoot when I pull up to the tiny private parking lot. Rebel is upset, but he makes some good points, reaffirming my decision to make him my right-hand man. And I'm so happy he and Troy have worked out their issues, because he's a different man. Lighter, happier.

So is Travis when he spots me, his eyes lighting up when I step into the room. Viola already noticed me coming in and said she'd ask the doc to stop by. Travis hugs me a little longer than usual. He's nervous, I guess, and so I reach for his hand, giving him the choice to take it, which he does, sending me a grateful look.

"Ryan had something come up at work," Travis says. "He was supposed to be here, but his colleague's kid got sick or something and he had to take his place in a presentation."

Sick kid trumps dying friend? I think not, but I don't say anything. It's not my place. "I'm happy to be here," I say, and much to my own surprise, I mean it.

"You looked a bit angry when you came in," Travis says. He's observant, that one. No wonder, since I found out he's a social worker who works in a juvenile detention facility. He's gotta be one tough cookie to do a job like that.

"Issues at work," I say dismissively.

"You mean issues with Pixie."

I shoot him an annoyed look. "Not everything is about Pixie."

He gently shakes his head. "I hate to break it to you, my friend, but there's only one person who's capable of eliciting such strong emotions in you."

A frustrated sigh forces itself from my lungs. "He got harassed during a photo shoot. This asshole touched him without his permission."

For a second, I'm worried Travis will make light of it, but his face darkens. "That is not okay. I'm so sorry. Is he all right?"

"I think so."

"What do you mean, you think so? You didn't talk to him?"

"God, Travis, I can't. Even hearing his voice would kill me. Knowing that he's hurting, it's..."

Travis lets go of my hand, his face uncharacteristically tight as he turns toward me. "Bear, you have to call him, talk to him. You need to make sure he's okay."

His words pile on the deep sense of guilt I'm already

experiencing for not contacting him. "You don't understand," I tell Travis.

Just then, Viola sticks her head around the corner. "I'm sorry, but Dr. McDonell will be a bit later. There's a resident who needs him."

"Thank you," I tell her. That's life for you in a hospice—the dying take priority over those still living, even if they're hanging on by a thread.

"So help me understand," Travis says, his voice soft but serious. "You keep telling me it's complicated, but what's the issue? It can't be just that he works for you."

I sag a little in my chair, my head spinning with the struggle of whether to tell him or not. If anyone can understand, it's this man, who's dying way too young himself.

"I grew up with a pair of hippies as parents," I start. "True flower power generation who were completely cool when I came out as gay when I was eleven. They gave me and my two brothers full freedom, sexually as well. I connected with a group of gay men through a guy who volunteered at our local youth center. They were all older than me, but I loved hanging out with them. They treated me as equal, you know? They were like a second family to me, even though my own family was nothing but loving and accepting. Then the AIDS epidemic hit..."

"Oh god," Travis whispers, and it isn't till then that I remember he's HIV-positive. Our talks have been focused on his lung cancer, which he attributes to an old two-pack-a-day habit that he finally kicked to the curb a few years back.

"I'm sorry," I say, shocked at my own insensitivity. "I wasn't thinking..."

"No," Travis says, gripping my arm with more strength than I would've thought him capable of. "We need to remember. We lost a whole generation of gay men, my generation. I lost so many friends. There were weeks when I had a funeral each weekend, each one with fewer people saying goodbye."

"I was just a teenager," I say, my throat aching with the memory of it. "And one by one, my friends got sick. They'd die alone, their families abandoning them out of fear of getting infected."

Travis wipes away a tear. "Yeah," he says, and that one word speaks volumes.

"Freddie was a cousin of one of my friends who died, and when we met, it was love at first sight. I'd just turned eighteen, and we fell hard for each other, even though he was fourteen years older than me. He was funny and kind and this big softie, and he was my everything. My parents and brothers loved him, and I thought we'd be together forever."

Travis takes my hand now, squeezing it gently. "He got sick."

"He never thought to get tested because he hadn't been that promiscuous, as he told me. He must've been positive for a while, because he was monogamous when we were together, but he just never had symptoms. But when it hit..."

"How long did he last?"

I swallow because my throat feels too tight. "Not even six months. I took care of him till the end, because his family abandoned him. I held his hand when he died. God, I had to fight like hell to even get him buried because the first five funeral companies I called wouldn't even take him. They were scared they'd get AIDS from even being close to his body."

"Oh Bear," Travis says, his voice filled with pain. "That's a heavy load to carry for an eighteen-year-old."

"I loved him...and I sat by his bed for weeks, watching

him die. I can't do that to Pixie, Travis. I can't. I barely came back from that experience, and I refuse to put him through the same."

"Wait," Travis says. "I'm confused. Are you sick?"

I frown, not following his line of thought. "No. Why do you ask?"

"Then who's talking about dying?"

"I'm over twenty years older than he is. We both know that statistically, I'll die before him. I don't want him to have to go through what I had to. He's not strong enough for that."

"Bullshit," Travis says with such force that he explodes into a coughing fit. All I can do is watch helplessly and hold out his oxygen mask to him, which he takes with shaking hands. It takes minutes before he's calmed down again.

"Let's forget about this," I say.

"Let's not," Travis counters.

"You shouldn't waste your energy on—"

"You know what your problem is, Bear?" Travis says, his voice soft but decisive. "I really like you, man, but you need to stop making decisions for everyone else. You can't decide for me what I'm willing to spend my last time here on earth on, and you can't decide for young Pixie whether or not he's willing to run the risk of you dying before him. You need to let people make their own decisions."

The look on his face softens as he holds on to my hand once more. "I get that losing Freddie was a traumatic experience for you and that it may have changed you forever in irreversible ways. You want to spare everyone else that hurt... But you can't. People die, Bear, and you have no control over that. You could die at the ripe old age of a hundred or be taken next year by a drunk driver. Who the fuck knows? I wasn't counting on dying this young, and yet here we are."

My head and my heart both hurt from the force of his words. They're like stabs to my core, this soft voice that slices through my heart like it's soft butter. But he's not done yet, and his parting shot stays with me even after the doctor finally shows up to tell us that he can't explain it medically, but that Travis is in a holding pattern. He's not deteriorating and not getting better, just circling in a holding pattern, the doctor says.

I ponder Travis's final words to me as I sit in my car, which steers its way over to Pixie's apartment all by itself. "You're so fixated on the possibility of dying, Bear, that you're forgetting to live."

12

PIXIE

I'm not sure I could be more pouty if I tried. With nowhere to be today, I never bothered to get out of my pajamas. After the rejection Bear dealt me, followed by that skeevy photographer the next morning, I think I've earned a day of crying while watching rom-coms and eating junk food.

I shouldn't be surprised about the Bear situation, and I guess I'm not really. I knew when I made the plan to seduce him that he didn't like to date employees, but I went for it anyway. It hurts like hell that it didn't mean more to him, but I can't bring myself to agree that it was a mistake.

My phone pings on the coffee table, and I pick it up to see a few messages on Grindr. I sigh and ignore them without looking. Stupid Bear and his stupid magical cock that I can't stop thinking about. Men like Bear should come with a warning: *will ruin you for other men, proceed with caution*.

Who the fuck am I kidding? I would've punched right through that warning sign and jumped into bed with him anyway. I wish there was someone I could talk to about all this. For once, it's not about not having friends, because Rebel, Brewer, and the rest of the guys *are* my friends, but know better than to tell them what happened in New York. And since I don't know anyone else in LA, my options are extremely limited.

Without thinking, I find myself picking my phone back up and typing out a text.

Pixie: Hey
Luke: Hey sweetie, how's it going?
Pixie: Meh

Right on cue, my phone starts to ring.

"Hi," I answer.

"What's wrong, baby?" Luke asks without skipping a beat. His concern warms me, but not in the way it used to. I like knowing there's someone who cares about me and worries about my wellbeing, but it doesn't make me want to cuddle up to him or kiss him anymore.

"I think I might've done something stupid," I admit.

"Tell me what happened," he prompts, and I can hear the shuffling sound of him making himself comfortable on the other end of the phone.

"There's this man..." I confess with a sigh. I'm sure there's nothing Luke can say to make any of this better, but maybe getting it off my chest will make me feel less alone.

"A potential new daddy?"

"I want him to be, but he doesn't want me."

Luke snorts a laugh. "Is he blind or just stupid?"

I giggle. "He's...um, he's kind of my boss."

"Oh Eli," he sighs, and I can picture him shaking his head at me. "Does he know how you feel?"

I tell him about New York and about the subsequent

rejection, leaving out the other drama that occurred, because if he knew about that I'm sure he'd be on the next plane out to LA to drag me back to Illinois.

"I hate to say this, baby, but he might've only wanted one thing from you," he says carefully.

"He's not like that," I argue. "He's a good man. Everyone says so, and I've seen it with my own eyes. He doesn't use people." I may be slightly more defensive than I need to be, but I can't stand anyone thinking Bear is a user or a creep.

"If you're sure he wasn't using you, then maybe he likes you more than he wants to admit. You can be a bit of a whirlwind, and not everyone is ready for that. He might need time to adjust to his feelings for you."

My heart beats a little faster this time. Maybe Luke is just telling me what I want to hear, but I *so* want him to be right.

"So, what do I do? Do I leave him alone or keep flirting until I break him down?"

Luke chuckles. "Without knowing him, it's hard for me to say, but I'd say don't give up on him just yet."

"Thank you. I really needed to hear that."

"No problem. Now, I hate to rush off the phone, but I have a date to get ready for."

"A date?" I smile to myself, glad to hear Luke isn't all by himself, still thinking about me.

"He's the sweetest boy you've ever seen, I think he might be someone special to me."

"I'm really happy to hear that. He's lucky to have you."

"Thanks, Eli. Take care."

"You too."

I hang up and lie back on the couch, thinking about what Luke said. I'm not going to give up on Bear. I just need to think about my strategy a little bit.

Before I can start plotting anything, my buzzer sounds.

Bear

I never let Pixie know I was coming, so I'm not even sure he'll be home. But when I ring the doorbell, my brain still fighting with itself over what I'm even going to say, Pixie is quick to open the door. He clearly wasn't expecting visitors, judging by his outfit—a pair of cute pajamas that make me want to reconsider the whole idea of *just talking*. Coming here was such a bad idea, but I can't back down now.

"Bear, what are you doing here?" he asks.

What *am* I doing here? God, I wish I knew. "Can I come in?" I ask.

He opens the door wide. "Sure."

There is an awkward shuffle as he closes the door behind me, both of us trying to keep our distance from each other. "Can I get you something to drink?" he asks, and he sounds like a stranger, some random hookup. This isn't what I want between us, but the problem is that I don't know what I *do* want.

"Are you okay?" I ask him. When he looks at me questioningly, I add, "I heard about what happened with the photographer."

His face tightens. "I'm fine."

It's not just that he's lying to me. It's that he's so bad at it. "You're not fine," I say softly.

I reach for his hand, but he pulls away, and I can't deny it hurts. It's what I wanted, what I asked him to do, and yet now that he honors my request, I feel bereft.

"No," he says. "I'm not. But it's really not your problem, is it?"

A spark of anger flares up inside me. "Of course it's my problem, not in the least because I'm your boss. This happened on my watch, on a shoot I sent you to. If that doesn't make it my problem, I don't know what does."

Pixie lets out a long sigh, then trots into the living room and nestles on the couch. I suspect that's where he was before, as there's a comfy-looking, baby-blue blanket he pulls over himself again, snuggling deep into the couch. I follow him and find a spot on the loveseat across from him.

"I'm shaken up," Pixie says after a moment of silence. "I wasn't expecting it, and I'll be forever grateful that Campy and Brewer were suspicious and stepped in. I don't know what would've happened if they hadn't."

I send him a soft smile, carefully keeping the anger from my voice. He can never, ever think this is his fault. "May be best not to dwell on that."

After a brief hesitation, he nods. "That's what I keep telling myself, but my brain is being a total bitch and trying to imagine worst-case scenarios for me. But anyway, I'm okay. I appreciate you checking in on me."

I hate the distance between us, the walls that he's throwing up. Or maybe they're my walls, and he's merely respecting them. I have no right to be upset about this, to be frustrated by the abyss that seems to separate us now, and yet here I am. I'm still struggling with what to say when Pixie says, "Are *you* okay?"

I frown. "Why wouldn't I be?"

Pixie's face softens, losing the polite, distant look. "You look a bit sad, like something's bothering you."

And as I look into his gorgeous eyes and see the genuine

concern there, I realize I have to be honest with him. "There's a reason why I can't start anything with you."

He leans back on the couch again, as if wanting to create more distance between us. "I know. You told me. I'm your employee, and you think I'm too young."

"There's more," I say with a deep sigh.

Travis's words play in the back of my head. Is he right, that I stopped living after Freddie died? It doesn't feel like it, even though I haven't had a serious relationship since. I've had boyfriends, just not any that lasted longer than a few months, maybe a year at most. But that's easy to explain, what with me being in porn first and then so focused on building Ballsy Boys from the ground up.

So maybe it's time to actively start looking for someone. But it can't be Pixie. I can't rob him of this innocence, this joy he has. My past is too heavy for him, too depressing. I would drag him down, no doubt.

Pixie waits patiently for me to speak again, his expression open. "When I was barely eighteen, I got into a relationship with an older man. His name was Freddie, and he was my everything. We were very much in love, and despite how young I was, I thought that he and I would be together forever."

"What happened?" Pixie whispers, his eyes never leaving mine.

What happened? It's the question of the century, isn't it? We never found out who he contracted the virus from. He did try to track down all his previous partners, but it wasn't easy. And when he got too sick, we stopped wasting energy and instead, focused on spending what little time we had left together.

"He died," I say. "He got HIV and it developed into AIDS.

It was a different time, before the meds were as effective as they are now."

Pixie's eyes fill with sadness. "How old was he when he died?"

Too young, I want to say. Way, way too young, like so many of our friends. It was such a horrible time for the gay community, so many men ripped from the prime of their lives by this unknown, deadly disease that spared no one.

"Thirty-three," I say. "He died within months of discovering he had the virus."

Before I realize his intention, Pixie rolls off the couch and scrambles onto my lap, hugging me tightly and pressing his soft cheek against mine. "Oh Bear, I'm so sorry," he whispers into my ear, and even though the words are nothing special, the genuine sorrow in his tone caresses my heart.

"Thank you," I say, breathing in his smell. How is it possible that he fits so perfectly in my arms, in my heart? How can fate be so cruel to give me this perfect boy that I can't have?

"But what does this have to do with me?" Pixie asks carefully. He leans back to meet my eyes. Then his expression changes into something alarming. "Are you telling me you're HIV-positive?"

I quickly shake my head. "No. Even though we were in a committed relationship, we always used condoms. Freddie insisted on it, and in hindsight, that probably saved my life. And ever since, I've not had sex once without condoms. No, I am fine."

Relief on his face is followed by more puzzlement. "Then I don't understand what this has to do with us."

"Watching him die was the single most horrific thing of my life. Dying of AIDS, it's a slow and torturous death that leaves you with no dignity. Everything is stripped away from you, including the support from family, even friends," I try to explain. "I don't want that for you, Pixie. With the age difference between us, statistically, I will die long before you, and I can't put you through that. Knowing that I almost couldn't bear it, how could I inflict that same sorrow upon you?"

Pixie's eyes fill with tears, and his bottom lip trembles a little as he speaks. "I don't like to think about you dying," he says, his voice all choked up. "You're not that old, Bear. We could have a long, happy life together before any of that even happens. And you're not gonna die like that."

I think of Travis, lying in his hospital bed, losing a battle with cancer he never had a chance of winning. He's right that I can't stop living out of fear of dying, but he's wrong about Pixie. He's not strong enough to survive that. He needs someone in his life who will be there for him to protect him and take care of him. Not someone who will leave him alone, grieving and forever changed by that loss.

I kiss Pixie on his head. "I envy your youthful optimism and naivete, baby boy," I say. "Sadly, life has taught me it rarely works out that well. I would love to be with you, because I think you're perfect, but I can't. It would forever hang over my head like a dark shadow, this deep fear of crushing your happy spirit by getting sick or dying. Even my past is almost too harsh to share with you. I don't want to rob you of your happiness and joy."

Pixie slides off my lap. "You can't protect me from everything. No one can. Haven't you ever watched *Finding Nemo*?"

I must look like an idiot, trying to figure out that reference. "Yes, I have seen that movie, but I have absolutely no idea what you're talking about."

Pixie puts his hands on his hips, and oh my god, he looks fierce. "Marlin, the dad. You know, the clownfish? He made this promise that he would never ever let anything happen to Nemo because his mom died, and he was scared that Nemo would die as well," Pixie patiently explains, but I still don't get it. "Remember what Dory says when Marlin tells her he made that promise? She said something like, if nothing ever happens to him, nothing would ever happen to him. You can't protect me or anyone else from bad things happening, because then nothing would ever happen to us. It's part of life, isn't it, the negative experiences? You don't get to experience the highs without taking the lows as well."

I open my mouth, but then close it again because I have absolutely no idea how to refute this.

"Also, I may want a daddy, Bear, but that doesn't mean I can't make my own decisions. You deciding for me what I'm strong enough for or capable of, that's a little insulting, if you ask me. I'll respect your wishes, but I think your reasons are bullshit, and you're just scared, just like Marlin was scared."

I blink a few times as it sinks in that I just got schooled on the philosophy of life by a little elf, young enough to be my son, using a Disney movie. Clearly, I am not quite as accomplished at adulting as I thought.

13

PIXIE

I'm not sure if my life could be any more tragic. Okay, maybe that's a *little* dramatic, but I'm still feeling down about Bear taking the time to come all the way over to my apartment last week to tell me yet again that we could never be together, right when I'd started to think I might be able to convince him otherwise.

And now, here I am after a day of team building for all the Ballsy Boys—how much closer you can get to someone than taking their dick up your ass, I'm not sure—standing in the hallway of my apartment building staring at the eviction notice pinned to my door. I thought I paid my rent this month. After the last time I was late, the landlord told me I'd be evicted, so I set a reminder in my phone so I'd be sure to pay.

I pull my phone out of my pocket and open my calendar. Sure enough, there's a reminder on the first of the month to pay my rent, and it's snoozed.

"Fuck," I mutter to myself, banging my head against the door just under the notice. I remember now. I didn't have *quite* enough to cover it on the first, so I snoozed the reminder so I could pay on the second after we got our paychecks. Annnnnnd then I forgot. "Fuck, fuck, fuck."

I look at the note again. It says I have thirty days to vacate the premises.

I tear the paper off the door and step inside, a hopeless pit opening up in my stomach. I don't have enough money saved for another security deposit or moving costs. Everything in LA is *so* expensive, and even though my Ballsy Boys paychecks are big, they seem to fly out the window as soon as I get them.

And now I'm going to be homeless.

I slide down the door and put my face in my hands. I would give *anything* for a daddy right now to make everything all better. A big, strong man to scoop me up in his arms and tell me everything is going to be okay. Maybe that makes me pathetic or a terrible adult. Fine, I'm both of those things.

The urge to call Luke and beg him to let me come home is nearly overwhelming. It would be so easy to get on a plane back to Illinois, move back into Luke's house, and let him be my daddy again. It would be so much easier than anything has been since getting to California. But Luke isn't the one I want, not really. I don't love him, not like a boy should love his daddy. Luke is a good friend, and he introduced me to the things I like, but we both knew it wasn't going to be forever.

When the tears start to fall, I'm not entirely sure if they're because I'm going to be homeless or because Bear doesn't want me. Probably both, but once they start flowing, I'm powerless to stop them. I cry into my hands until my eyes are sore and my nose is so runny I can hardly breathe. It's a full-on ugly cry, nothing cute or pretty about it whatsoever.

I'm not sure how long I sit there wallowing in self-pity, but eventually it's too pathetic to let go on any longer. I drag myself up and head to the bathroom to wash my face. While I'm cleaning myself up, the thought of going out to a club tonight flits through my mind. I don't want to be lonely right now; I want to be taken care of, even if it's only for tonight.

With my mind made up, I hop into the shower to wash the day off me and then get myself ready to go out—perfect hair, hot as fuck clothes, no shadow of my misery showing in my eyes. When I'm ready to go, I look so hot even I'd fuck me.

I decide on Vibe. I did an appearance there not too long ago with Tank chaperoning me, and it was a fun night. And there were even men there who were more my type, rather than the largely twenty-something crowd at Bottoms Up.

The Uber drops me off in front of Vibe, and the bouncer recognizes me from the last time I was here, waving me in immediately so I don't have to wait in line. I feel like a celebrity.

As soon as I'm inside, I head straight for the bar to get a drink and get catcalls and greetings from even more people. Clearly, there are a lot of regulars at Vibe who remember me from last time.

Multiple men buy me drinks and flirt, effectively helping me forget my problems under the flashing club lights and pounding bass. I get a few offers for bathroom blowjobs, which I kindly decline. I lose track of how many drinks are bought for me, but when I stand up from the bar stool to head out onto the dance floor, I wobble on my feet, a stranger's hand steadying me before I can fall.

I weave my way into the massive crowd of sweaty bodies on the dance floor, receiving enthusiastic greetings and being groped at every turn. I couldn't begin to guess how many hands grab my dick or my ass through my jeans; points for creativity to whoever tweaks my nipple through my shirt. Maybe being objectified like this should bother me, and if I was more sober or less lonely, it might. But right now, the attention feels better than a hundred orgasms all at once. These people might not even know me, but they fucking love me.

I move my body to the music, getting lost in the pounding bass and flashing lights of the club, all the bodies writhing around me like waves in the ocean. Damn I'm philosophical when I'm drunk.

My eyes fall on a man dancing less than a foot away. He looks like he's in his forties, broad shoulders and a few gray hairs making him look stupid hot. He's wearing a nice, black button-up shirt and designer jeans that hug his legs and ass perfectly. I always love a man with style. I dance closer to him, tilting my head and batting my eyelashes at him. Our bodies meet, and I smile when I feel his substantial bulge press against my stomach.

His smile is nice as his arms surround me and we find the rhythm of the music together.

I get up on my tiptoes to whisper in his ear, pressing my hands to his firm chest and getting hard from the feeling of his strong arms wrapped around me. It feels so fucking good to be held like this.

"You're the hottest guy in this whole club," I whisper to him, grazing my teeth against his earlobe and feeling the vibration of his laughter in his chest.

"You're quite a flatterer, aren't you?"

"Just calling it like I see it."

His cock gets harder against me as we dance and flirt, laughing and grinding against each other shamelessly. It would be easy and fun to let this man take me home and make me feel special and loved. He has kind eyes. I bet he would help me forget about Bear for a few hours, maybe even longer. But as soon as I think the name Bear, going home with anyone else feels every kind of wrong.

"Are you okay?" the man asks, probably noticing my sudden shift in mood.

"I'm not feeling so well." It's not a lie. My stomach is churning and my head is starting to spin.

"Do you want to go sit down or step outside where it's more quiet?" he offers, a look of genuine concern in his eyes.

"Thanks, but you stay and dance. I'll be okay."

The ground beneath my feet feels a little like the tilt-a-whirl by the time I make it outside. Maybe I should've actually kept track of how many drinks I had.

"Fuck," I mutter to myself, sagging against the rough brick side of the building. I need to call for a ride, but my legs are a bit too unsteady under me, so I slide down onto the ground, my back still against the building.

"You okay?" someone asks, and I nod, swallowing the bile that rises in my throat at the movement.

"Need to call an Uber," I mutter.

"Don't call an Uber when you're this drunk. You might get a creepy driver. You should call someone you know."

Huh, good point. I pull out my phone and dial the first person who comes to mind.

"Pixie? It's late. Is everything okay?" Bear asks as soon as he answers.

"Mm-hmm, went dancing."

"Sounds like there was more drinking than dancing. Where are you?"

"Vibe."

"Okay, stay right where you are. I'm coming to get you to take you home."

"Thanks, Daddy Bear," I mumble, and I hear him sigh on the other end of the phone before hanging up.

"Goddammit." Bear's growl snaps me awake, and I blink a few times, trying to focus my surroundings and figure out where I am.

"Daddy Bear," I say happily, pushing to my feet unsteadily.

"This is a nightmare I'm having, right? You're not really asleep on the sidewalk outside of a club, right?" he grumbles, putting an arm around my waist to help me, and I let myself sag into him.

"We should go in and dance," I suggest, swaying a little against him to the faint sound of music coming from inside the club.

"I'm taking you home, and possibly looking into putting a tracking device on you so I'll know if you're doing something dangerous like this again."

"Aw, you worry about me," I tease, grabbing a fistful of the front of his shirt and tilting my head to look up at him. The concern in his eyes warms me all over, and that's not just the alcohol talking.

"Of course I worry about you. Come on."

He leads me to his car, his arm around me the entire time, and then helps me into the passenger seat. He leans in, his mouth-watering scent filling my nose as he buckles my seatbelt for me before closing the door and going around to the driver's side.

"If you're going to be sick, tell me so I can pull over," he says, and I nod my head.

"Are you mad at me?" I ask.

Bear sighs and doesn't respond at first. I lean over and press my forehead against the glass of the window, watching as the city passes us by.

"You scared me when I found you sleeping on the sidewalk like that. Anyone could've done anything to you."

"I didn't mean to fall asleep."

"Please don't go out by yourself like that again."

"Okay, Daddy Bear," I agree, closing my eyes again.

When we pull up in front of my building, a new wave of loneliness washes over me at the thought of going up to my bed all alone. I unbuckle my seatbelt and turn toward Bear, who's gripping the steering wheel and not looking at me.

"There was a man I thought about going home with tonight," I tell him, and his jaw ticks. "But then I thought of you, and I couldn't do it."

"Eli..." He says my name like it's a prayer and a curse at the same time. He releases his grip on the steering wheel and looks over at me, his eyes full of wanting, his self-control clearly hanging on by a thread.

Alcohol and neediness make me bold, and I lean across the center console to press my mouth to his. Bear's lips mold around mine, his rough stubble scratching my skin as I dart my tongue out to lick at his seam. He moans, a deep rumble that vibrates against my mouth as his hand finds the back of my head, his fingers grabbing onto my hair to tilt my head back and deepen the kiss. His tongue licks deep into my mouth, tasting and claiming me all at once. I pant and whimper, wrapping my arms around his neck, desperate to get closer to him.

When he pulls back from the kiss, I nearly cry, wanting to chase his lips but being held in place by his hand still pulling my hair.

"Go up to bed, Pixie," he says with an air of finality in his voice.

"Daddy," I complain.

Bear kisses the tip of my nose and then releases my hair.

"Good night," he says again, and it's obvious there's no arguing with him.

I climb out of his car and shuffle to my building while he waits and watches. When I get up to my apartment, I turn on the light in my living room and go look out the window. His car is still sitting there. I put my hand to my lips, still able to feel the intense kiss lingering there.

After another minute, he drives away, and I watch until his car disappears before stripping out of my clothes and falling into bed with thoughts of Bear to keep me company.

14

BEAR

I'm worried about Pixie. I can't put my finger on it, but something is wrong. He's distant, not his flirty, bubbly self. Almost moody, and that's so not Pixie.

The whole gang has gathered at the studio on a Saturday for a photo shoot. We like to update the pictures on the site from time to time, and we'd planned this shoot for months, making sure everyone could be here. And everyone includes not just the boys who I consider the heart of Ballsy Boys, but all our regulars. Some boys do a shoot a month, others a shoot every quarter, but they're all part of our extended family.

Jody, the photographer, is a friend of mine, and she's set up in the main room of the studio, making the last adjustments to her lighting. She's using Brewer as a model, who's his usual self, flirting and goofing around. He doesn't give a flying fuck that he's naked with close to fifty people around him. Then again, there's little that fazes him, with the exception of Tank, maybe, who's watching him with hungry eyes from his position against a wall. You could power up an entire city with the electricity between those two.

But Pixie isn't frolicking around as I had expected. Granted, he's always a little more shy when he's on set, but I barely recognize the withdrawn, quiet boy who's perched on a sofa and not interacting with anyone. What's wrong with him?

As Jody starts her shoot with Brewer, I keep a half eye on Pixie. Did something happen to him? My mind goes to that night a week ago when I picked him up from that club, completely wasted. I shouldn't have kissed him. It was stupid, and I regretted it immediately, but it was so hard to resist him when he looked at me like that. He was so needy, so desperate for my attention, my...guidance.

God, that boy needs a daddy something fierce, and my heart makes this painful thud in my chest as I realize once again it can't be me. That voice is getting weaker though, every time it pipes up. I don't know how much longer I can fight this overwhelming need to take care of him.

"Boss, is everything okay with Pixie?" Rebel asks me, his voice soft.

I spin around to face him. "Why would you ask me?" I snap at him.

He holds his hands up in mock surrender. "Because you're our boss and you make it a point to know what's going on in our lives?" he says, and the sarcasm is strong with this one.

I let out a sigh. "Sorry. Bad mood."

"Yeah, no shit," Rebel murmurs. "But seriously, what's wrong with him?"

"I don't know."

Rebel looks at me funny. "You don't know," he repeats. "Have you tried your usual approach?"

"What's that?" I ask, fighting to not snap at him again.

Sexual frustration does not become me, that much is

clear. Maybe I need to score myself another hookup. I haven't gotten laid since New York and that was... And we're back at Pixie again. Damn my one-track mind.

Though in all fairness, it's not just sexual frustration. I wish it were, because cold as it sounds, that's a relatively easy fix. You just fuck it out of your system. No, this obsession with Pixie is much more. Yes, I want him, but for so much more than just sex. I want to take care of him, make sure he'll never fall asleep drunk on a sidewalk again, spank his cute little butt when he's naughty, pamper him... There's so much I want to do to him.

"Bear, you still with me?" Rebel asks.

I let out a sigh that seems to originate in the deepest parts of my soul. "Yeah. What did you say my usual approach was?"

Rebel gives me an exasperated look. "Talk to him? You know, like you always do with us when you see something is wrong?"

I jam my hands in the pockets of my jeans, barely able to look Rebel in the eye. "Can't you talk to him? You two get along, right?"

"Sure, but technically, I'm not his boss. Why won't you talk to him?"

There's speculation in his eyes, and I know there have been rumors about me and Pixie since New York. These guys aren't stupid. Sex is what they do for a living, and they recognize sexual tension a mile away.

"I can't," I say, hoping he'll understand. "I need to keep my distance."

Rebel studies me for a few seconds with narrowed eyes. Then his face relaxes, and he shrugs. "Sure, I'll sit with him for a bit and chat, see what I can find out. If I do, do you want me to tell you?"

"Of course," I say with more force than intended, and I can't blame Rebel for rolling his eyes at me like a pro.

"Whatever you want, boss," he says. Yeah, like I said, the sarcasm is strong.

Rebel doesn't make it obvious, bless him, but works the room for a bit, chatting with various people before sitting down on the couch next to Pixie. I try not to watch them too much, but my worry over Pixie eases a bit when I see the two of them talking for a while.

Then Jody asks me to look at some pictures to make sure I'm happy, and I have to focus on that. Time flies as we get great shots of all the boys, and finally, it's Pixie's turn. He sends me a shy smile as he steps in front of the camera, and my heart does that crazy fluttering thing in my chest it always does when he's around.

I almost wish I could say I'm worried about arrhythmia, but I'm not that stupid. I know damn well what the problem is, and it's standing right there in all his perfect, magnificent, sparkly glory. He's not completely back to his flirty self, but he's chatting with Jody, and when she starts calling out suggestions for poses, he responds to every one.

My urge to walk away is strong, but I stay, determined to act like everything is okay and like it doesn't pain me to see him. It's this mix of desire and dread, like seeing something you really want but knowing you shouldn't because it's bad for you. Or in this case, bad for him.

"He says he's fine," Rebel speaks up softly near my ear.

"He's not," I say.

"I know, but when I asked what was wrong, he said he just hasn't been sleeping well."

I turn my head to look at Pixie again. "He does look paler than usual. Maybe he's sick?" The thought alone makes it hard to swallow.

"I don't think he is. He's worried about something, but he won't tell me what. Maybe you should try to talk to him. You have a way of making us say shit we think we want to keep to ourselves."

I face Rebel. "I do?"

Rebel laughs. "You have this quiet authority that makes people want to obey you. Well, me at least, and I'm about as vanilla as it gets when it comes to shit like that. But seeing as how you know stuff about all of us, I figure I'm not the only one. You'd make a great daddy."

It's like a stab to my heart, that last line. As much as I want to deny it, I can't. That, at least, has become more and more clear to me. The daddy instincts in me are strong. I just need to find someone closer to my own age who's into that stuff. And more than anything, I need to stay the hell away from Pixie, because if he keeps flirting with me like he does, I won't be able to hold out for much longer.

"Not to him," I say, putting every ounce of finality in my voice I can muster. "He'll have to find someone else."

Rebel doesn't say anything, but the sigh he lets out speaks volumes.

∼

Pixie

I'M NOT GOING to cry, I tell myself firmly even as I feel tears burning my eyes, my throat aching, and my bottom lip starting to quiver. Rebel's front door opens, and a sob escapes my chest in spite of how hard I'm fighting it.

"Pixie, what's wrong?" he asks, putting an arm around

my shoulder and leading me inside while I quickly wipe the tears from my cheeks and command myself to stop crying. "Did something happen? Did someone hurt you?"

"No, nothing like that," I assure him. "I'm sorry, I know you asked what was wrong before and I lied and said everything was fine. Now everything's falling apart and I didn't know who to go to and I should've figured something out sooner but it was so overwhelming and I feel so stupid."

"Pix, calm down, take a deep breath," Rebel says, and his boyfriend Troy appears in the hallway looking concerned as well.

"You want some weed? It might help you chill," Troy offers.

"No thanks, pot makes me really horny, and that's the last thing I need right now," I say, and then because I can't help it, I add, "That shirt is really boxy on you. Something more formfitting would make you look a lot hotter. Also, that orange color washes you out. You need earth tones."

Troy looks down at his shirt with a frown, and Rebel seems to be fighting a laugh.

"How about some water instead?" Rebel suggests, and I nod, following him into the living room and sitting down on the couch while Troy goes to get me water and Rebel rubs a comforting hand up and down my arm.

"I got kicked out of my apartment," I manage to explain without breaking into more tears.

"What happened?"

"I kind of, um, forgot to pay my rent." I don't think I could feel like more of a child if I tried. I can't even manage the most basic adulting possible and, if I'm being honest, I don't *want* to. I miss having a daddy to worry about these things for me. I miss someone taking care of me.

"They can't kick you out for paying your rent late once," Troy says, returning with a glass of water and handing it to me.

"It was more than once. The renter guy said if it happened again, he was going to evict me, and then it happened again."

"Okay, this isn't that bad," Rebel assures me. "How long do you have before you have to be out? It should be thirty days I think, right?"

"It was, but that was twenty-nine days ago," I admit miserably.

"Oh, Pix," Rebel sighs. "I wish you would've said something sooner."

"I'm sorry, I just didn't want to think about it. I kept hoping if I didn't think too much about it, eventually it would go away. But now I have to be out tomorrow and I have no place to go. I'm going to end up living under a bridge."

"You're not going to live under a bridge," he assures me. "We're going to go to your place and help you pack up your stuff, and then you'll stay here until we figure things out."

"You don't have to do that," I argue weakly, even though it's exactly what I was hoping Rebel would say when I showed up at his door.

"It's no trouble," Troy assures me.

Both of them put their shoes on, and before I know it, we're climbing into Rebel's car.

"How much stuff do you have? Do we need to stop and rent a storage unit or a moving truck? Do I need to call the other guys for a hand?"

"I don't have a lot. The apartment came furnished, so it's pretty much just my clothes and personal items."

We swing by Target to get some bins, and Rebel decides we should call the other guys because his car won't be able to fit more than two bins in the trunk once they're full of my stuff.

"I don't want Bear to know," I plead as he pulls out his phone to make the first call.

"Why not?"

Because I don't want him to be disappointed in me. Because if he doesn't want to take care of me, I don't want him to feel bad for me. Because it's fucking embarrassing enough as it is.

"I just don't. Please?"

"All right, I'll call everyone *except* Bear."

He manages to get everyone else to agree to meet at my place *and* not mention it to Bear.

When we get back to my apartment, all the guys are waiting on the sidewalk outside my building. I can't decide if I'm touched they all showed up or completely mortified at the reason for it.

"Hey, thanks for coming," I say to them as we get out of Rebel's car, carrying all the empty totes we got.

"No problem. Any reason it was so impromptu?" Brewer asks while I unlock the door that lead us up to my apartment.

My face heats, and I'm sure I'm blushing every shade of red imaginable.

"I'm an idiot," I admit. "I got evicted."

"You're not an idiot, Pixie. This was your first time living on your own, right?" Campy asks.

"Yeah."

"It can take some getting used to, making sure you know when to pay your bills, budgeting, all that stuff," Tank assures me, and I start to feel a little better that they don't all think I'm the stupidest person alive.

"Tank and I will start in the kitchen," Brewer offers while Campy takes the bathroom and Rebel, Troy, and I hit my bedroom.

Troy pulls open the top drawer of my dresser to start packing it up and grins. "Very nice collection."

Rebel joins him, looking over his shoulder. "Impressive," he agrees.

"Yes, I have a lot of sex toys. I don't think that's exactly shocking."

"Not shocking, just interesting," Troy says. "Are they safe to touch?"

I roll my eyes. "They're all clean. I wash them thoroughly after each use. I'm not an animal."

While they pack up my dresser, I start pulling clothes out of my closet and folding them neatly. *Oh my god, everything is going to get so wrinkly being stored in plastic bins for god knows how long.*

Packing everything up goes more quickly than I expected, and I think I *really* underestimated the amount of clothes I own because there seems to be way more full containers than I anticipated. I wonder if all this is even going to fit in Rebel and Troy's apartment while I try to figure out getting my own place again.

When all the guys start carrying my stuff down to their cars, Brewer pulls me aside and hands me the Mastercard bill I forgot was still on my refrigerator.

"It's probably none of my business, but if you ever need help making a budget or anything, I've gotten pretty good at making my money stretch."

Hot embarrassment washes over me again as I take the bill from him and fold it up to shove in my pocket.

"Thanks," I mutter.

We head back to Rebel and Troy's place with my stuff, and the guys make quick work of bringing everything inside and stacking it all in Troy's office.

I thank them all, and when Brewer assures me *it's what friends are for*, I nearly burst into tears on the spot.

I stand in the doorway of Troy's office, looking at all my things in buckets, taking up almost all the free space in the room, and I feel terrible for invading their home like this.

"It's going to be fine," Rebel assures me again when he sees me on the brink of more waterworks.

"Come on, let's find a movie and relax," Troy suggests, putting an arm over my shoulders and leading me into their living room.

I plop down on the far end of the couch, and they take up the rest. Rebel picks a movie while Troy rolls a joint, lighting it and sticking it between his lips. I've never really been a big pot smoker, but right now, it sounds like a great way to escape my miserable life.

"Can I have some?" I ask, and Troy readily passes it over, along with his lighter.

I take one toke and start to cough as the smoke burns my throat and makes my eyes water. Rebel pats me on the back until I stop coughing and takes the joint out of my hand to give back to his boyfriend.

"That's probably enough for him."

"It's not my strong stuff. He'll be fine," Troy promises.

With only one hit, I don't feel super loopy, but my body does settle into a warm, relaxed place. The movie plays, and I barely pay any attention to it, my mind instead going to its favorite place—Bear.

It's been a month since I kissed him in his car, and if I thought he was avoiding me after New York, it was nothing compared to this. He hasn't been on set for any of my scenes, he's missed every group get-together, and he hasn't held any team-building activities. If I didn't catch occasional glimpses of him around the studio, I'd think he skipped town.

Maybe it's the tiny bit of weed in my system, or maybe it's that I'm super bummed about what happened with my apartment, but I pull out my phone and type out a text.

Pixie: I'm sorry I kissed you. If I promise not to do it again, will you stop ignoring me?

It shows as read right away, and the little dots pop up to show he's typing back before disappearing, reappearing, disappearing again. I hold back a frustrated sigh, and eventually a response appears.

Bear: I'm not ignoring you
Pixie: I'm not stupid
Bear: I know you're not stupid
Bear: Fine, I was avoiding you a LITTLE. I'm sorry.
Pixie: I wish you wouldn't. I miss you
Bear: You can't miss me, I'm your boss
Pixie: But I do anyway
Bear: What am I going to do with you, Pixie?
Pixie: Do you want actual suggestions, because I can probably come up with a few ;)
Bear: Tell you what. I'll stop avoiding you if you promise not to flirt

. . .

I sigh, making a face at his offer before typing a response.

Pixie: No deal

15

BEAR

There's something deeply satisfying about watching Tank ravish Brewer's ass, besides the obvious. I have to admit, I thought Rebel was absolutely out of his fucking mind when he paired those two up. But damn, that initial scene was so fucking explosive, and the idea he came up with for the rest was nothing short of brilliant.

The dynamics between them have changed though. There are still fireworks, but it feels different. It's softer now, with a level of tenderness that wasn't there before. Tank brushing Brewer's hair off his forehead, Brewer's hand that caresses Tank's biceps rather than merely hanging on for dear life, the slow kisses... They're in love. Not fake in love, but the real thing. And for some reason, despite the fact they wanted to kill each other mere months ago, it makes total sense.

What doesn't make sense, however, is the way Rebel is avoiding me. We're both observing this shoot, and he's as far away from me as possible. After I noticed, I even discreetly sniffed my pits, wanting to make sure I wasn't radiating garlic or something. But I'm not, and yet he's avoiding me, not even meeting my eyes when I try to make eye contact.

As if that in itself wouldn't be cause for alarm, Brewer is even worse. Tank usually ignores me, because that's how he rolls, but Brewer is known to be chatty on scene. Today, Brewer has this permanent look of guilt whenever he looks at me in between shooting. And Brewer never feels guilty about anything, so that tells me all I need to know.

They're hiding something from me, and they suck at it, and it doesn't take a genius to figure out it has something to do with Pixie. I *knew* something was wrong with him. I've known it since that shoot three weeks ago, and I'm pissed at myself for actually keeping my distance from him this time. I haven't been ignoring him exactly, but I've certainly not gone out of my way to talk to him either. It's just too damn hard, because every time I see him, I want to do so much more than talk.

As soon as the scene is done, I corner Rebel, who looks at me as if he's a deer and I'm the hunter. He's not far off. "What's going on?" I ask, skipping the niceties.

"I don't know what—" he starts, then stops when my eyes narrow and a low grumble originates from my chest.

"Don't," I say. "Don't even try to lie to me. What the fuck is going on? Is Pixie okay?"

"How did you know it was Pixie?" he asks.

I cross my arms. "Because you and Brewer suck at pretending and lying, and there's no reason why you'd hide anything from me, unless someone specifically asked you to...and the only one who has reason to do that is Pixie. And I asked you to talk to him weeks ago and find out what was bothering him...and to report back to me. Now, start talking."

"I promised him I wouldn't say anything," Rebel says sheepishly, and I know I've got him.

"Whatever I need to say to put enough pressure on you to cave, consider that said," I say. "That way, you can tell him I made you tell me."

He scoffs. "I'm not that much of a coward."

"Rebel..." My voice takes on a growl as I'm seconds away from losing my patience. My stomach weighs a ton as my mind considers what could possibly be wrong with Pixie.

He jams his hands into the pockets of his shorts. "He got evicted from his apartment."

"What?"

"He missed rent a few times, apparently, and they kicked him out."

I have to take a breath before I can say anything, my heart rate jumping through the roof. "He's homeless?"

Rebel shoots me a look. "Of course he's not homeless. We took him in, me and Troy."

I picture the apartment Rebel lives in and how stuffed it was even before Troy moved in. I can't imagine what it must look like now, with Pixie's stuff added. "That's not sustainable for long."

"Yeah, no kidding. Do you have any idea how many clothes that kid owns?"

"But..." I try to wrap my head around it. "I don't understand. We pay him well, and he's gotten a few bonuses since his scenes did so well."

Rebel's face softens. "Did you see where he lives? I think he needs more help in figuring out his finances."

Come to think of it, I *did* wonder how he could afford that, but I figured he'd get a roommate or something. Or that he had money saved up. Dammit, I should've checked in on him, should've made sure he knew what he was doing.

LA is an expensive city to live in, and I knew he wasn't accustomed to it. I failed him again.

"I'll sit down with him," I tell Rebel. "Explain some things to him about the costs of living."

Rebel hesitates, but then says, "I think he needs more help than that. We found some other unpaid bills as well that point toward him racking up debt. He's drowning, Bear. He doesn't just need a lifeline; he needs someone who'll teach him how to swim."

I hold up my hands, almost automatically taking a step back at his suggestive tone. "That's not gonna be me. He's my employee, and I wanna make sure he's okay, but that's where my responsibility ends."

"You're awfully concerned and invested for someone who's merely looking out for an employee," Rebel points out.

"You may wanna stay out of it," I say with a dark look in his direction, but this time, Rebel isn't so easily intimidated.

He raises himself to his full height, and a look of determination fills his eyes. "I get that this is your personal life," he starts.

"Damn right it is," I growl, and god help me, I sound like Tank.

Rebel holds up a hand, and much to my own surprise, I find myself respecting it. "He's my friend, Bear, and he's vulnerable. You didn't see how crushed he was, having to admit he needed our help. And I heard him on the phone with someone, a friend of his named Luke, and he was crying. I only heard one end of the conversation, but it sounded like Luke was asking him to move back home."

I open my mouth to say something along the lines of hell, no, he's not going anywhere, but Rebel isn't done yet.

"And this weird dance between you two? It's not helping.

He likes you, and you may have reasons why you're keeping your distance, and I respect that, but he needs you. He needs someone to help him. God, Bear, he's one bad decision away from disaster, and I need you to promise me you're either gonna step in and fix this or back off and let someone else step in. You can't refuse to help him and then get mad when others do."

My cheeks grow hot at his words, because he's so right it's not even funny. And then he leaves me with his parting shot.

"Make up your mind: are you in or out?"

∽

Pixie

THE TEXT BEAR sent me was ominous to say the least. All it said was *come down to Ballsy, we need to talk*. Is he firing me? *He can't be firing me. I haven't done anything wrong and the fans love me*, I reassure myself as I pull open the outside door and step inside.

"Hey, Pixie, you're not filming today, are you?" Joey asks when he spots me.

"Nope, just here to talk to the big boss man," I say as casually as I can manage. *I'm totally not getting fired. It's going to be fine.*

I hear the distant sound of Tank and Brewer arguing, otherwise known as foreplay for those two ever since they started dating. When I reach Bear's office door, I chew my bottom lip, clenching and unclenching my shaking hands a few times before working up the courage to knock.

"Come in," Bear calls.

I step inside to find Bear sitting behind his large desk with a frown on his face, looking as sexy as he always does. I want to kiss the unhappy expression off his lips and then sink to my knees between his legs to take his thick cock into my mouth. I could be such a good boy for him. I could make him so happy. God, even when I'm about to get fired, all I can think about is sex with my Daddy Bear.

"You wanted to talk to me?" I say stupidly, but in my defense I have *no* clue how to act right now and whether I'm in trouble or blowing things out of proportion. *Annnnnd now I'm thinking about blowing again, dammit.*

"I should spank your ass is what I should do," Bear threatens, and my cock perks up, my eyes going wide at his statement.

"Okay," I agree breathlessly.

"I didn't mean it like that," he corrects himself, and I deflate, sinking into the chair in front of his desk.

"Tease," I grumble.

"You should've told me you were having trouble with your living situation."

Shame washes over me, and I sink down in the chair, wishing I could disappear through the floor. I can't believe one of the guys told him.

"It's fine. Rebel is helping me out for now, and I'll be back in my own place soon. I'm fine, I can handle this." I lie my ass off instead of crawling across the desk and begging him to take care of me.

"Rebel and Troy live in a shoebox."

"It's a little tight, but I'm going to be out of their hair as soon as possible."

Bear levels me with an assessing look. I can see the wheels turning behind his eyes. It seems like he's at war with himself for several tense seconds as the muscle in his jaw twitches and his frown deepens.

"I have a guest room. You're going to come stay with me," he says with an air of finality. He's not asking, that much is crystal clear. I'm torn between wanting to throw myself at him and thank him, and telling him where to shove his guest room. It's been hard enough to suffer his repeated rejections when I could go home to my own apartment to lick my wounds—what will it be like to live with him? Will I have to see him bring other boys home to play with?

"I don't—"

"It's not up for discussion." He cuts me off, and fuck me if his firm tone doesn't make me hard as steel. "You can stay with me as long as you need to, and I'm going to look over your finances to set up a budget for you."

"Okay." I'm back to breathless and agreeable.

"I'll send a couple of guys over to load up your things from Rebel's and bring them to my place."

"Thank you," I say quietly, sitting forward on the edge of my seat. Taking a chance, I reach across the desk to touch his hand—large and strong under my delicate one.

He tenses and pulls back. "I'm sorry, but it doesn't change anything else."

"Right." I pull my hand back and force a smile as I absorb yet another rejection from him. "Well, I guess I'd better get back to Rebel's to get everything together. I'll see you tonight."

Getting up, I turn toward the door and stride out of his office with my head held high and a relaxed expression on my lips. As soon as the door closes behind me though, I sag against it and let just one tear fall before wiping it away and pulling myself together. Bear is doing something nice for me, and I'm not going to be a brat about it just because he doesn't want me like I want him.

On my way out of the studio, Rebel stops me with an apologetic look.

"I'm so sorry. I didn't mean to rat you out. Bear could tell we were keeping something from him, and I totally caved under interrogation."

I sigh and pat him on the shoulder. "It's fine, I understand."

"Are you moving in with him?"

"Yeah, he didn't exactly ask. He pretty much told me that was how it was going to be."

Rebel frowns a little. "Is that okay with you? I know there's a certain dynamic between you two, and he's your boss, but you don't *have* to move in with him if you don't want to."

"Honestly, I do want to," I admit.

"Okay, as long as it's what you want."

"Thanks, Rebel. I've gotta go meet Bear's moving guys back at your apartment, so I'll see you later."

Like Bear promised, three men show up a few hours later to Rebel's place and load all my things into a small moving truck, and then one of them offers to drive me over to Bear's place.

We ride a little way outside the city proper to a neighborhood full of nice homes. Anywhere else in the country it would be a middle-class neighborhood, but in LA I have no doubt these houses cost a small fortune. We pull into the driveway of one of the houses, and the driver of the car hands me a key for the house and tells me that they'll bring my things in.

I take it upon myself to explore the house a little as they put my stuff in the spare bedroom...my bedroom for the time being. It's a beautiful house, and I'm not sure why it didn't occur to me before, but Bear is clearly *very* well off. I guess that makes sense after years making good money in porn and now owning the most popular gay porn studio in the country.

I find myself outside a set of double doors that I'm sure lead to the master bedroom. My curiosity is too much to bear as I reach out and turn the handle to peek inside. My stomach flutters a little as I slip into his bedroom. It's *so* Bear —decorated in rich colors and tidy. The carpet feels thick and lush under my feet. It's the kind of carpet that could hardly cause any rug burn if you got fucked on it. Not that I have a lot of experience with that kind of thing, *snort laugh*.

The scent of Bear's cologne hangs in the air, making my cock hard as memories of burying my face against his chest while he fucked me fills my mind. I creep forward and run my hands over his bedsheets, soft and luxurious to the touch. I wonder if Bear likes to sleep naked. He clearly paid a lot for these fancy sheets, so he should.

I hear the sound of the front door, and my heart jumps. I'm sure it's the moving guys, but if it's Bear, I definitely don't want to get caught in his bedroom. I hurry back out as quickly as I can, clicking the door shut quietly behind me.

Living with Bear isn't going to be easy, that much is clear.

16

BEAR

Pixie is nervous as he sits across from me at my dining table, biting that luscious bottom lip of his. And he looks so scared that I'm gonna yell at him that my heart fills with tenderness.

"What happened?" I ask, forcing myself to leave off the terms of endearment that want to come out.

His eyes fill up, and my heart squeezes painfully. "I'm not mad at you, I promise," I say, my voice soft and warm. "I'm gonna help you get back on your feet."

"Y-you sounded angry before," he says, gesturing with his hands. "When you told me I was moving in with you."

"I was upset you didn't come to me," I say.

His eyes narrow. "You know, for someone who says they don't want me, you sure seem to expect me to come running to you at the first sign of trouble."

His words sounds awfully close to what Rebel pointed out as well, and I can't deny they're true. "I never said I didn't want you, Pixie. God, you have to know I do. I said I can't have a relationship with you. Doesn't mean I don't care or that I'm not worried when I hear you've been evicted."

He cringes, and I remind myself to tread lightly. "I just don't know where I stand with you anymore," he whispers, and when he peeks at me with those baby blues, it takes everything I have not to gather him on my lap and hold him.

"Consider me a friend, baby boy. A close friend you can tell everything."

He lets out a soft sigh. "I didn't realize how expensive everything was," he starts.

Fifteen minutes later, I have a good overview over the sad state of his finances. He hands me a crumpled collection of notices, bills, and statements that I quickly scan. Let's just say it's a lot worse than I thought.

He missed rent twice in a row, but worse, he doesn't have enough money in his account to even pay it. He has two older credit cards that he's paying off the balance of every month—and boy, he knows how to spend money—but combined with his unlimited phone plan including a brand-new phone he's paying off, his utilities, which are on autopay, and his insurance payments, that doesn't leave him enough for rent. And he hasn't even started off paying the debt on three new cards he took out.

In hindsight, it's a good thing he got evicted this quickly, because if that hadn't happened, he would've been able to hide this from me much longer. In that sense, I kinda have to be grateful his landlord was on the ball with his rent situation.

"You have racked up quite the credit card debt," I say, making myself sound as friendly as I can manage. It's not him I'm angry at. It's myself. How could it have gotten this far? His credit score has taken such a hit that it's gonna take him years to recover.

"I thought I wasn't paying interest yet," Pixie says,

looking puzzled. "Like, they're all new credit cards, and you don't have to pay anything off till, like, six months later."

"It's been six months," I say gently. "So you should've started paying and you haven't, which means you're not only racking up interest, but fines as well."

"But...shouldn't they tell you when you need to start paying?"

I could tell him that it's all there on his monthly statements, but there's no sense. He already feels small enough, no need to rub it in. "We'll sort it all out. I promise."

"Do I have any money left?" he asks in a quivering tone.

I debate lying to him but then realize that's not gonna help him. "I'm not sure you had any money to begin with. That apartment, baby boy, the things you bought...you spent more than you earned from the get-go."

A big tear trails down his right cheek, and he looks absolutely gutted. Everything in me screams at me to hold him, but I can't. Touching him is my kryptonite.

"I'm such a failure," he says, all choked up. "I thought I could make it here in LA, but I can't. I'm not cut out for this."

"You're not a failure," I say. "You just need a little more help to figure it all out."

He looks at me with tear-stricken eyes. "How am I ever gonna climb out of this debt? I don't have any money, so what will I live off?"

"I've got you, baby boy. Here's what we're gonna do. I'm gonna look at all your finances, okay? Then I'm gonna pay off everything you owe so you're not increasing your debt. Instead of paying you your paycheck, you're gonna get an allowance from me. No more credit cards, just a debit card linked to a bank account where I'll deposit your allowance each week. When that's gone, you're out of money. I'll use the rest to pay off your debt to me and to start a savings account for you. You're staying with me till you're back on your feet, so you don't have to worry about rent and food."

He slowly shakes his head. "You can't do that, that's way too much. We're talking about a lot of money. You can't pay all of that off for me."

"Of course I can...and I will. We'll get you back on your feet, baby boy."

The look he gives me is pure hopelessness. "And then what? I'll fuck it up all over again. I don't want this kind of independence. I'm not cut out to be on my own. Daddy Luke was right, I should move back home."

My heart skips a beat. "Daddy Luke?" I ask, my tone sharper than I intended.

"Well, I have to call him just Luke now, since he's not my daddy anymore, but—"

"You had a *daddy* before you moved here?"

The thought of him with another daddy unsettles me, but I can't explain why. It wasn't like I didn't know he was into older men, but I guess I thought it was more like a hookup role-play for him, not something he'd be interested in doing full time in a relationship.

Pixie looks at me, blinking a few times. "You didn't know? I was with Daddy Luke since I was eighteen."

It wasn't casual, then. Somehow, that both comforts me and sends a stab of jealousy through me. "He let you go to LA on your own?"

"He knew I wanted to try and make something of myself. He made me a whole budget and everything, which I clearly ignored." His bottom lips quivers a little. "I haven't been a good boy lately, and he was upset with me when I told him what had happened."

"And what would he do if you'd been bad?" I can't stop myself from asking.

Pixie's look changes, his eyes growing heavy and that bottom lip going from quivering into seductive in a nanosecond. He's *so* got my number. "He'd spank me..." His hand travels underneath the table, and I can all but feel him rub his pretty butt. "Until my ass was all red. And he'd put my cock in a cage and then he'd fuck me, so I'd remember who was in charge."

My hand slips under the table as well to rearrange my dick. Pixie's little smirk tells me he knows exactly what he's doing to me. "Did he have to spank you often?"

I have no right to ask these questions, and god knows he shouldn't answer them, but I can't stop myself.

Pixie nods. "I'm not always a good boy..."

I swallow. "Something tells me you didn't mind those spankings so much."

He looks as naughty as a little imp can be, his eyes sparkling. "It's the best feeling in the world. Unless Daddy Luke was genuinely upset. There was nothing worse than the feeling of disappointing him. God, I miss having a daddy..."

The sadness in that last statement hits me deep.

"Do you love him?"

The question is out of my mouth before I can think it through. Pixie's eyes grow a little sad, forlorn, even. "I thought I did, but when the urge to leave became stronger than the urge to stay, I realized I didn't. Not like he loves me. I was happy with him, but it wasn't like it's supposed to be. It was comfortable, like a pair of sweatpants that are out of style and baggy and yet you still want to wear them because they're comfortable and make you feel relaxed."

I frown, trying to follow his line of thinking. "Love shouldn't be comfortable?"

"Love should be like a new Gucci bag that you can't wait

to use and show off to everyone. Even looking at it makes you go all fizzy and bubbly inside. Or a pair of skinny jeans that are a size too small but that make your ass pop in a way guaranteed to get you laid by the best dick in the room. That excitement, that rush, that's what it should feel like...like you're scared and excited and feel amazing all in one."

My heart does a funny dance inside my chest at the longing in his voice. How I want to be that person for him, with him, especially now that I know that it's what he wants. He's not looking for hookups with older men. He wants a relationship with one. If I keep rejecting him, he's gonna find himself another daddy who will take care of him, another daddy to cuddle with him and spank him when he's been bad and to protect him and spoil him just a little.

And those reasons I have for keeping my distance, for not wanting to have a relationship with him, they don't even make sense anymore. Why do I keep fighting this? Those reasons I had, they sound like bullshit now compared to the prospect of losing him. I keep turning it over and over in my head that night, but I can't reach a conclusion that makes me feel at peace. And knowing that he's just two doors down from me makes it even more complicated.

∽

Pixie

When Bear laid down the new rules about my allowance, it was all I could do not to climb into his lap and kiss him senseless. But I knew that wasn't what he wanted. He'd made it abundantly clear where things stood between us, and I knew if I was going to being staying at his house, I needed to respect that.

That was two weeks ago, and let me tell you, it's so much easier said than done.

We seem to dance around each other, avoiding each other while pretending we're *not* avoiding each other. We eat dinner together most nights, except when Bear goes somewhere else after work. Where he goes, I have no idea, but he always comes home sad.

I'm lying on the couch, half watching *Project Runway* and half listening for the front door to announce Bear's arrival home. If he comes straight from Ballsy, he usually gets in around five, if not a little earlier. I glance at the clock telling me it's half-past eight, which means he went wherever it is he goes.

It's another fifteen minutes before I hear the front door finally open. Bear's footfalls are slow and shuffling. I hear him take off his shoes, and then there's a rustling and thumping sound as he picks up the shoes I left haphazard in the hallway and lines them up on the mat like he likes. I wait every time to see if he'll scold me, but he never does, just sets them straight.

I sit up and turn off the TV as he nears the living room. I wonder if he's just going to pass by and go straight to his bedroom like he often does on nights like this, or if he'll stop to make small talk for a few minutes, ask if I ate dinner, if I had a nice day, tell me about the scenes they filmed today.

I hold my breath as he slows to a stop just outside the living room. I can see him through the doorway, but he doesn't come inside. When he turns and looks at me from the hallway, my breath catches at the pain in his eyes.

"Bear?" I get up slowly off the couch and move toward him. "Are you okay?"

"I'm fine, baby boy," he says, but the broken sound of his voice tells me a different story. His shoulders are hunched and his eyes are red rimmed like he's been crying. *Where the hell does he go on these nights?*

"Have you eaten anything?" I ask instead of the question I really want to.

"I'm not hungry."

I frown. Maybe I should let it go. He's clearly not interested in my help, but he looks too ragged to let walk away. He looks like he's hanging on by a thread, in desperate need of someone to pull him back onto the ledge.

"Come on." I reach for his hand and, to my surprise, he doesn't pull away. I lead him to the kitchen and pull a chair out at the table for him. He eyes me for a second before sitting down. "I'm not a great cook or anything, but how does soup and grilled cheese sound?" That's comfort food, right?

He gives me an almost smile. "That sounds good, thank you."

Bear sits quietly while I make his dinner, questions buzzing in my mind that I'm afraid to ask in case it upsets him more or sends him running for his room instead of staying to let me take care of him.

"How was work? Was it Campy and Heart filming together today?" I ask instead as I stand at the stove with a spatula in hand.

"Yeah, Rebel did most of the on-set work while I got paperwork done. Pretty soon, he's going to be running that place, and there will be no more use for me," he jokes, still sounding down, but with a little more life in his voice now than there was before.

"That wouldn't be so bad. You could retire and let him worry about everything while you collect your checks and travel the world or something."

I turn around to see Bear grimacing. "I'm old but I'm not *retirement* old."

I snort a laugh and shake my head. "I didn't mean it like that. I just meant that it wouldn't be so bad to take more time for yourself and let Rebel do the heavy lifting."

"I like working hard."

I plate the finished sandwich and pour the now hot soup into a bowl, then carry both over to the table to set in front of him.

"This is very nice, thank you."

"You're welcome." I stand beside him and wait for him to take the first bite to make sure everything tastes okay. "Would you mind if I rub your feet while you eat?" I ask shyly, unsure if I'm pushing it with that suggestion.

Bear's eyes go wide, and he stops with his spoon halfway to his mouth. "You don't have to do that."

"Can I if I want to?" I tilt my head down and hit him with the eyelash look that I know he won't be able to say no to.

"Sure, thank you," he agrees, and I smile, dropping to my knees and crawling under the table, giggling at the gasp he makes.

"You know, there's a lot of fun I could have under here," I muse playfully. "But for now, I'll just rub your feet."

I make myself comfortable, sitting cross-legged, and pull his left foot into my lap. Tugging off the sock, I toss it to the side. I don't have a foot fetish or anything, but Bear's feet are just as sexy as the rest of him—strong and manly with a little bit of hair on the knuckle of the big toe. I'd put money that he gets pedicures because his skin is all soft and free of calluses, and his toenails are neatly clipped. I take his foot between two hands and knead it, eliciting a deep moan from him.

It's strangely relaxing, sitting under the table in the semi-darkness, rubbing his feet, the only sounds from him eating or the occasional moan of pleasure. I wonder if he'd let me make this a regular thing. There are so many things I'd love to do for Bear if he'd let me.

One thing I learned from Luke was that boys can take care of their daddies too sometimes. Not that Bear is my daddy—he's made that extremely clear—but it's still nice to take care of him after all he's done for me.

After I finish rubbing both his feet and it sounds like he's done eating, I crawl back out from under the table and clear his dishes. He doesn't say anything as I rinse each one and place them neatly into the dishwasher, and when I turn back to look at him, the warmth in his eyes washes over me.

"Can I do just one more thing for you?" I ask.

"What do you want to do?" he asks, sounding more relaxed now.

"Can I draw you a hot bath? I have these *amazing* bath salts that I could add, maybe light a few candles for you to help you relax."

He hesitates for just a second before nodding in agreement. I smile and hurry to my bathroom to get my bath supplies, bringing them to the master bathroom. His tub is *huge*, like, you could definitely fit at least three full-grown men inside. I start the water and sprinkle in the salts so they can dissolve while the tub fills and then I light a few candles.

Bear steps into the bathroom in nothing but a towel, and memories of New York become difficult to resist. My cock gets hard, and I notice the front of the towel tenting as well.

But when I drag my gaze up to meet Bear's, there's hesitation and resistance there, not heat like I want to see.

"It should be all set for you. Do you need anything else?" I ask.

He swallows, and I see his throat bob. His grip tightens on his towel, and I can see a war going on in his eyes, just like last time. As much as I'd love to push him past the edge, to strip and slide into the tub with him to see where things go, it's obvious he's too emotionally raw tonight. If I throw myself at him, he'll probably say yes, but tomorrow he'll push me away again, and I can't take anymore rejection from him.

"Enjoy your bath," I say quietly, slipping past him to get to the door. I reach for the handle and stop, turning to look at him one more time. "Why do you go wherever you go if it makes you so sad?"

"I'm keeping a promise."

I nod in understanding before leaving.

17

BEAR

"Bear, it's so good to see you."

I haven't seen Hunter Tronco in two years, but his hug feels as familiar as if we saw each other yesterday. It's a funny thing to say, but the man gives the best hugs, with full body contact and two strong, furry arms wrapped tight around you. He's not afraid of intimacy, this guy, and it shows in everything. Then again, there is a reason why he goes by the moniker *Daddy* now.

"Right back at you, Hunter," I say.

He lets go of me with one last squeeze and shoots me a wink. "You're not going to use my nickname?"

My grin is wide. "Dude, I'm not calling you *Daddy*. Hell to the fucking no."

"Fair enough. But you have to admit, the name suits me."

I give him a good once-over, from his tight-fitting T-shirt to the jeans that hug his tree-sized thighs and the sturdy boots. Oh yeah, he's got the daddy vibe down to a T. "You look hot as fuck," I say. "If I were, you know, twenty years younger, a bottom, and a cute little twink, I would bend over for you in a heartbeat. Sadly, I'm none of those, so you're shit out of luck here."

He slaps a strong hand on my back, and I have to brace against the impact. "I wasn't proposing."

"I didn't think that's why you were here. So, why are you here? Last I heard, you were living it up in New York."

Hunter owns a well-known club in New York that caters to a wide range of kinks within the gay community. He's a Dom himself, though from what I know, not one whose preferences fall on the extremes of the spectrum.

A flash of something clouds his eyes. "New York isn't working for me anymore. I'm looking to make a fresh start."

I resist the urge to ask questions. I've known Hunter for a long time, and if he wanted me to know, he would tell me. "Here in LA?"

He shakes his head, leaning back in his chair and folding his hands behind his head. "Las Vegas."

I whistle between my teeth. "From the cold Northeast to the desert, huh? That's quite a change."

"That's the whole idea," he says. "Something new, something fresh. Building it from the ground up. And that's where you come in as well."

He's got me curious now. "You want to open a new club in Las Vegas?"

"Not a club, a porn studio. And I would love to have your help."

I lean forward, resting my arms on my desk. "Okay, I'm listening."

"My idea is to set up a very specific type of porn studio. Gay porn, obviously, but catered toward the kinky elements in our community. I know there is a market for it, but I also know it's hard to get it right. A lot of the supposedly kinky porn is either laughable because it's so bad or doesn't follow the accepted standards."

"You mean safe, sane, consensual," I say.

He gestures with his hand to indicate that's not quite what he meant. "I prefer the term RACK—risk-aware consensual kink—but I think we're referring to the same thing. If we're gonna show kink, especially where there's any kind of power imbalance, we have to show it right. I want to create high-quality videos that show how beautiful kink can be, but that also demonstrate how to do it consensually. And I would love for it to be affiliated with the Ballsy Boys, considering the reputation you've already built."

My first reaction is that it's a brilliant idea and that he's absolutely the right person to bring this to life. Hunter and I go way back, having first met when we were both doing porn. He knows the business, but he also knows a lot about kink in its broadest definition.

"How do you see that working, being affiliated with the Ballsy Boys?" I zoom in on the aspect that will most directly affect me.

"Look, Bear, I'm here for two reasons. The first is that I would never start a porn studio without your approval. We'd be competitors, even if my targeted niche is different from yours. I respect you and what you've built way too much to go behind your back. But more importantly. I would love to utilize your experience and knowledge of the industry. I want to do this right, and the way you've built your business, I have nothing but respect for that. You have a fantastic reputation and treat your boys well, and you deliver a high-quality product. That's what I want, so it would make sense for me to work together with you. The details, that's something we can talk about, but I'm envisioning something where you would get part of the profits in exchange for allowing me to be affiliated with the Ballsy Boys."

I rub my hands at that last sentence, my face splitting open in a wide grin. "I like the sound of this. I've thought about expanding the studio, but I simply lack the manpower. And hiring people to run something like this, that's not easy. It would have to be someone I trust explicitly. Someone like you."

An hour later, we have the rough concept of a business plan, and with every idea we jot down, I get more excited. This could be a fantastic way for me to build upon the name and reputation I've created with the Ballsy Boys, while letting someone else do the hard work. And no one would be better suited for this than Hunter.

Hunter extends me his hand. "Let's shake on this formally, Bear, like men do."

I chuckle. "Is that what men do? Kinky fuckers like you, they're content with shaking hands? If that's what you do, you're in the wrong business, man."

But I shake his hand anyway, and we both grin like idiots at each other. I reach for the bottle of Jameson I keep in my cabinet drawer for special occasions. So far, those have mostly consisted of me either celebrating something or needing to get shitfaced, and I think today falls in the first category.

I pour two generous amounts in mugs I keep there and hand one to Hunter. We toast, clinking our mugs together. "To the Kinky Boys," Hunter says.

"To the Kinky Boys."

We sit for a while, sipping our whiskey like the old men we are.

"I'm honored you'd want to do business with me," Hunter says. His eyes meet mine. "You may hear some rumors about me at some point. Just remember that you know me, okay? You know the truth."

I nod. "You know me, man. I never believe rumors. If I hear anything, I'll verify with you, okay?"

He sends me a grateful look and takes another sip of his drink.

"For my first video, I wanna do something special," Hunter says. "Something that will put me on the map right away."

"I can see if one of my boys would be willing to star," I say, my mind already going over the options.

Heart might be a good fit, since he's usually open to pretty much everything. Though now that he's with Lucky and Mason, I'm not sure how long he'll be staying. I'm expecting Campy's resignation any day now, what with him and Jackson being together. My boys are growing up, I think, my heart suddenly full of emotions.

"How about Pixie?" Hunter asks, and my heart doesn't feel so full anymore.

"Pixie?" I say, my voice sounding strangely hoarse.

"God, that boy is perfect. I don't know where you found him, but I could watch him for hours. In fact, I may just come out of retirement myself to shoot that first video with him. That would certainly break the Internet, don't you think? Is he the type to appreciate a little daddy lovin'?"

I've never been possessive of my boys, ever, but the thought of Pixie with Hunter is enough to make my vision go hazy with this weird anger. I have no rights to him, none at all, and I would never stand in his way, but *god*, why him? Out of all the boys that work for me, why did Hunter have to choose him?

My mouth is sour, and I have to swallow before I can speak. "I don't know," I lie. "I'll have to ask him."

Pixie

I CAN'T HELP WONDERING who the man is who showed up at Ballsy studios today to talk to Bear. I shamelessly listened at the door but it was difficult to make out what exactly they were saying. I caught a few words like *porn* and *daddy*, so maybe the man owns his own porn studio? Or Bear is hiring him to work here?

As he steps out of Bear's office and the two of them shake hands and then give each other a hug, I tilt my head a little, admiring the view. Obviously, Bear is off-the-charts hot, but whoever this other man is, he's yummy as hell too. His hair is a little more silver-gray than Bear's, quaffed in a pompadour like fancy Elvis. He's a little taller than Bear, with broad shoulders and a confident swagger as he turns to walk away, Bear watching him with a friendly smile.

The man's eyes land on me assessingly, and his smile widens. He slows his steps.

"Well, aren't you even cuter in person," he says, extending a hand in greeting. "I'm Daddy."

A giggle bubbles past my lips. "Of course you are." I shake his hand, his palm warm as it engulfs mine. "I'm Pixie."

"I know who you are," he assures me. "It's nice to meet you. I'm sure this is terribly forward, but I'm only in town for a week or so, and other than bothering the hell out of my old buddy, Bear I've been spending my time pathetically alone."

"That's quite a shame," I flirt, my eyes darting back to where Bear is watching us with a scowl on his face.

"It is," he agrees. "Maybe you could put me out of my misery and let me buy you dinner one night?"

My heart gives a little flutter, and I look over at Bear again. If Bear wasn't in the picture, the answer would be easy. Of course I want to let a handsome, charming man take me to dinner and make me feel all kinds of special. But ever since the night in New York, all my heart wants is Bear. *It's not fair*, I sigh internally. *Bear doesn't want me.*

I look Daddy up and down, feeling the simmer of want buried deep under my longing for Bear. Maybe it's time I stop waiting for Bear to want me. It's not like letting Daddy take me to dinner means we're getting married or anything anyway. I can let him make me feel special and taken care of for just one night.

"Sure, I'd like that," I agree. "How about Friday night?"

"That sounds perfect." He reaches into his pocket and pulls out a business card to hand to me. "Text me your address, and I'll pick you up at seven."

"Great," I agree, taking the card and tucking it into my pocket.

Bear's door slams shut, the bang echoing loudly through the hallway, making me jump. Daddy looks back over his shoulder at Bear's closed office door.

"Uh-oh, did I just step on some toes?"

"He's made it abundantly clear that he's not interested in me," I assure him somewhat bitterly.

"In that case, I'll see you Friday."

~

I'M SITTING at the kitchen table, using Bear's laptop to look at the fashion design program at the College of Art and Design, when I hear the front door open. I close the website and shut the laptop quickly. Bear told me I'm allowed to use it—he even set up my own profile with a password so I could have some privacy when using it—but for some reason, I don't want him to know about my dream of becoming a fashion designer. If he doesn't want me, then I'm certainly not going to bear my soul to him.

His heavy footfalls come down the hallway, and my stupid heart goes crazy the closer he gets, excited to see him. He enters the kitchen and stops to look at me with a small frown. I actually forgot about meeting Daddy and the date I agreed to until I see Bear looking so sour about it.

"Hi, how was work today?" I ask sweetly.

"Great," he answers in a slightly clipped tone, his shoulders tense as he crosses his arms. "What were you and Hunter chatting about?"

I paste on an innocent expression and resist the urge to give Bear the finger, because fuck him if he thinks he can blow so hot and cold with me and then get all jealous if someone else shows interest.

"Not much. He asked me on a date for Friday, and that was about it."

Bear's jaw ticks. "Did you agree?"

"Um, duh, have you *seen* him?"

"He's too old for you," he points out, and I let out a harsh laugh, getting up from the table and standing directly in front of Bear. I'm close enough that I have to tilt my head to look up into his eyes, his stance relaxing a fraction, but all the tension still there. I can feel the heat radiating off him, and it's all I can do not to rub myself all over him like a cat.

"I *like* older men," I say firmly. His arms drop from their crossed position, and I press myself against him just a little as I reach up to run my fingers through his hair. "I like gray hair." I drag my hand down to his bicep. "I love strong, daddy arms to hold me tight," I continue, moving my hand to the front of his jeans. "I can't get enough of a big daddy cock splitting me apart."

"Eli," Bear groans in warning.

I pull my hand away and take a step back. "You don't want me, and I have to accept that, but you can't keep me from finding someone who *does* want me."

Bear opens his mouth, no doubt to tell me again about how we can't be together because he's too old, or whatever bullshit excuse he wants to give me today. I don't want to hear it again, so I push past him and go straight to my room, closing my door behind me more loudly than necessary. Okay, fine, I totally slammed it like a brat.

My heart is pounding as I listen for Bear's footsteps, imagining him coming after me to punish me for the way I acted in the kitchen—teasing and touching him and then storming away and slamming my door. I would give anything for Bear to come in here and spank my ass red for the way I behaved, to cage my cock and fuck me until I'm full and dripping with his cum. The want is so much it nearly chokes me as I lean my back against my door.

I don't hear any sounds from Bear. Whether he's still standing stunned in the kitchen or he's gone to his own end of the house, I have no idea, but it's clear he's not coming after me. The disappointment is heavy in my chest as I drag myself over to my bed and crawl under the covers, pulling them over my head to block out the world.

18

BEAR

The last time I saw Travis, he didn't look so good. It's not like he ever looked healthy for as long as I've known him, of course, but his eyes were lifeless, and that was new. I recognized the signs from the countless patients I'd known before, so it doesn't come as a surprise when one of the nurses calls me the next day to tell me Travis is deteriorating rapidly.

Pixie is hanging out with Rebel and Troy, so I send him a quick text message I'll be home late, then fire one off to Rebel with the instructions to drive him home personally. Knowing Pixie is taken care of, I jump into my car and drive over to the hospice. It takes me longer than usual because of the evening traffic, and all that time I worry that I'm gonna be too late.

It's a miracle he's clung to life for this long. On average, residents in the hospice last two weeks. There are outliers, of course, the people who pass away within days or even hours, and those who hold on to life much longer. Travis fell in the latter category, and his doctor was amazed that his decline had come to an unexpected stop. He wasn't doing well, but he wasn't deteriorating either.

It got to the point where the hospice director had to have a conversation with Travis about alternate arrangements, because he'd already been there for months. But apparently, Travis has money, and a generous donation from him ensured he could stay in his lovely garden room. He told me he'd expected to die within weeks, so he'd already sold his house and had nowhere to return to. But now it seems his time has come after all, which doesn't surprise me after our last few visits.

When I rush into his room, I am taken aback by the sight of another man sitting next to his bed, holding his hand. For one second, I fear that I am indeed too late, that Travis has passed already, but then I hear the sound of his labored breathing, a strangely comforting noise. But who is the man holding his hand? I've never seen him before.

He gives me a quick once-over, then sends me a tired smile. "You must be Bear," he says. "Travis has told me so much about you."

And then I know who he is. "You're Ryan," I say, and he nods.

I shake his left hand, since he's holding onto Travis with his right. "How is he holding up?" I ask.

A deep sadness fills Ryan's face. The man is beautiful, I have to admit. A California surf boy in his fifties, that's what he looks like. Tanned, sun-kissed golden locks, wrinkles around his eyes, a trim and athletic physique. "He's having trouble breathing. The doctor says it won't be long now."

I nod, not surprised by Ryan's words. "Have you ever been through something like this before?" I ask as gently as possible. Part of our job is to prepare and support family and friends as well.

Ryan shakes his head. "No. My parents are still alive. I've lost my grandparents, but I wasn't there when they passed away."

"In that case, you need to prepare yourself. It could still take hours, maybe even days. I've seen patients bounce back unexpectedly and hang on for days more. There is a lot doctors still don't understand about the process of dying and why some people seem to last when there's no reason to and others pass away much faster than expected. Death is one of the last remaining big mysteries of life."

He takes my words in with a seriousness that warms my heart. I don't know what happened between them, but it's obvious that he cares for Travis a great deal. "He's not in pain, is he?" Ryan asks.

"No, the doctors are making sure he's as comfortable as possible. As his breathing grows more labored, that might cause discomfort for him, from what I understand, as much mentally as physically. But they'll up his meds if they need to, and he can also ask for a sedative when the time is there."

A sad smile plays on Ryan's lips as he softly shakes his head. "He won't accept it. You're talking about a man who's never backed down from a fight in his life. He'd consider that cheating."

"Damn right," Travis croaks, blinking a few times and then opening his eyes.

I smile as I bend in to kiss him on his forehead. "Hey, handsome."

The fact that he only sends me a warm look rather than joking back tells me how tired he is. He reaches out with his other hand, and I take it. "I'm here," I say simply.

It's about a minute before he speaks again, and all that time, his slow, raspy breaths echo through the room. "You can go now if you want," he says to Ryan, who immediately starts shaking his head.

"I am not going anywhere," he says, and despite all my reservations about the guy, he just jumped a few places in my ranking.

Travis falls asleep again soon, his breathing slowing down even further. I know I told Ryan it could be days, but I know that won't be the case. Travis has hours at most. I know that's a morbid thing to say, but when you spend as much time with the dying as I have, you simply know. I've learned to recognize it by the breathing, by the way the life seems to slowly leave the body. He's close now, and the thought fills me with a bone-deep sadness.

It's about an hour later that I really need to use the bathroom, and when I walk back, I run into Ryan in the hallway outside Travis's room, finishing up a call. "Just updating my wife," he says, and an irrational anger fills me that he couldn't love that wonderful man. It makes no sense, because you can't force love, but I've seen how much Travis loves him, and I can't help but be a little upset that a love that grand was never returned.

"I don't know how you do it," Ryan says. "Spending so much time with people, knowing they're going to die. How do you do it?"

My usual answer is some platitude, since most people don't really want to understand. They just want me to say something to make them feel better about the fact that they couldn't do it. So my standard reply is something along the lines of *it's not for everyone*. Which is kind of true and at the same time absolute bullshit. But in this case, I find myself giving an explanation that's awfully close to the truth.

"I lost a great number of friends over the years, many of them dying alone because their families abandoned them.

When my boyfriend died, he made me promise that I would do whatever was in my power to not let anyone die alone."

Ryan cocks his head, studying me with an intense look. "That's a pretty big thing to ask of someone."

I shrug. "Both of us watched many of our friends die without their family present. It changes you."

"I can totally see that, but I'm just saying, that's an awfully big ask to make of someone in such a situation. It's not like you were in a position to deny a dying man his last wish."

All these years, I've been volunteering to keep my promise to Freddie, and no one has ever questioned my reasoning. I started in hospitals that had an AIDS wing first. Volunteers were scarce back then, everyone too scared of contracting the virus. I was too, but I had promised Freddie, and so I did it anyway, always using every precaution.

When being around dying gay men got to be too much for me to bear, because most of the patients were gay men, I switched to volunteering in a few hospices before I settled with Almost Home. Granted, not everyone knows the real reason why I do this, but I haven't made a big secret of it among the volunteers here. And no one has ever said anything negative about it, until now.

My first instinct is to tear Ryan a new one, but somehow, I can't. Part of the reason is the knowledge that the man dying in the room right next to us loves him more than anything in the world. I respect Travis too much to dishonor his love by attacking Ryan. But it's more than that.

Somehow, Ryan's words hit home. I've never thought about it, never even questioned it, this promise Freddie asked of me in the last hours before he died. He was a shadow of himself, nothing but skin and bones at that point, half delirious at times. But his request to me was so passionate that I couldn't refuse.

And let's face it, I would've done anything at that point, would've given him the world if I could, promised him anything he'd asked for. And so I did. I made the solemn promise that I would never let another person die alone if it were in my powers. It's been the driving motivation for me to volunteer here all this time. And I've never questioned it until now.

"I'm sorry," Ryan says. "I didn't mean to offend you or question your motives for volunteering here. I think you're doing amazing work here, and I'll be forever thankful that you were there for Travis."

I shake off my acute sense of discomfort that makes me question myself after his remark and focus on his words. "I'm grateful I got a chance to get to know Travis," I say, meaning every word. "He's a wonderful man, and you have been blessed to have him in your life for so long."

I don't mean anything by it other than a referral to their friendship, but Ryan's eyes sharpen as they meet mine. "I know he's in love with me," he says, his voice dropping to a whisper.

He must've seen the involuntary surprise on my face, because his lips curl up in another one of those sad smiles that makes him even more beautiful. It's easy to see why Travis fell for him.

"I'm not stupid," Ryan says. "I've known for a long time."

I decide keeping up pretenses is useless now. "Why didn't you ever say anything?"

"And then what? Lose his friendship over the inevitable estrangement that would follow that conversation? The awkwardness and discomfort we'd both experience, knowing that what we had has forever changed? What good would that have done? At least now he could pretend I didn't know, and we could both pretend that we were the same."

There's not a single argument I can come up with to refute that logic. "You didn't want to lose him," I say.

"He's my best friend," Ryan says. "And don't think I've never been tempted. There have been times where I came so close to saying something to him, to breaking that last thin barrier between us, knowing that if I wanted to, I could have him. There was a period when things were rough between me and my wife, and you have no idea how much willpower it took to not run to Travis and ask him to console me."

My admiration for him grows by the second, I'm not ashamed to admit. "So why didn't you?" I ask, even though I can already guess the answer.

"Because for me, it would've been curiosity to see what it would've been like. Attraction, sure, but not on the same level as his love for me. And I could've never forgiven myself had I broken his heart. So in the end, I decided that ours was to be a friendship, and nothing more. There's not been a single moment that I regretted that decision, until tonight. Knowing that these are the last hours I will ever spend with him, I regret not knowing what it is like to be with him."

His voice breaks, and a single tear escapes from his cloudy eyes. I reach out for him and grab his shoulder with my hands. "I know we don't know each other, so this may mean shit to you, but you did the right thing. At the end of the day, Ryan, love is love, whether it's friendship or more. And by what you did, you protected that love between the two of you. You may not know what it would've been like to be with Travis, but you're allowing him to die knowing that he was loved by his best friend. Trust me when I say that's worth a hell of a lot more than sex."

I give him a few minutes to compose himself after that, and then the two of us walk back into Travis's room. He's still asleep, though he wakes up minutes after we both take his hands again.

"How's Pixie?" he asks me, sounding remarkably lucid. And my heart drops in my chest, because I recognize this phase too. Not all patients have it, but some do. It's the last effort of the body, the last bit of lucidity before it gives in. And because of that, I can't lie to him. A dying man deserves the truth.

"He's perfect, like he's always been. You have no idea how hard it is to have him around me and not give in to the temptation to be with him, knowing that he wants me as much as he does."

"You're an idiot, Bear," Travis says, his voice crystal clear. "I've been sugarcoating it so far, trying to be nice to you and give you advice, but I'm running out of time. That kid is the best thing that ever happened to you, and you're a complete idiot if you let him go because of some misplaced idea that you need to protect him."

I can't help but laugh at his directness. "The best thing that ever happened to me?" I say, and my thoughts immediately wander off to Freddie. It's not fair to compare the two, Freddie and Pixie. And yet somehow, I want to. Because my feelings for Freddie were so big, so deep, that I wonder if what I feel for Pixie could ever measure up.

"You may not realize it, but every time you mention his name, your face lights up. I know losing your boyfriend at such a young age was a harsh blow, but to me it feels like you've been somewhat dead inside since then. I know it looks on the surface like you've lived a great life, what with your career and everything, but you've never opened your heart again, too scared of getting hurt again."

He has to catch his breath, and I let his words sink in. They hurt, like darts hitting the bullseye dead on.

Travis sends me a warm smile, maybe to compensate for his deadly accuracy with words. "It's not Pixie you're protecting, you big idiot. It's yourself. You're projecting your own feelings onto him, but it's your own heart you're worried about. But he's good for you, Bear. He makes you feel alive again. He makes you *feel*. You can't let that go."

It's quite the speech, and by the time Travis is done, he's panting. But every word is like a blow, painful and yet liberating. It's as if he's removing veils that covered my thinking, that I never realized were there. With every sentence, he reveals a new truth, and I can barely keep up.

He's absolutely right. It was never Pixie I was worried about. It was my own heart, too scared of having to endure another loss of that magnitude. How did I miss this all these years? I thought I was just busy with work, with my career, and couldn't find a boyfriend that fit in with that, with me. But it was never that. It was me not letting anyone too close because I was too scared to lose them.

"God, you're right," I say, my thoughts scrambling in my head. "How did I not see this?"

Travis squeezes my hand. "That's the one good thing about dying," he says. "It changes your outlook on living and it helps you see what really matters. And what matters more than anything…"

His voice is getting weaker and weaker, trailing off at the end. I squeeze his hand, knowing this is it.

"What matters is love," he finishes, barely audible now.

And Ryan, god bless him, leans in to plant a soft kiss on Travis's cheek. "I love you, my friend," he whispers. "Smooth sailing."

Travis's face lights up like a fucking Christmas tree, and

the love that shines out of it is so big that I should look away because it feels too private to witness. His eyes flutter shut, and he never says another word as his breathing drifts away into silence.

I lift his hand and kiss it, knowing that I owe him everything. He's set me free in a way that I never realized I needed.

19

PIXIE

Bear's text earlier didn't seem like a happy one, so I'm not surprised when Rebel drops me off to find the house empty. I'm still not sure where Bear goes a few times a week, but wherever it is, he always comes home looking sad and drained. He hasn't let me take care of him again like he did the night he came home so upset, but I can tell part of him wants to.

I only have two hours until Daddy will be here to pick me up for our date, so I shake off thoughts of Bear and head into my bathroom to take a shower. My stomach is fluttering with nerves as I wash myself up, spending extra time on all my fun bits, because you never know.

As usual, it takes me ages to pick something to wear, and it doesn't help that my mind keeps wandering to Bear, wondering if he's going to come home sad tonight and how he'll feel when I'm not here. Eventually, I manage to settle on an outfit and get my hair styled, but my heart isn't fully in it. I almost consider texting Daddy to cancel, but by the time the thought occurs to me, it's already seven o'clock.

The sound of the doorbell announces his arrival, so I put

on a smile and shove my phone and wallet into my pockets and go to greet him.

Daddy's eyebrows are raised when I open the door, a confused look on his face. "You live with Bear?"

"Um...yeah."

"When you texted the address, it sounded familiar, but I didn't realize this was Bear's place until I pulled into the neighborhood. I guess that explains why he insisted on meeting me at his office this visit instead of coming over to grill steaks and have a few drinks like usual."

"Sorry, should I have said something?"

"No, it's fine. I'm just trying to figure out what I'm doing here," he admits with a laugh.

"Oh, it's not like *that* with Bear," I say. "He's made it *abundantly* clear," I grumble, mostly to myself.

"As long as you're sure?"

He's giving me an out, a chance to beg off this date without feeling bad. But, in spite of the fact that I'd been considering bailing just a few minutes ago, I really do want to get to know Daddy better. I deserve to be taken out on a nice date, wined and dined a little.

"I'm sure."

Daddy smiles, showing off some sexy dimples hiding in the gray scruff on his cheeks. Damn, he's so hot. He offers me his arm, and I take it, closing the door behind me and then letting him lead me down the walkway to his shiny, silver Jag in the driveway.

He's the perfect gentleman as he opens my door and leans in to buckle my seatbelt, but all I can think about is when Bear buckled me in when I was drunk. Daddy smells nice, like Old Spice and cinnamon gum, but he doesn't smell like Bear.

He closes my door and goes around to the driver's side,

sliding in and shooting me a smile before putting the car in reverse and backing out of the driveway.

"I made a reservation at my favorite seafood place in LA. I hope that's okay?"

"I love seafood," I say. "I grew up in Illinois, so I never had good seafood until I moved out here. The freshness of the fish makes *such* a difference."

"Oh yeah, I won't eat seafood anywhere without a coast," he agrees vehemently.

While we drive to the restaurant, we make small talk about favorite food and places we've lived, nothing earth-shattering. It's been so long since I've been on a real date, I forgot how nice it can be. Of course, Daddy opens my door again when we get to the restaurant and puts a hand on my lower back as he leads me inside. With my permission, he chooses a wine and orders me a dish he swears is the best thing I'll ever eat. It's turning out to be the absolute perfect date...and still my mind keeps wandering back to Bear.

"How did you come to work for Bear?" he asks after pouring each of us a glass of wine. I take a sip and hum happily at the taste.

"Bear picked me up at a club," I say, giggling when Daddy's eyebrows go up again. "Not like *that*," I explain. "Although, I did think that's what he wanted. But I guess he thought I had a look viewers would like, so he gave me his card and told me to call for an audition, and the rest is history, I guess."

"Do you like it?"

"What's not to like?" I joke. "The guys are great, the job is fun, and Bear is an amazing boss. He really cares about all of us. It never feels like we're just a product he's selling. He sees us and makes sure we're always happy."

Daddy narrows his eyes a little at my praise of Bear

before giving me a small smile and taking a sip of his own wine.

"Bear's a great guy," he agrees. "Between you and me, I'm planning to open a porn studio myself, and I've seen how well Bear has treated his models over the years, which is why I came to him for advice."

Our meals arrive, and Daddy tells me more about the studio he's planning to open, based out of Las Vegas and focusing mostly on various kinks. It sounds intriguing, and we end up talking about it through the rest of the meal. In spite of the overtly sexual nature of the business we're discussing, it ends up feeling more like a professional conversation than a date as I give him some tips from a model's perspective and help him brainstorm about which kinks he should focus on most heavily—we agree that bondage, pet play, Daddy/boy, and impact play need to feature.

When the meal ends and Daddy leads me back to the car, my brain starts racing with a gentle way to let him down easily, to tell him I think we should be friends but I'm not interested in more right now. We reach the car, and his hand moves from my lower back to my hip, spinning me to face him.

"Daddy, I—"

"It's okay," he cuts me off, giving me an understanding smile. "But listen, if you ever get tired of waiting for Bear to pull his head out of his ass, let me know."

I giggle. "I will."

He leans in and brushes a brief kiss to my cheek before opening my door and helping me in again.

Bear

I DIDN'T REALIZE how much I was counting on Pixie being home until I come home to an empty, dark house. And then I remember. He's on a date. With Hunter. His possible new daddy.

My first instinct is to go straight for my liquor cabinet and get absolutely blinding drunk. How I wish I could numb the pain inside me with alcohol. Oh, I could, and I'm dead sure it would work too. Wouldn't be the first time I reach for the bottle. The problem is that it doesn't fix anything, as I know from experience. I would only wake up with the mother of all hangovers tomorrow, and the pain would still be there.

Instead, I make a cup of lavender tea, laughing at myself for choosing this hippie, new age approach over a bottle of whiskey. My mother would certainly be proud of me. Maybe she has an essential oil or two that can cure heartbreak. It wouldn't surprise me, considering her vast collection of shit like that.

I settle on the couch with my tea, not even bothering to turn on the lights except for a little reading lamp I can reach. My throat is hurting from the grief that grows inside me, and the only sound audible in the room is my rapid breaths. I haven't felt this empty inside in a long time.

In the many years that I've volunteered in the hospice, I've encountered death almost on a biweekly basis. Travis hung on to live a hell of a lot longer than any of us had expected, himself included. I'd love to say that's why his death impacts me more than any of the other residents I've accompanied on the last leg of their journey in this life. But I know that's not the reason.

When you do this work, the veteran volunteers tell you there are two ways to survive. The first is to make sure that you stay in a somewhat professional mode, even if you are friendly with the residents and their family. You keep yourself emotionally detached, and you certainly don't become friends.

The second way is to allow yourself to become close, but accept that it will break your heart every single time someone dies. Doris, the seventy-five-year-old lady who showed me the ropes when I started doing this work, said she'd never seen anyone sustain the second approach for long. That's why I chose the first method.

I've always been good at keeping my emotional distance, but I failed miserably with Travis. I don't know if it's because he was gay or because he had HIV or because our characters simply matched. He became a friend, and I didn't realize how much I had started to appreciate his company until tonight. It's a sad reminder of the old adage that you don't know what you've got until you lose it.

And maybe that's true for Pixie as well. Even though I never truly *had* him, I did have his desire, his devotion. But now he's out with Hunter, and I can't imagine the two of them not clicking. Hunter is a fantastic guy, and he would be the perfect daddy for Pixie. Fuck knows Pixie craves one.

As much as it hurts to think about the two of them together, how could I not be happy for Pixie? I've rejected him so many times that I don't even blame him for moving on. It's not his fault that it took me this long to realize the truth. And the sad reality is that without Travis pointing it out to me, it might've taken me even longer.

God, he was so right. All these years, and all this time with Pixie, I was telling myself and him I was keeping my distance to protect him. There was a certain nobility in it, in being the better person who was making sure his heart wouldn't get broken.

But the sad truth was that all along, I was just protecting myself. It was never about him. It was always about me being too scared to love again, to lose again. On some level, I've always known that Freddie's death impacted me deeply, but I never realized how traumatized I'd become.

I knew about the obvious effects, the ones I struggled with for years after. The nightmares after he passed away, after I watched god knows how many men die in similar ways. The fear of getting sick as well that led me to stay celibate for two years after he died, until I let science convince me that condoms did protect. I never, ever went bareback after that. Ever.

There was irony in me going into porn, of course, considering my fear at first of contracting something. But I'd always been sexually active, even as a teen. Hell, I've always loved sex. I still do. In the end, rational thinking prevailed and I vowed to stay safe. I never deviated from that principle, not even when barebacking could've earned me twice as much. Even now with Ballsy Boys, safety is my number one concern, and I'm proud of the reputation we have.

No, those effects, those I was well aware of. But the emotional consequences, what I now recognize as the trauma of what I've been through...that, I totally underestimated. I thought I was happy by myself, with my string of hookups and casual boyfriends, with my life, my friends, my volunteer work... In reality, I was deadly afraid, literally, all along. Deadly afraid of loving again the way I loved Freddie, because it would leave me open to hurt again the same way as when I lost him.

It's like Psychology 101 and yet, I missed it, all these years. It hurts, not just for me, but for Pixie as well. I kept him at bay, rejecting him again and again, when it was all about me being scared. How sad is that? God, I hope he'll give me one last chance, even if I've done nothing to deserve one. But am I too late now that he's met Hunter?

I must've sat in the near dark for close to two hours, grieving and pondering the stupidity of my life choices, when I hear the front door open.

"Bear?" Pixie calls out hesitantly. "Are you home?"

For some reason, the sound of his voice brings tears to my eyes. I want to be near him more than anything, but the thought of witnessing the happiness on his face his encounter with Hunter must've brought him may be too much for me.

"I'm here," I say, my voice close to breaking.

Pixie steps into the room, frowning at the darkness surrounding me. He turns on the lights, though dimming them to the softest setting. "Are you okay?" he asks, and how I love that his first concern is for me.

I don't deserve him, but I'm not gonna make the same mistake twice and decide for him. It wasn't just Travis who was right. Pixie's analogy with Nemo's dad was spot on as well. Even if I were his daddy, there are certain decisions I can't make for him. I can't protect him from everything...and myself either.

"How was your date?" I ask. "Did you have fun?"

After a short hesitation, he sinks to his knees in front of me, his sweet face full of worry. "What's wrong, Bear? What happened?"

I shake my head, needing to know where we stand first. "Please, baby boy. I know I don't deserve it, but will you please tell me if you and Hunter are together now?"

The worry on his face changes into annoyance. "You're right. You don't deserve to know. You can't do this, Bear. You can't keep pushing me away and then get jealous when I start seeing someone else."

I hang my head. "I know." It comes out barely more than a whisper. "I did you wrong, baby boy."

I can't even look at him, his face too much of a reminder of what I have lost due to my own screw ups.

"What are you saying, Bear?" Pixie asks, and there's something in his voice that makes me look up and meet his eyes. Maybe, just maybe all hope isn't lost yet, judging by the look on his face.

"I fucked things up with you. I kept rejecting you and keeping you at a distance, even though I wanted to be with you more than anything else."

Pixie rolls his eyes at me. "Yeah, because you're scared of me surviving you and having to watch you die. We went over this, and for the record, I still think it's total bullshit."

"It is," I admit, and I watch his eyes go wide.

"What?" he says rather inelegantly.

I reach for his hands, encouraged when he allows me to take them. "As a friend pointed out to me today, I've been an idiot. I kept pushing you away, not because I was scared for you, but because I was scared for me. I don't even think I fully realized it myself, but losing my Freddie the way I did, it damaged me. I got scared of loving again, of ever opening up myself to that potential pain."

Pixie swallows, his eyes firmly trained on mine. "What are you saying?" he asks, and this time, there is no denying the hope in his voice. It pierces me, that after everything I've done to him, he would still want me.

"I'm saying that I'm so sorry for hurting you. I'm saying that I was an idiot, even though I didn't realize it and thought I was doing the right thing. I'm saying that I want to be with you…if you still want me."

And Pixie, my strong, sweet Pixie, cocks his head as he narrows his eyes. "Define *be with me*."

I can't help but smile. He's so right to ask more of me than some vague term. "If you'll have me, I want to be your Daddy. Not just for sex or hookups, but for a relationship. You and me, baby boy, together."

A gasp flies from Pixie's lips, and then his eyes fill up, stabbing my heart once again. I vow that if he forgives me for being such an asshole, I will spend the rest of my life cherishing him.

"I thought you'd never ask," Pixie whispers, and then he's in my lap, those two slender arms wrapped tightly around my neck as he presses his sweet face against mine.

For a minute or so, I simply hold him, my head too full of emotions to even think beyond the fact that he said yes. But then I have to ask, just to make sure. "What about Hunter?"

Pixie leans back and gives me a sweet smile. "We both realized I wasn't meant for him."

The relief that fills me is a sweet reprieve, but there's more we have to talk about. "I lost a dear friend tonight," I say.

Pixie nestles himself on my lap, maybe sensing that I need to get this off my chest. "Is that who you've been visiting? You came home so sad every time."

"Yes. His name was Travis."

And then I tell him about the hospice and about Travis and our friendship and how my dying friend called me an idiot for not being with the boy who made me smile.

"I make you smile?" Pixie asks.

"You do. Just being near you makes me feel better, even now when I'm hurting so much."

He presses a soft kiss on my cheek. "I'm sorry, Daddy Bear. He sounds like a wonderful guy."

"He was. I'll always be grateful I met him, even if it was so short."

We sit for a bit, and I'm not lying: Pixie's mere presence does soothe the raw hurt inside me. He's so sweet, my perfect boy.

"We'll need to talk more about what we both want from this relationship," I say after a while. "And we're gonna lay down some rules for you."

Pixie grins. "You're just looking for an excuse to spank me," he teases.

I reach around him and squeeze that bubble butt. "Damn right, though I don't need an excuse, now do I? If I told you to strip and present your ass to me for a spanking, you'd do it, wouldn't you?"

His cheeks flush and he licks his lips. "Yes, Daddy."

My cock grows hard, as it usually does when he's around, but this time I realize I don't have to hide it. I don't have to hold back anymore or restrain myself. He's *mine*.

20

PIXIE

"I'm taking you to bed now," he says firmly.

"Yes, Daddy."

Bear wraps his hands around my thighs and stands up, holding me as if I weigh nothing. Compared to him, I guess I don't, but the show of strength makes my cock tingle and my heart beat faster. This is really happening.

I wrap my legs around Bear's hips, my arms around his neck, and I brush our noses together with a smirk on my lips.

"What are you waiting for Daddy?" I tease, darting my tongue out to flick against his lips.

"Don't borrow trouble, baby boy. Any more sass and I might have to punish you."

I groan and wiggle against him, my cock trapped inside my tight jeans, pressed against his stomach. I can feel his denim-clad erection brushing against the curve of my ass. I consider for a second if a punishment might be worth it. Imagining Bear dropping me on the bed, pulling down my pants, and spanking my ass red before taking me hard and rough, using my hole for his own pleasure until

I'm begging for release, has precum wetting my underwear.

Bear squeezes my ass cheeks in his hands and tilts his face toward mine.

"Give Daddy a kiss."

Not needing to be told twice, I press my lips to his, letting out a little surprised squeak against his mouth as he starts to carry me toward his bedroom. His tongue pushes into my mouth, and I moan around it, happy to have any part of him filling me. Unlike the other kisses we've shared, it doesn't feel like Daddy Bear is holding back anymore. He's kissing me fully, deeply, hungrily, like he can't get enough, like he's claiming me for his own. I make little thrusts against him, my cock and balls already aching for relief.

"Such an eager boy. Are you going to behave and let me play with you?"

"Yes, Daddy." I nod eagerly, gripping him tighter as he lowers me onto the bed, not wanting to let go.

I whine as he eases my arms and legs from around him and steps back, standing at the foot of the bed and looking down at me.

"Strip for Daddy," he commands, his eyes dark with lust, the bulge in his pants making me want to beg and whine until he fills my needy hole. But I can be a good boy for Daddy...tonight at least.

I grab the hem of my shirt and slowly drag it upward, exposing my little belly, my peaked nipples, and finally pulling it over my head and tossing it aside. I unbutton my jeans and start to shimmy them down until I'm left in nothing but my black jock, tented with my erection.

I slip my hands into the waist of the jock, but Bear stops me. "Leave it on for now."

"Yes, Daddy."

His eyes flare with even more heat, his hand rubbing up and down the front of his pants.

"Roll over for me. I want to lick your pretty hole."

I nearly break my neck rolling over so fast. I tilt my hips and stick my butt up in the air like the little cock slut I am, wrapping my fists around his soft, expensive sheets and turning my head to look at Bear over my shoulder.

He licks his lips, looking down at me with hungry eyes. He unzips his pants and reaches inside, stroking his cock without pulling it out. I whine in protest, wanting to be the one playing with his big, sexy cock.

He brings his free hand to my ass cheek, kneading it before drawing back and giving me a quick slap. I moan at the sharp sting, humping the bed.

"Still, baby boy," he commands. "Daddy's going to take care of you."

"Yes," I pant, forcing myself to hold still, my eyes still glued to Bear's hand working himself up and down inside his boxers.

"You want a little taste?" he asks.

I whimper. "Yes, please, Daddy."

He pulls his hand out, his fingers glistening with precum, and brings them to my lips. I open my mouth, and he shoves his fingers inside, my tongue licking over them eagerly as I suck the salty taste of his arousal off them.

I whine when he tugs his fingers out of my mouth, but it turns into another moan as he uses both hands to spread my cheeks apart to look at my hole. He drags his wet fingers from the top of my crack, over my pucker, and down to my balls, making me shiver and push my hips back in search of more.

"This has to be the prettiest little hole I've ever seen," he praises, getting close enough that I can feel his hot breath on my cheeks and fluttering over my entrance.

I gasp at the first touch of his hot, wet tongue as it drags over my hole. With his hands grabbing both of my cheeks, he licks me hungrily. My body trembles as I do my best to hold still and not fuck the mattress again, no matter how much my cock drips and throbs, my balls tight and aching. I grunt and moan and whimper as his tongue pushes inside my ass, opening me with his tongue, fucking me.

"Please Daddy, please Daddy, please," I beg. He slaps the same ass cheek again, and I cry out as pleasure rolls through me, a shadow of the orgasm to come, lighting up every nerve ending in my body.

He pulls his tongue out and reaches toward the nightstand, opening the top drawer and pulling out a bottle of lube and a condom. I want to ask if we *need* the condom. He's seen my test results already and knows we always use condoms on set as well as being on PrEP. But he already knows all that, and if he thinks we need a condom then I trust Daddy to know what's best.

The sound of the lube cap clicking open makes my hole clench eagerly. I tilt my hips up again, begging without words, and get another slap on the ass for it, my skin prickling where his hand connects.

"I'd love to play with you for hours, tease you all night long, bringing you to the brink and then pulling you back over and over until you're nothing but a trembling mess of need." Bear says, and I whimper, both wanting and dreading what he's describing. "But not tonight."

I let out a relieved breath, and his slicked finger slides against my hole while he presses kisses to the back of my shoulder and down my spine before finally pushing it inside. He has nice, thick fingers, but it's not nearly enough.

When a second finger joins the first, I clench around them, wanting to feel more full, wanting to feel split open. Bear groans and crooks his fingers to hit my prostate, sending a jolt of electricity from my head to my toes.

"Are you ready for Daddy's big cock?"

"Yes," I moan.

He pulls his fingers out and, with his hands on my hips, flips me onto my back. I watch as he opens the condom and rolls it down his cock, my whole body buzzing with want, my cock dripping a steady stream of precum and soaking my jock.

Bear grabs the waist of my underwear and drags them down my legs, my cock slapping against my stomach as he does. I spread my legs wide for him, looking up into his eyes and feeling warmth spread through my body from the way he's looking back at me—like he wants to take care of me, like he *needs* me, like I'm his boy and he's my Daddy.

He pushes my legs up to my chest and lines himself up. The fat head of his cock nudges my entrance, and I grip his firm bicep, looking deep into his eyes.

"Tell me it's real this time, Daddy?" I beg, panting as he starts to push inside.

"It's real, baby boy, I promise it's real," he grunts, leaning down and burying his face against my neck as his impossibly thick erection splits me apart. I moan, wrapping my legs around him.

He slides in deep, filling me until I swear I can't breathe because it feels so good. The pain of being stretched turns quickly to pleasure as he rocks his hips, his cock moving against my prostate and tugging at the sensitive rim of my hole. I can feel every inch of him inside me, his huge body hovering over me, his eyes watching my every expression, and it all feels incredible.

I dig my fingers into his arms, holding on for the ride as he draws back and then thrusts into me harder, fucking me the way we've both been dying for him to. He grunts with each thrust, the deep rumble in his throat the hottest thing I've heard in my life. My eyes flutter closed, my head falling back.

"Open your eyes," Daddy Bear commands gruffly, and I snap my eyes back open. "I want you to watch as I make you fall apart."

"Yes, Daddy," I moan.

"I want you to come for me, baby boy."

I reach for my cock, but he pushes my hand away. "I know you can come hands free. Come on Daddy's cock."

"Oh god," I moan as he fucks me harder, hitting my prostate with every thrust, lighting me up as heat pools in my stomach and my balls throb. My cock drags against his stomach, and I dig my nails into his shoulder blades as pleasure rolls through me. My channel clenches around him, making his erection feel even bigger inside me. I let out a desperate cry as my cum pumps out of my cock against his skin, my ass pulsing around him until his thrusts become more erratic and his muscles tense. Daddy Bear lets out a roar worthy of his name, and his cock throbs inside me. I can feel the heat of his release even through the condom, and I wish it was inside me.

He sags against me, and a happy giggle bubbles past my lips.

"It's not good for a man's ego to laugh at him while he's still balls deep," he admonishes playfully.

"I'm not laughing at you, Daddy. I'm just so happy." I wrap my arms and legs around his body again, holding myself close to him until he pulls out and rolls us onto our sides facing each other.

"I'm happy too, baby boy." He cups the back of my neck and pulls me in for a slow, sweet kiss. "I'm going to get you cleaned up, then we're going to go to sleep, and in the morning we'll talk some more."

"Yes, Daddy," I say with a yawn.

21

BEAR

Waking up with Pixie is my arms is the stuff dreams are made of. It takes me a few seconds to realize I'm awake and yet my boy is still in my arms. He's plastered against me, half on top of me, as if he's scared I'm gonna sneak out on him. It dims my joy just a little to know it's gonna take time before he fully trusts I'm committed now. I've rejected him too many times for him to believe everything will be fine now. That's on me, and I'll do whatever I need to to make up for it.

His face is tilted in my direction, and my heart does a funny stumble in my chest when I take in his flawless skin, his smooth cheeks, and those luscious lips that are puckered even in his sleep. His is the face that inspires lofty poetry, if I were the type of man to write that shit. My style is more debauched, I reckon, but damn if I don't wanna make a really pretty video of him jerking off and pleasuring himself...just for my private viewing pleasure.

Pixie lets out a soft whimper, and then his eyes flutter open. As soon as he spots me, the little pout on his lips curves up into a sweet smile. "Good morning, Daddy," he says, and my heart stumbles again.

There's something about the way he says that word, with so much joy and contentment. It's not forced or acted, but this natural reverence that makes me feel so strong and protective. "Good morning, baby boy," I say.

Morning breath be damned, I reach over for a quick kiss. Well, that was the intention anyway, but once those soft lips brush against mine, I need more. Pixie is game, rolling on top of me and rubbing his body against me like a cat while allowing me to plunder his mouth, exploring every nook and cranny until we're both panting for breath.

"Daddy Bear," Pixie whimpers when I break off the kiss.

There's just enough of a whine in his tone to make me smile. "What is it, baby boy?" I ask.

His lips pucker into a cute pout. "You can't stop now, Daddy." He rubs his hard morning wood against me as if to underscore his point. "We were just getting to the good stuff."

My hands wrap around him, possessively claiming his ass. I squeeze those two luscious globes gently, reveling in the smooth skin under my rough hands. "Is my boy feeling needy this morning?"

He nods. "I have an awful lot of need stored up for you." Then his pout changes into a bit of a worried expression. "You don't think you'll get tired of that, do you?"

I shouldn't laugh at him, not when it's clear he's serious, but the question is so ridiculous I can't help it. "I don't think you'll have to worry about that. Every time I so much as look at you, I want to do things to you. Bad things. Naughty things. Things that involve bending you in a whole lot of different positions and seeing how deep I can get inside you."

Pixies smile is blinding. "I'm pretty flexible, did you notice?"

As if to prove his point, he's spreading his legs wide, and my right hand slips between his cheeks. "I did," I say, finding his entrance with my index finger. He's still slick from last night, and I slip inside him easily, aided by a little extra saliva. His eyes flutter as a soft moan flies from his lips. "But I can't wait to test out your flexibility myself."

After just a few strokes, I'm able to add a second finger, and Pixie drops his head against my shoulder, whimpering as he pushes back against my fingers. I love watching him, his expressive face showing everything he's feeling. It's easy to tell when I hit the right spot inside him, his eyes rolling back slightly and his mouth opening in a little O.

And oh, the sounds he makes. He's not loud, but it's more like this constant stream of soft sounds, little breathy intakes and moans, this whimpering he does when he really likes something, the way he clicks his tongue when he gets impatient for more.

"Daddy," he says, pleading.

Then there is that, the beautiful way that he begs. It makes me want to bring him to this point and keep him hovering there forever, just to hear him plead and beg. A man could get high on that, just saying.

"Daddy, please," he says again, lifting his head and shooting me a desperate look.

"I think we need to work on your stamina, boy," I tell him, fighting hard to keep my face straight. "You need to learn some orgasm control so you don't come as fast and easily. I thought now would be a good time to start with that."

Desperation changes into indignation in under a second. "You wouldn't," Pixie tells me.

My fingers, which have been fucking him steadily, stop, and I narrow my eyes at him. "Excuse me, baby boy?"

"No, no, no, please, Daddy Bear. You can't stop now," he pleads. He's wriggling his ass, clearly trying to get me to move again.

"I think we need to go over the rules," I tell him. "Because clearly, you're confused as to who's in charge in this relationship."

He shakes his head adamantly. "No, sorry, Daddy. You are. You're in charge. I'm sorry."

"Does that mean you get to tell me what I should or shouldn't do? Or what I would or wouldn't do?"

He shakes his head again, biting his lip. "No, Daddy."

I honestly can't tell if he's being serious or playing along, but either way, I love this dynamic between us. The idea of being in charge, of making decisions for him, it's exhilarating. And not just the sexual decisions, though I can't deny that power makes me heady and feel like a total caveman. I have two fingers shoved deep inside him, and the fact that I get to decide whether he can come or not, whether we continue this or not...I love it.

I start moving my hand again, but slowly, with deep, perfectly aimed thrusts that hit his sweet spot perfectly. "I'm not sure what you were used to with Daddy Luke," I say conversationally and watch his eyes shift to me instantly. "But I'm pretty sure he was in charge of your orgasms, wasn't he?"

Pixie nods, whimpering at the pleasure my fingers are bringing him. He's such a bottom, getting such pleasure from even my fingers. "Yes," he manages.

"So he would give you permission to come, right? And if he didn't, you couldn't come."

Pixie hesitates, even as he shifts his ass again, seeking more. "He would usually let me come," he confesses.

I laugh. "It's not hard to understand why. You're pretty damn hard to resist when you beg."

He blinks twice, and then a slow smile spreads across his face. "I like begging," he says, his eyes twinkling.

"I like it when you beg," I tell him. "So beg me, baby boy. Convince me to let you come."

His smile widens, growing mischievously. He brings his mouth close to my ear and whispers, "Daddy Bear, will you please put your fat cock inside me?"

My breath catches in my lungs, my already significant erection growing iron hard at the sound of those words.

"Pixie," I grumble, only half in protest.

He nips my earlobe with his teeth, sending sparks down my spine. "I love how full you make me feel, how your big cock splits me wide open. I want to ride you, Daddy, pleasure myself until we both come."

I all but yank my fingers out of him, rolling the both of us over so I can reach for the condoms and more lube on the nightstand. As soon as I'm ready, I push inside him, his face lighting up with pleasure as he lets me in.

"Ungh, so good," he says breathily.

And true to his word, the second I'm balls deep inside him, he pushes me on my back and starts riding me. My hands are on his hips, but he doesn't even notice. His head is thrown back, his eyes closed as he takes his pleasure from me.

He wasn't lying when he said he loved being split wide open by me. It's such a tight fit, his hole clenching around me, and it's the best feeling in the world. His hands roam my chest, holding onto my chest hair for leverage at times as he rises up and down, snapping his hips and angling them just right for maximum pleasure.

He's beyond beautiful, almost a dream come true, a vision if not for the very real sensations he's evoking inside me. My pulse is racing, my skin breaking out in a fine layer of sweat, which is funny, because I'm barely doing anything. It's all him, using me for his own pleasure, as if my enjoyment is an afterthought. And somehow, that's the most erotic thing I've ever seen.

He's moaning, groaning, swearing when his muscles get tired and he needs my hands to help him lift and slam down. I hold him tightly, then start whipping my own pelvis up in hard thrusts, creating even more friction. The wet slaps of flesh against flesh roll through the room, mingling with our rapid breaths and grunts.

He reaches for his cock, but I slap his hand away. "That's mine," I grunt, enveloping his pretty dick in my hand. He's wet with precum, and I love how perfectly he fits in my hand. He likes it rough, I know from watching his videos, so I don't hold back as I jerk him off.

I don't need him to tell me he's close. I can sense it and the way his muscles tense up, and the uncontrolled way his body is coming down now, ruthlessly seeking that last push to send him over the edge, almost uncoordinated.

I allow him to fly, then let go of the hold on myself and tumble right off the cliff with him, my orgasm barreling through me. Now *this* is how I like to start my days.

∽

Pixie

. . .

AFTER SEX, we doze again for a little while, and I wake up sticky with cum and sweat, plastered to Daddy Bear's side. I smile and snuggle closer, his arm tightening around me as I do.

"You awake again, baby boy?" he asks in a sleep rough voice.

"Mm-hmm," I murmur with a yawn.

"How about I make you breakfast, and we can have a talk about rules and expectations?"

"Sounds good, Daddy. Can I shower first?"

"Of course. Go shower, and I'll get breakfast ready." He kisses the top of my head, and I giggle happily, rubbing my nose against his shoulder and gripping him tightly for a second before crawling out of bed. I can feel his eyes on my ass as I saunter out of the bedroom with a little sway in my hips for his visual enjoyment.

I shower quickly, replaying the events of last night and this morning over and over until my cock is hard. I wrap my sudsy hand around it and stroke myself more than strictly necessary for cleaning purposes, a little moan falling from my lips as I get even harder.

We haven't talked about rules yet, but I have a feeling not touching myself without permission will be one of them, which makes it even more exciting to do it. Would Daddy spank me if he found out? I moan again and force myself to let go of my hard cock and rinse off before I can get myself into any trouble.

Getting out of the shower, I dry myself off and dress quickly, the smell of bacon and coffee wafting down the hallway and beckoning me to hurry as my stomach growls. I get dressed and pad barefoot down the hall and into the kitchen. There's a plate with bacon, eggs, and toast, as well as a glass of orange juice waiting for me on the table when I get there, Daddy Bear at the stove dishing up a second plate.

"Have a seat, dig in."

"Thank you, Daddy," I say politely as I slide into my seat and pick up my fork.

He joins me at the table and we eat in companionable silence for a few minutes until Daddy Bear clears his throat.

"It's time we discuss our expectations for what our relationship will look like," he says, and I nod eagerly. "I've played with boys before, but I've never had a boy full time. Is that what you want? To be my boy outside of the bedroom? Or do you see the daddy dynamic as purely sexual role-play?"

I study his face, considering my answer. He doesn't give anything away with his expression about what the right answer is, so I decide honesty is the best policy.

"I want to be your boy all the time, Daddy. I like knowing you'll take care of me, remind me to be responsible, look out for me and always know what's best for me."

He nods. "I'd like that too, baby boy." He reaches over and puts a hand on mine. "I'll be honest, having a boy full-time may be a little bit of an adjustment for me."

I snort a laugh. "Daddy, you've been daddying me since the day we met. You'll be fine."

He gives me a wry look before going on. "I don't see myself being a very strict disciplinarian Daddy. There will be rules because I care about my boy and want to make sure he knows what's right and wrong, but I don't want to control your every move or punish you often."

I smile even wider. "I like that, Daddy."

"Good. I'm glad we're in agreement," he says. "Are you ready for your rules?"

"Yes, Daddy."

"The first rule is put your shoes on the mat where they belong when you take them off," he says, fixing me with a stern look that makes me giggle.

"I knew you were going to say that."

"If you knew I was going to say it, then it shouldn't be hard to remember."

"Yes, Daddy," I agree sweetly.

"The second rule is no coming or touching yourself without permission."

"What about during filming?" I ask, my heart sinking a little as I realize he may ask me to quit Ballsy Boys.

"You can come during filming, but outside of that I expect you to get permission first. I know this is a little unorthodox, since we work in porn, but outside of the work on set, no one touches you but me. You're mine."

"Yes, Daddy," I agree happily. "What happens if I break the rules and touch myself? Will I get a spanking?"

"Do you like getting spankings?"

"Very much, Daddy."

"Then that's not much of a punishment, is it, baby boy?" he asks with amusement.

"No, Daddy," I pout.

"Tell you what, if you want a spanking, why don't you ask? And we'll have to figure out something less fun for when you *do* misbehave."

"Thank you, Daddy."

I scoop up another bite of eggs and put it into my mouth.

"Why don't you come over here, baby boy," Daddy Bear says, patting his lap.

I light up, scrambling out of my chair and into his lap without a moment's hesitation. He reaches over to grab my plate, one hand on my hip to keep me in place, and brings it over so I can reach it.

"Are those all the rules, Daddy?" I check, nibbling on a bite of toast.

"For now. We'll find our way as we go," he says, kissing my shoulder, one arm around my waist while he uses the other to eat. It's the best morning ever.

"I have one more question, Daddy."

"Go ahead."

"Do we have to keep this a secret at work, or can we tell everyone?"

Daddy Bear chews a bite of eggs slowly, seeming to consider the question carefully.

"I need to think about that," he admits after what feels like forever.

"I have a scene in two days, so should I pretend we're not together?"

"Just for now while I think about how best to approach it."

A slight feeling of disappointment settles over me. I was hoping he'd say he didn't want to hide our relationship, that we could shout it from the rooftops. But if he doesn't want the other guys at Ballsy to know, then I guess I'll have to keep my mouth shut for the time being.

"I have an idea. After breakfast, why don't we go spend the day at the beach?"

"Really?" I light up at that suggestion. "That sounds like so much fun, Daddy."

"Good. Eat up then so we can go."

"I'll have to decide which swimsuit to wear. I have four."

He shakes his head and smiles at me. "I'm sure you look great in all of them."

"Thank you, Daddy."

22

PIXIE

Bear's eyes on me during filming have always been my favorite part of doing a scene. But now that we're *together*—really, truly together—it's even better. He stands outside the view of the camera like he always does, and I keep my eyes on him as I ride Heart's cock into an explosive orgasm.

Since we haven't decided whether we're telling the guys right away or not, Bear disappears as soon as the scene ends, heading to his office like he always does, while Rebel hands me a towel and Heart gives my ass a friendly slap and tells me I did a great job today.

"I've gotta hurry up and shower. Mason and Lucky are waiting for me," Heart says as soon as I climb off him.

I wipe myself down and then grab my underwear off the floor to put them back on while Heart disappears to the locker room and Rebel talks to Joey and looks at the footage we just filmed. I edge in the direction of Bear's office rather than toward the locker room, keeping an eye out for anyone paying attention to me. When I'm satisfied that no one gives a good goddamn what I'm up to now that the scene is over, I quietly hurry down the hall to the office.

I tap on the door, and Bear calls out for me to come in. Stepping inside, I eye his large desk like I've done every time I've come into his office, and I imagine how much fun we could have in here, just the two of us. The difference is, this time it has the potential to be more than a fantasy.

Bear is sitting behind his desk, looking so in charge and sexy as fuck.

"Hi, Daddy," I say, giving him a sweet smile and batting my eyelashes at him.

"Hello, baby boy," he replies with a hint of amusement. "What can I do for you?"

"I was thinking more along the lines of something I could do for you." I waggle my eyebrows suggestively, and Bear lets out a deep, rumbly laugh that heats me up inside.

"Is that right?"

Crossing the small office, I lower myself to my knees at Daddy's feet. Evidence of his arousal tents his pants, showing how much it turned him on to watch me on set. I lick my lips and look up at him through my eyelashes, putting my hands on the rough denim covering his thighs. I trail my index finger along the inner seam of the pants as he spreads his legs, looking down at me with heat and amusement but not giving me explicit permission yet.

"Did you like watching Heart fuck me, Daddy?"

"I like seeing you feel good."

I consider the evasive answer for a few seconds, still running my hands up and down his thighs.

"I wasn't sure if it would be uncomfortable now that I'm yours," I admit.

"Eli." He says my name gruffly, taking my chin between his thumb and forefinger and tilting my head so I'm looking him right in the eyes. "You've been mine since the minute I laid eyes on you. I was just too stubborn to accept it."

My heart flutters, and I smile up at him. "Yes, Daddy," I agree.

"Now, be a good boy and suck Daddy's cock," he says, and I wiggle excitedly at his feet, reaching up to unzip his pants so I can get my hands on him. I haven't had a chance to taste him yet, and I've been dreaming of having his big, thick cock filling my mouth, fucking into my throat, gagging me and making me feel so sexy.

He lifts his hips so I can pull his pants and underwear down, his erection springing free, dark and swollen, his foreskin peeling back to expose his tip, glistening with a little bit of precum already. Bear wraps a hand around the base of his cock and brings it to my mouth. I part my lips, but instead of pushing inside, he drags the head of his cock along my lips, painting them with precum like lipstick. I whine impatiently, darting my tongue out to gather the salty taste, my hands gripping his knees, waiting for Daddy's instructions.

"Mmmm, such a well-behaved boy, so eager for my cock," he praises, and I nod rapidly, opening my mouth wider, hoping to entice him to fill it.

Even though I only came a few minutes ago with Heart, my own cock is already growing hard again as Daddy runs the fingers of his free hand through my hair, holding me in place as he continues to tease me with just his tip.

I'm so engrossed in what's happening that it takes me a second to register the sound of the office door opening.

"Bear, I was thinking—" Rebel's voice cuts off. "Oh shit."

Bear releases his grip on my hair, hurrying to pull his pants back up. I turn my head and give Rebel the stink eye.

"Ever hear of knocking?"

"Knocking would've meant missing the live porn show in here. Damn, Bear, you're packing some serious heat."

"Rebel," Bear growls, fixing him with a warning look that probably shouldn't turn me on as much as it does.

"Sorry. I would've knocked if I'd had any idea what was going on in here. I figured you were still pretending you weren't crazy about the kid," he explains, tilting his head in my direction so there's no doubt about who *the kid* is.

"He just pulled his head out of his ass two days ago," I explain.

"Are you looking for a spanking, baby boy?" Daddy warns.

Still kneeling near his feet, I turn my gaze back on him and bat my eyelashes again. "Maybe, Daddy."

"Fuck, that's hot," Rebel says. "You should totally come out of retirement and film a scene with your boy."

Bear chuckles, but my eyes go wide. "Oh my god, that would be *so* fun. Can we, Daddy?"

"I don't think anyone wants to see an old man like me on screen."

"It would be hot," I argue. "Please, Daddy? Pleeeeease?"

He sighs. "I'll think about it."

"Fans would love it," Rebel adds helpfully. "You know, it might even be a great intro video for the Kinky Boys studio you were telling me about. It would really solidify the connection between our two studios and give your friend a great opening boost."

"I'll think about it," he says again.

"Great. So, is this supposed to be a secret? Or can I round up all the guys so we can go out and celebrate? I'm pretty sure money is owed for bets placed between some of them about whether you'd ever work your shit out," Rebel says. "Speaking of which, what happened in New

York? Because if you two fucked then I owe Brewer fifty bucks."

"We're not keeping it a secret, and we can go out and celebrate, but if you think I'm giving you details about our sex life, you're sorely mistaken."

"Fair enough," he says with a smirk. "I'll send everyone a text while you two finish up what you were doing." He backs out of the office, shooting me a wink before closing the door behind him.

Bear lets out a breath once we're alone again.

"Sorry, Daddy, I know you weren't sure yet if you wanted everyone to know." I chew my bottom lip, worried this is going to spook Bear into pulling away again.

"Not because I'm ashamed of us," he assures me. "I didn't want anyone to think there was anything inappropriate going on since you're my employee. I wanted time to think of a way to explain it."

"Anyone who knows you knows you would never do anything inappropriate. You're the most upstanding man I've ever met." I crawl up into his lap and take his face between my hands. "You're a man of your word, and you always do the right thing. That's why I wanted you to be my Daddy so badly. Well, that and you're sexy as fuck."

He smiles and pulls me in for a kiss, one hand on the back of my head, the other cupping my ass through my underwear. I melt into the feeling of his tongue caressing mine, his lips firm and commanding, his hands on me steady and sure. My heart beats a little faster, and a giddy feeling bubbles in my chest. I know it's fast, but I think I'm falling in love with him. I think this is what love is *supposed* to feel like, and it's *so* much better than sweatpants.

"Why don't you go take a shower, baby boy," he says when the kiss ends, giving me a little pat on the butt.

"But I wanted to blow you," I pout.
"Later. Do what Daddy says."

***

Bear

The sound of laughter fills the private room of the Mexican restaurant where we're gathered. Our group has grown over the years, and as I look around the room, I couldn't be more proud. There's Rebel and Troy, a match made in heaven if I've ever seen one. They are perfect for each other, this surprisingly solid couple that supports and complements each other.

I think Rebel is ready for even more commitment, but he's smart enough to take it slow. Troy has come a long way, from what I understand, but he's still skittish at times. He's slowly building a relationship with his mother, and I'm happy every time Rebel gives me an update that it's going well.

Sitting next to them is our threesome. Mason is parked on Lucky's lap—probably to stop him from knocking more stuff over since he already spilled a whole pitcher of water—while Heart is leaning against him from the other side. That's the union that surprised me the most, but it's also the one that makes me happiest, I think. To see Heart so loving and carefree with his two men, it's a thing of beauty.

He's working hard on his education, reducing his scenes to prioritize getting his degree. And Lucky and Mason support him every step of the way, which I think is amazing. Heart has changed so much, losing that dark, edgy look he had, which has been replaced by a deep inner peace and joy. Being cleared from his previous conviction certainly helped, but at the end of the day, it was his men who changed him.

Tank and Brewer still bicker and banter most of the time, but it's easy to spot the love underneath. On the surface, they're probably the most unlikely pairing, but when you dig a little deeper, it makes total sense. I love seeing how big, gruff Tank can get so sweet and caring with Brewer. And more surprisingly, Brewer lets him. He has the bad habit of taking shitty care of himself, but Tank forces him to.

I'm expecting their resignation any day now, what with the two of them graduating and moving on. It's a bittersweet feeling, losing this group of boys. It's an inevitable part of being in porn, since it's not something most people do for long. But how can I not be happy for my boys, seeing how much they've grown, watching them fall in love and find happiness?

Campy and Jackson showed up as well. He quit shooting with us a while ago now, but he still gets invited when we hang out. And his transformation rivals Heart's. Campy was always closed off before, clearly hiding something, but now he's this open guy who is so secure in his own identity and the love of his man.

Jackson's fame has grown exponentially, and his series is still a big hit. It's amazing to realize that when you see him hanging out with a bunch of porn stars, something his publicity agent still doesn't like, but Jackson refuses to hide his association with us. It speaks volumes to his character, and his fans love him for his unwavering support of LGBTQ rights.

My sweet Pixie climbs on my lap, yanking me from my

thoughts about the happiness of my boys and making me focus on my own joy. He's quickly become my everything, this ray of sunshine. And since we got caught in my office, everyone knows we're together anyway, so there's no need to hide it anymore. None of the boys have an issue with it though. Apparently there were several bets going on regarding what was happening between us. *Fuckers.*

I'm still not entirely comfortable being in a relationship with one of my employees, though it's hard to think of Pixie like that when he's so quickly become my everything. But after finally coming to terms with my fears, I wasn't about to let work hold us back even longer. I did ask Rebel to schedule all his shoots, do his performance reviews, and sign off on all payments to Pixie, just so he can make sure I'm not favoring him in any way that would be unfair to the others.

I nuzzle his neck. "Hey, baby boy," I say softly. "Did you miss Daddy?"

Pixie lets out a soft sigh as he nestles himself on my lap, rubbing his cheek against my chest as he so often does. It's this gesture of comfort for him, like reorienting himself on my body every time. "I always miss you when you're not holding me, Daddy," he says, and my heart totally melts over that cheesy line.

The thing with Pixie is that he means it. His devotion to me is so pure and complete, it has no limits. My arms around him tighten for a second, letting him feel I need him too. "I love having you close," I tell him. "If it were up to me, you'd be on my lap all day. You know that."

"When are you going to make an honest man out of our Pixie?" Brewer calls out, teasing as usual.

Does he really think I'd ever risk letting my beautiful boy go? No chance in hell. I just want to wait a little longer before getting quite *that* serious, maybe encourage him to get an education first. He's so young, but I don't doubt his love for me anymore. It radiates off his face all the time. But someday, he'll be mine officially...and I won't wait too long.

Before I can say anything, Campy clears his throat. "On that note, Jackson and I have an announcement."

With an intro like that, it can mean only one thing, and my heart soars with happiness for them. Campy reaches for Jackson's hand, and the look the cowboy sends him is so full of love it brings tears to my eyes. He's done well, our Campy, but then again, so has Jackson.

"Jackson has asked me to marry him, and I said yes," Campy says with audible pride and happiness.

The cheer that rolls through the room is loud enough to rattle the glasses, and we all jump up to congratulate them. When it's my turn, I give Campy a tight hug. "You did good, kid," I tell him. "I'm so fucking proud of you."

He hugs me back, then kisses me on my cheek, a rather unusual sign of affection from him. "Thank you for everything, Bear. I wouldn't be who and where I am today without you and the boys."

Gah, he's gonna make me tear up all over again. "So, when's the wedding?" I ask.

Jackson steps close to Campy and pulls him against his body. "It's gonna be a private wedding with a very small group of friends," he says. "You're all invited, but we ask you to not reveal the date or location to anyone. We don't want the press to get a hold of this."

That makes total sense, considering Jackson's Hollywood status.

"Jackson's agent was able to close an exclusive deal with a magazine for the story and pictures. With them, we know they're gonna put it in a positive light, rather than focus on the fact that we're gay or that I used to do porn," Campy says.

It's clear this is something he's stressing about, and I'm glad to see they've found a way to handle it well.

"We'll be there," I promise him. "We wouldn't miss it for the world."

23

PIXIE

I nuzzle into Daddy's side, melting into the warmth of his touch, and I wonder if I should wait for him to tell me he loves me first. I've never been very good at not saying exactly what I'm thinking, but I'm also afraid to scare him if I say it too fast. It took long enough to get him here; the last thing I want is to spook him. It's only been a couple of weeks since we've officially been together, and I'm sure he would think that's too fast for me to love him. But I do.

"What are you thinking about, baby boy?" he asks, running a hand gently up and down my bare back. I fling one leg over his hips, loving the feeling of his big, hairy body against mine.

"The future."

"Oh yeah?" he sounds a little cautious, but curious all the same. "What about the future? What are your dreams? I'm assuming you didn't come all the way out to LA to work for Ballsy Boys."

I giggle. "No, but it's certainly been a worthwhile detour."

"I agree." He kisses the top of my head, and I smile against his chest.

"It's probably silly," I admit. "And with my bad money management, it's going to be awhile before I can actually do it."

"Tell Daddy," he says.

"I've always wanted to be a fashion designer. I came out here to go to design school, but then everything was so expensive and overwhelming, I got off track."

"Fashion design? I can definitely see that."

"You can?" I ask hopefully. "Do you think I'd be good at it?" I push myself up to look at him.

"Baby boy, you have so much fire in you, I think you'd be incredible at anything you set your mind to." He cups the back of my neck and pulls me in for a peck on the lips. "Did you pick a school yet?"

"I've looked at a few, but only their websites. I haven't done any tours or talked to admissions or anything."

"Okay, here's what we're going to do. Tell me your top three favorites, and we're going to make an appointment to visit them and get more information. Then we're going to get you enrolled for the next available semester."

"Really?" I smile brightly. "But how will I pay for it? I could apply for a scholarship or financial aid. Do you know how to do any of that?"

"Don't worry about that, that's Daddy's job."

"Thank you, thank you, thank you." I crawl on top of him and kiss all over his face. "You're the best Daddy ever."

He chuckles and holds me tight. "I don't think you'll have time to work at Ballsy if you're focusing on school," he says once I stop kissing him.

I deflate a little at that. Doing porn may not have been part of my plan, but I really do like it. I like all the guys at the studio, and I love the fans. It's fun and exciting. I know all the guys are moving on with their lives too, so soon there will be all new models. It makes me sad to think of this time of my life ending. I've never had friends like them before. I never thought I could love a job like this before. I know everyone moving on doesn't mean we aren't still friends, but it's still sad. It's the end of an era.

"Do I have to quit completely? What if I only filmed occasionally?" I ask, not quite ready to completely walk away.

"Is that what you want?"

I nod rapidly. "It really is."

"Okay, then that's what we'll do."

"Thank you, Daddy." I kiss him again, and this one turns heated quickly, my lips parting to let his tongue in as he grips my ass cheeks in both hands. My cock hardens against his stomach, and I squirm impatiently.

"What do you want, baby boy?" Daddy Bear asks me, like he so often does. Daddy Luke always took care of my pleasure, but nothing can compare to how much it means to Daddy Bear. It makes me feel like the luckiest boy in the whole world with the very best Daddy.

"You said I could ask if I wanted a spanking?"

"That's right," he says, squeezing my cheeks in his hands. "Is that what my boy wants? A spanking?"

"Please, Daddy?" I beg breathlessly.

Without warning, he sits up, and I giggle as I do my best to hold on so I don't fall backward.

"Spin around and show Daddy that pretty little ass of yours so he can redden it."

"Yes, Daddy," I gasp, scrambling quickly to turn around in his lap so my ass is facing him and my hands are planted on either side of his calves, his feet stretched out in front of me. He kneads my cheeks between his hands again, parting and squeezing them, my cock growing harder as it bobs in the air.

"I'm not going to be rough with you, baby boy, so I don't think we need a safeword. If it's too much and you want me to stop, just say so, okay?"

"Yes, Daddy."

His hands continue to rub my skin, warming it, relaxing me into his touch as my anticipation builds. He pulls one hand back and lands a loud smack against my right butt cheek, and I yelp at the sting, my cock jerking excitedly.

He rubs the spot for a few seconds before pulling back again and delivering another slap, on my other cheek. The contact heats my skin and makes my balls draw tight, precum leaking from my slit onto Daddy Bear's legs.

"My boy likes that, doesn't he?" he praises, squeezing the globes of my ass again before giving me another spank, another jolt of excitement that makes me whine and thrust my hips involuntarily.

"I love it, Daddy." I pant as another blow comes, and a sob falls from my lips.

"Your pretty little cock is so hard right now, isn't it?"

"Yes, Daddy," I groan as he swats the upper part of my thigh where it meets the swell of my ass.

"Touch yourself, baby boy. Come while I'm spanking you."

I groan and reach between my legs, taking my erection in my hand and squeezing it as he gives me two slaps in quick succession.

"Your skin is so sensitive, all nice and pink for me without having to spank you too hard," he says, rubbing my cheeks and parting them again. I can feel his gaze on my hole, and it fills me with heat and need. I tug my cock faster, my balls tightening as more precum dribbles from my slit.

"Please, Daddy, please." I'm not sure what I'm begging for—maybe I'm caught up in the pure pleasure of begging.

His thumb brushes my hole while his other hand lands another slap on my ass, and pleasure washes over me, cum pumping into my hand as I moan and cry his name over and over.

Daddy Bear pulls me into his arms and cuddles me close again as I come down from the high of my orgasm.

"Thank you, Daddy Bear," I murmur, burrowing my face against his chest again, feeling his coarse hair against my cheeks and drowning myself in the smell of him.

"Anything for you, baby boy."

I love you is right on the tip of my tongue, and I weigh the pros and cons of saying it first until I drift off for a nap.

When I wake up, the light coming through the window has changed, and I'm pretty sure it's been more than a few hours.

"Why if it isn't Sleeping Beauty, finally awake," Bear says. I realize I'm no longer lying on top of him, so I lift my head to find him sitting up with his back against the headboard and his laptop in front of him.

"Sorry, did I sleep a long time?"

"A few hours. It's okay though. I had some bookkeeping to get done anyway."

I yawn and stretch, a small ache still in my ass from the spanking. My stomach growls, and Daddy Bear closes his laptop.

"Go hop in the shower and get ready, I'm taking you out for dinner."

I brighten, sitting up quickly and hopping out of bed. "Do I need to dress fancy?"

"Do you *want* to go somewhere fancy?" he asks with amusement.

I tap my chin, considering the question. "How about medium fancy?"

Bear raises an eyebrow at me, and his lips twitch. I can tell he's trying not to laugh at my antics. "Medium fancy it is."

"You know, Daddy, you might spoil your boy if you give in to his every whim," I warn sagely.

"I'll be on the lookout for that," he says. "Now go get ready before I change my mind."

I scurry into the bathroom as quickly as I can. The day we came home from celebrating with Rebel and the rest of the guys a few weeks ago, Bear told me to move all my things into his room because it was *our* room now.

Our bedroom, our gigantic bathroom with a jacuzzi tub, our house, our life…together.

I can't stop smiling as I shower and get ready to go out. I meant it earlier when I told Daddy Bear this unexpected detour in life had been worth it. I wouldn't trade what I found along the way for anything in the world.

Bear takes me to a nice French restaurant where I can't pronounce, let alone understand, anything on the menu. It's okay though because Daddy takes the liberty of ordering for me, and if I thought he couldn't get any hotter, I was completely wrong. Daddy Bear speaking French, even if it *is* just to order snails or something gross, is literally the hottest thing on the planet.

I sip the wine Bear ordered me and smile contentedly at Daddy, boldly sliding my foot up his leg as he hands our menus over to the waiter and then gives me a warning look.

"You're playing with fire, baby boy," he warns sternly.

"I don't know what you mean, Daddy," I say innocently, batting my eyelashes.

"Uh-huh." He takes a sip of his own wine. "Don't think I won't remember you being naughty once our meals come and you want to know what exactly it is on your plate."

I gasp in mock horror. "Devious Daddy," I accuse, and he laughs, filling my chest with warmth and making me love him just a little bit more.

∽

Bear

These past few weeks have been wonderful. Being with him is everything I imagined it would be, and I've found a freedom in being his daddy that is almost unreal. In hindsight, I can't believe I've been such a stubborn ass for so long. I'm damn lucky my sweet boy proved to be even more stubborn than me...and that he's got such a big, forgiving heart.

We're cuddling on the couch while watching *Queer Eye*. Pixie's running commentary and excited squeals are even more entertaining than the show itself, and there's a deep sense of peace and joy in my heart.

Then my phone rings, and Pixie pauses the TV so I can take the call.

"Hello?" I say, not recognizing the local number.

"Maxwell, it's Ryan Hannah, Travis's friend."

"Ryan, how are you?"

He lets out a sigh before he replies. "I'm okay. I miss him terribly, but I'm okay. The judge has signed off on Travis's will, and he's left you something. Would it be okay if I stopped by today to give it to you?"

"Sure."

I give him my address, and he promises he'll be there in under an hour.

"He left you something?" Pixie asks after I've ended the call.

"It seems so. We never discussed it, so I have no idea."

Pixie accompanied me to Travis's funeral, despite me insisting I could go by myself. I didn't want to expose him to my grief, but he insisted, and I was beyond grateful to have him there. It's been the hardest funeral of a resident I've ever attended, and having him by my side made it a little less painful.

He takes as much care of me as I do of him, just in different ways. His foot rubs are the best in the world, he gives wonderful back massages as well, and he loves pleasuring me with a blow job as much as he can.

Me, I love taking care of him in other ways. I paid off all his debts, and he has a budget now with a debit card that has a maximum spending limit. I still treat him to stuff all the time, but that's my discretion, and he loves it like that. He's submitted fully and with joy to my care, and I love seeing him blossom. Even the guys have commented on it, how much happier he is, and how he thrives in our relationship. We both do, and I've no intention of ever letting him go again.

Ryan shows up as promised, but when I ask him if he wants to come in, he declines. "I promised my wife I'd be back soon to spend some time with the kids. They miss their uncle Travis as well, and it's hard on us as a family."

I nod in understanding.

He grabs an envelope from his pocket and hands it to

me. "Travis wrote you a letter and asked me to hand deliver it to you. I don't know what's in it."

I take it from him, grief filling my body. "I miss him too," I tell Ryan and watch his eyes fill up.

"I still wonder, you know, if I made the right call. But then I think about what you said, how love is love, no matter what form it takes, and I know it wouldn't have mattered," Ryan says, his voice breaking at the end.

I reach out and put a hand on his shoulder. "You would've missed him just the same. Be grateful for the time you had together. In the end, it's all that really matters. Love."

He nods, then sends me a watery smile. "I was happy to see you with your boy at the funeral. I didn't have the chance to say anything then, but I'm happy for you."

"Yeah, I finally pulled my head out of my ass, thanks to Travis. I owe him everything."

Ryan's smile widens, even as there's still sadness. "He'd love that."

We say goodbye with a firm handshake, and I close the door behind him, looking at the envelope in my hand. Pixie steps in for a hug, sensing I'm sad, and nestles his head against my chest.

"Are you gonna read it, Daddy?" he asks.

"Yeah. Wanna come sit with me while I do?"

Fuck knows I'll need his sweet presence. We settle on the couch again, Pixie draped all over me as I open the letter.

DEAR BEAR,
There's so much I want to say to you, but my time is running

out. I hope we'll have the opportunity for a last heart-to-heart, but if not, I need to say this to you.

Thank you. Your friendship has meant the world to me these last months and has brought me so much joy. If circumstances had been different, I know we would've been lifelong friends.

So as a friend, allow me to speak some truth into your life. People often say that we only have one life to live, but we don't. We only have one death, but we live every day. Sometimes I fear that you've forgotten how to live. You spend so much time with the dying that you've forgotten you're still alive and in your prime. So live, Bear. Live life to the fullest every day.

I know you promised your dying boyfriend you'd be there for the dying, and God knows that you held that promise. I'm now releasing you from it. You've fulfilled your promise. You've had enough. Go live, Bear. It's another dying friend's last wish.

Love,

Travis

PS And for fuck's sake, open your damn eyes and see how perfect that sweet boy would be for you before he finds himself another daddy. You idiot.

THE TEARS COME FAST, and I'm not even ashamed when I fall apart in Pixie's arms. He's holding me tight, whispering sweet words as I let out a mountain of grief. I don't even know what I'm crying for but it's way more than just Travis.

He's right. I've paid my debt, if I even ever had one. I fulfilled my promise to Freddie. The sad truth is that he died, but I'm still alive, and I want to live with my Pixie by my side. All I need to do now is convince him I love him and will love him forever.

Pixie

I CLUTCH Daddy Bear's hand tight as we walk into the hospice. Sadness hangs in the air along with the smell of antiseptic and illness. It's easy to understand now why he always came home so sad after his visits here, and it makes me even more in awe of him. If anyone in the world needs someone to care, it's the people here, and Daddy Bear gave them that, even when it took something from him.

I squeeze his hand harder and let him lead me down the busy hallway. He clearly knows his way around this place, and I guess that makes sense considering how long he volunteered here. All the nurses seem to know him, giving him smiles and waves when they see us. A few of them check him out shamelessly. I edge closer to Daddy Bear until he's nearly tripping over me, so no one can question whether he's available or not. He's *my* Daddy, and I'm never giving him up.

We slow to a stop in front of one of the rooms, and Bear brings his hand up to knock at the door.

"Come in," a frail, female voice answers.

He opens the door and leads me inside.

"Hi, Helena." He greets the woman who is sitting halfway up in bed, looking just as weak as she sounded. Her whole face lights up at the sight of Bear, and my heart flutters a little with even more adoration for him.

"Maxwell, I'm so happy to see you. I remembered that recipe I wanted to give you last time, and I wasn't sure if you'd be back to see me before...well, if I'd have the chance to give it to you."

"I appreciate that. I've been craving a good apple crumble since you mentioned it," he says warmly, pulling two chairs from the corner of the room up close to her bed. "I brought someone special to meet you today. I hope you don't mind."

She smiles at me and I give a shy wave.

"This is my... This is Eli," he introduces me.

"He's cute. Is he your boyfriend?" Helena asks with a small smile.

"He is, but between you and me, I feel like I'm a little old to be calling anyone a *boyfriend*," Bear confesses, sitting down and patting the other seat for me to do the same. Helena laughs and shakes her head at him before lapsing into a coughing fit. Bear calmly reaches for a small bucket on the tray near her bed and holds it under her mouth so she can spit some phlegm into it. Then he grabs a few tissues and offers them to her.

"You're such a sweet man," she says. "And if you're too old for a boyfriend, then I think you ought to make an honest man out of this one. He's too cute to let get away."

Bear chuckles, his cheeks pinking, and I can feel my own heating as well.

"You should listen to the woman, she sounds smart," I joke.

The three of us chat for a while after that. It turns out the sweet old lady in the bed led quite a wild life in her time. She regales us with tales of following her favorite band on tour one summer when she was eighteen and all the trouble she got into. It seems like Bear has heard these stories before, but he doesn't seem bored or put out by listening to them again. He laughs in all the right places and helps Helena sip water when her throat gets dry.

"I'd better give you that recipe before I fall asleep on you," she says after a little while. "Grab a pen and paper so you can write it down."

Bear does as she says, writing down her *very* detailed instructions word for word as she gives them.

"Thank you for this. I'm going to have to make it for Eli as soon as we get home." Bear puts a hand on Helena's in thanks.

"Don't mention it. My daughters can't cook worth a damn, and *someone* should have my family recipe to enjoy."

"Well, I'll certainly enjoy it, and I'll think of you when I do," Bear promises. "I wanted to let you know before I go that this is going to be my last time volunteering here for the foreseeable future."

"Oh?"

"A friend here helped me realize it's time to change my priorities a little. I've spent all my time here for over a decade. It's time I focus on other things." He shoots a look at me out of the corner of his eye, and Helena follows his gaze with a smile.

"I think that's a good plan. There's a lot of life out there to live, Maxwell. Don't let it pass you by."

"I won't." He pats her hand one more time, giving it a squeeze before letting go. "Take care, Helena."

"You too."

He takes my hand again and leads me out of the room and into the hallway.

"Daddy," I say softly, tugging at his hand so he stops. The feelings that have been growing for him for months feel too big to hold back a second longer after seeing this side of him. He's an incredible man, and I can't believe he's really mine.

"Is everything okay, baby boy?" he asks, a look of concern flashing through his eyes.

I step closer, tilting my head to look up at him, putting

my free hand on his chest, where I can feel his steady heartbeat.

"I love you, Daddy Bear."

He drags in a sharp breath, his eyes going wide and his lips parting in surprise. His grip on my hand tightens, and he brings his other hand to my face, gently running the pads of his fingers along my cheekbone and over my nose, then tracing my lips with them.

"You're too perfect to be real," he murmurs as if to himself. "I love you so much."

I smile so big it makes my cheeks hurt as I launch myself up to plant a smacking kiss on his lips.

24

BEAR

This is absolutely crazy. I am absolutely crazy. Why the fuck did I ever allow myself to get talked into this?

"Nervous?" Hunter asks me as I walk onto the set, which consists of a living room with a sturdy couch. We're really not gonna need more, so it'll work.

I shoot him a dark look. "I'd like to see you shoot a porn at our age," I say.

A porn. I'm shooting a freaking porn video. I'm bare chested, dressed only in a pair of ripped jeans that, according to Pixie, make my body look like a god. I'll take his word for it. They're not gonna stay on long anyway, according to our script. I can only hope I'll perform half as well as he's expecting me to. I'm certainly going to need some more help getting into the *mood*, as I'm only half hard right now.

Hunter shrugs. "It wasn't my idea, man."

"No, but you certainly didn't object when Rebel suggested it."

Hunter's face breaks open in his signature cheeky smile.

"Why the hell would I say no to *that*? It's brilliant marketing."

That, I can't deny. With my permission, Hunter asked Rebel for his input to market his new website, and Rebel came up with some genius ideas. One of them was the spontaneous suggestion he made that day in the office when he caught Pixie giving me a blow job: that we would shoot a scene together.

At first, the notion was too ridiculous to even consider. I am forty-five, for fuck's sake, way too old to be shooting porn. But then Hunter made a request again to use Pixie for his first scene, and I just couldn't. I have no problem at all with him still shooting for Ballsy Boys, but somehow, it's different for Hunter's site. Don't ask me to explain, because I can't. Must be some weird protective thing, I don't know.

The only solution I could come up with was to shoot a scene with him myself, and here we are. Hunter was over the moon when I told him, since his research shows daddy kink is super popular. Somehow, that doesn't make me any less nervous. My god, it's been what, fifteen years since I did porn?

"This should be interesting," Joey comments, and I swear, he's literally rubbing his hands together.

He gets an even darker look from me, not that I expect it to have any effect. "Not. One. Word."

"Damn, Papa Bear, you are one hot motherfucker," a gleeful voice calls out.

A voice I know all too well. A voice that shouldn't be here, because he announced his retirement weeks ago.

I turn around to find not only Brewer, because of course it was him who made that remark, but the other boys as well. Tank, Heart, hell, even Campy is standing there. And they're all sporting identical grins as they take in my half-naked body. Let me tell you, few things are more effective for losing your erection than facing a firing squad like this.

I throw up my hands in a dejected gesture. "Really?" I ask. "I mean, guys, really? You all had to show up to witness my humiliation?"

I can't even be upset with them, because let's face it, in their position, I would've done the exact same thing. They've had to shoot hundreds of scenes with me always watching, so of course they'd jump at the opportunity to get back at me.

"We're just here for moral support," Campy quips, because of course, *that's* why they're here. *Right.*

"And we brought some Viagra, just in case," Brewer pipes up again. Even Tank laughs at that joke, and I have to work hard to prevent my lips from curling up into a smile. I can't give him that satisfaction.

But then my sweet Pixie walks onto the set, naked and uninhibited, immediately seeking my embrace. "Hi, Daddy Bear," he says softly, then offers his mouth for a kiss.

And as soon as my arms wrap around him, I forget about everything and everyone else. It's just him and me, my precious boy and his Daddy. "Hey, baby boy," I say, pulling him tight against me. "How are you feeling about this?"

I know the answer, but I want to check anyway and give him the opportunity to pull out if that's what he wants. Of course, if anyone of us is going to be pulling out, it's gonna be me—pun intended.

Pixie must've asked me ten times if I really was okay with doing this, and even now, I'm still not sure. I know there's a market for older men in porn. Hell, I saw the research. I know the numbers. But why does it have to be *this* older man?

"I'm excited, Daddy," Pixie says, almost bouncing in my

arms. "I want to show everyone how sexy you are and how good we are together."

When he puts it like that, it's hard to resist. I kiss him one last time. "Okay, baby boy. Let's do this."

We break apart, and just when I want to walk over to the couch, Hunter grabs my arm. "Bear, all joking aside, if you really don't want to do this, it's okay to say no."

I respect the hell out of him for saying this, especially at this stage. I grab him by the shoulder and give it a squeeze. "Thanks, but I'm good."

He nods, relief visible on his face. "I know you're a pro at this, but I also realize it might be hard for you to relax now that you're in front of the camera rather than behind it. So just try to let go and focus on your boy, okay? We want it to be as natural as possible. You don't have to signal for anything, unless you need a break. We'll be close with the cameras to capture everything, so just keep it flowing naturally."

I nod. "Gotcha."

And then I sit down on the couch and grab the book I'm supposed to read according to the very loose script we created for this scene. Joey does a last check on the cameras and the lighting, and then everyone quiets down as Hunter calls out that were rolling.

I take a few deep breaths to center myself, then focus on whatever book I'm reading. It's a gay romance novel, I discover, and I can't hold back a soft smile. Nice touch from Rebel right there.

After ten seconds or so, Pixie trots in to the scene, immediately kneeling at my feet. I ignore him, according to my instructions. He bows his head, waiting for me to acknowledge him.

I take my time, and then address him. "Why are you here, baby boy? I thought you were going to take a bath."

Pixie bites his lip. "I've been naughty, Daddy," he says, his eyes twinkling with mirth. He knows what's coming, and judging by how excited his cock is, he can't wait.

Still, we have a part to play before we get there. "Naughty? That doesn't sound like a good boy. What did you do?"

Pixie looks at me from between his lashes. "I touched myself, Daddy."

Oh, he plays it so well. "Touched yourself where, baby boy? Did you play with your pretty nipples?"

He shakes his head.

"Did you give yourself the stomach rubs Daddy always gives you?"

Another shake of his head.

"Show Daddy where you touched yourself."

He shuffles back on his knees slightly, spreading his legs. His right hand trails from his collarbone downward, meandering down his body until he reaches his pretty little cock. He only taps it, never saying a word, though his heated look at me speaks volumes.

I look at him as sternly as I can pull off. "Did you touch yourself on your cock?"

He licks his lips, knowing what's coming. "Yes, Daddy."

"Are you allowed to touch yourself there?"

"No, Daddy."

"Who does that gorgeous cock belong to?"

"To you, Daddy. I'm so sorry, Daddy. I didn't mean to, but I was undressing for my bath and I got excited and... I touched myself."

I shake my head at him, frowning. "Daddy is disappointed in you, baby boy. You know you're not allowed to touch yourself without Daddy's permission. That means Daddy is going to have to punish you."

Pixie nods solemnly, and how he pulls that off when we both know how much he wants this, I have no idea. "Yes, Daddy."

"Position yourself on Daddy's knee," I tell him, and Pixie doesn't waste a second in draping himself over my knee, that gorgeous round butt sticking out.

From the corner of my eye, I notice Joey moving in with the handheld camera, even as two other cameramen are getting wide and medium shots from other angles. I try to close them out of my mind and focus on how soft Pixie's skin feels under my hand as I rub his ass.

"Are you ready, baby boy?" I ask, even now checking in with him for his permission.

"Yes, Daddy. I deserve to be punished."

I let my hand come down on his ass cheek, leaving the first red spot behind. It's quickly followed by more, as I rain down slaps on his butt, covering both his globes in a slow, random pattern. Hunter warned me not to go too fast, as viewers needed to see his ass grow red. That's not hard, since I always like to take my time spanking him. It's simply too much fun and pleasurable to rush.

Pixie moans, gasping as his skin grows more red with every hit. He takes it beautifully, like he always does, almost leaning into my touch.

I don't hit him that hard. This is a pleasure spanking, even if it's supposed to look like a disciplinary one. Fortunately, Pixie's skin is super sensitive, so even with light slaps, he reddens beautifully.

After a few minutes, his ass is all hot and red, and I keep rubbing in between smacks to stimulate the blood flow. I'll admit I tease his hole a little every now and then, but I don't think anyone will mind. Hell, I doubt anyone could resist that perfect, pink star that's right there in front of me.

When I think he's had enough, I stop. Pixie's body trembles with a heavy shudder, and I slowly rub his behind a bit more, playing it up for the camera. "I hope you learned your lesson, baby boy, though I will admit, I'm partial to the sight of your well-spanked ass."

Pixie slides off my lap onto his knees, looking up at me with dark eyes and cheeks flushed with desire. "Thank you for punishing me, Daddy. You take such good care of me. I'm so sorry I disobeyed you. Can I please make it up to you?"

I lean in for a soft kiss, which wasn't in the script, but how can I resist? "What did you have in mind, baby boy? Do you want to make Daddy feel good?"

Pixie's hands are already on my jeans. "Yes, please, Daddy. Let me suck you. I love your thick cock in my mouth."

From anyone else, that would sound fake and cheesy as fuck, but Pixie means it. You can't act the way he greedily unzips my jeans and the gasp of pleasure as he takes in my cock—which is now almost fully erect, much to my relief.

I lift myself off the couch for a few seconds to allow him to drag my jeans down to my ankles. Of course, I went commando. No need to make things harder than necessary.

Pixie nuzzles my cock. It's one of those things he does, breathing in my smell. He says it's comforting and makes him feel loved and treasured. Again, I'm aware of the cameras moving around me, but then Pixie takes me into my mouth, and I forget about everything else.

∽

Pixie

. . .

This isn't anything like the other scenes I've filmed. It's so much better. I look up at Daddy Bear from my place on my knees, his big cock stretching my lips, and it's easy to forget there are a dozen people standing around, just outside my peripheral vision, watching us, filming us. I bet we look amazing together like this. My cock gets harder at the thought of watching our video later, knowing other people will be getting off watching it too.

I take Daddy Bear's cock with long, sloppy sucks, the mics no doubt picking up the wet sounds my mouth makes. He groans, his eyes fixed on me the entire time, one hand in my hair, the other cupping my jaw, fingers tracing the shape of my stretched lips.

"Such a good boy, taking Daddy's cock so well," he praises.

I pull off with a pop and smile up at him with wet lips. My skin is hot where Bear's hand reddened it, and I can't wait to watch this later to see how hot it looks. I flick my tongue along Daddy's shaft, down to his balls. He spreads his legs farther apart, and I take each of his heavy balls into my mouth one at a time.

"Daddy wants to see your pretty hole, come up here and show me," Bear says, patting the couch beside him.

"Yes, Daddy." I crawl up into his lap and place a quick kiss on the tip of his nose, earning me a sweet smile, before turning sideways on the couch to drape myself over the arm, spreading my legs so he—and the camera—can get a good view of my entrance.

Since we discussed beforehand that we weren't going to do cuts during the scene, I skipped the plug, opting to take some time *right* before coming on set to prep myself. Daddy

Bear's big hands part my cheeks, a little sore from the light spanking, and he groans at the sight of my hole. He traces a finger down my crease and over my pucker, drawing a moan from my lips as I wiggle my hips, desperate for more.

"I think you weren't being honest, baby boy," he accuses.

"I was Daddy, I told you I touched myself," I whine as he teases the rim of my hole with the pad of his finger.

"You told me you touched your pretty little cock, but I can tell you played with your hole too. It's all slick and open for me."

He pushes his finger inside, and I gasp, my response getting lost as my brain scrambles and I push back to get him deeper faster. He works his finger in and out at a leisurely pace.

"More, please, Daddy," I beg.

"Such a greedy boy," Daddy Bear says. "I'm not sure if such a naughty boy deserves more from Daddy."

"Please, please, I'll be a good boy from now on," I promise, struggling to hold myself still to prove I can behave.

He kisses my shoulder and then down my spine, pulling his finger nearly all the way out before pushing back in with two this time. I moan and dig my fingers into the arm of the couch to force myself to stay still.

"I have a bad habit of spoiling my boy, don't I?" he teases.

"Yes, Daddy," I answer obediently with amusement.

He pulls his fingers out and reaches for the condom stashed in the couch cushion, making quick work of putting it on while I wait impatiently. Most porn studios edit out the part where someone puts on a condom, but it's something that's always remained in all Ballsy Boys videos. I used to wonder about it, but knowing about Bear's past living through the AIDS crisis, I get it now. My Daddy, doing his best to save the world, one day at a time.

"Come here, baby boy," he says, and I let go of the arm of the couch to crawl back into his lap. I straddle him, my hole fluttering with excitement as his erection brushes against the curve of my ass, his hands grabbing my cheeks and parting them.

"Take me nice and slow," he instructs when I feel the nudge of his head against my pucker.

I suck in a sharp breath as I lower myself onto him, the familiar sharp sting of the first inch making me bite my lip. Bear cups the back of my neck, pulling me in for a kiss as I take him deeper, little by little. His tongue sweeps gently over mine. It's not like the porn kisses I learned from Rebel and have perfected with all the other Ballsy Boys. This is a kiss from Daddy to me, just like all our other kisses.

I take him all the way to the hilt, his hands tightening on my hips as I moan into his mouth, swiveling my hips to revel in the fullness.

"Hang on, baby boy, I'm going to take you for a ride," he warns, and I grab on to his arms and smile against his lips.

"Use me, Daddy."

For all his nerves about age and stamina over the past few days, Daddy Bear fucks me like it's an Olympic sport, picking me up and moving me into a different position every time I'm close to coming too soon.

I drag my tongue along his sweat-drenched forearm next to my head, grazing the tendons with my teeth afterward. My legs are pushed up to my chest as he pounds into me rhythmically, pegging my prostate with every deep thrust. My balls ache with the orgasm that's been so close to the surface for what feels like hours, but is probably more like half an hour.

"So good, Daddy, so good," I pant, clenching my hole

around him and moaning as heat sparks all my nerve endings.

"Be a good boy and come for Daddy," he says, and I nearly sob with relief. He thrusts deeper, pushing my legs up farther. Incoherent sounds fall from my lips, my eyes screwed closed as my channel clamps tight around Daddy Bear's big cock and my release shoots all over my stomach, erupting so hard some of it hits my throat and chin.

"That's Daddy's good boy. You're so pretty when you come for me."

"I love you, Daddy Bear," I cry, digging my fingers into his biceps as my orgasm goes on and on until I'm completely drained.

"I love you too, baby boy," he whispers near my ear before pulling out, stripping off the condom, and tugging his cock until his release joins my own, coating my stomach and throat. He collapses forward with a groan.

I giggle and wrap my arms around his neck, nuzzling my nose against his throat as our combined cum sticks us together and likely works its way into all of Daddy Bear's chest hair.

"Cut," Rebel calls, and loud cheers and applause erupt from the rest of the guys watching us from off set.

"Damn, Papa Bear, you've still got it," Brewer calls out, and I notice a little blush rising in Daddy Bear's cheeks.

"Don't you forget it," Bear quips back, throwing a smirk at them over his shoulder.

Normally after a scene, I feel a little awkward, getting dressed as quickly as possible. But with Daddy being naked right beside me, it's hard to feel anything other than sleepy and sated.

"I'm just going to nap here," I joke, curling up on the couch and closing my eyes.

"Aw, you broke him," Heart says. "Clearly the rest of us failed to go hard enough, because we've never fucked Pixie into a coma before."

"Come on, baby boy, let's get you a shower." Bear scoops me up, and I wrap my arms and legs around him, resting my head on his shoulder and yawning.

"Thanks, Daddy."

I wave at the guys, and they all playfully catcall as Bear carries me off set and toward the showers.

25

BEAR

Rebel and I sit in my office, and he ends the call he made in my presence. "Byron will be here in a few minutes," he announces. "He's already on his way in an Uber."

"Remind me, how do you know this guy again?" I know he gave me a brief explanation, but I've been so busy the last few days with helping Hunter launch his Kinky Boys that I'm drawing a blank.

Rebel grins. "Troy and I met him on a road trip to visit my parents a while back. We overheard him saying he'd been stood up for some bachelorette thing for his cousin. So we offered to take him, and I swear, it was the most fun I'd had in forever. His bitchy cousin and all her equally bitchy friends were the nine circles of hell, but we had a blast."

There's something in his tone that suggests they had more fun than just drinking and painting. "Did you guys have some *adult* fun as well?" I asked, wiggling my eyebrows.

Rebel's grin widens. "Trust me, I wanted to, but I was drunk off my ass, so Troy and Byron killed that plan. Troy and I talked about it later, hooking up with him at some point, but it never got anywhere."

"So how did he contact you now?" I ask.

Rebel shrugs. "He reached out to me through my fan page. Said he'd run into some financial trouble and wanted to ask if I thought he would be a good fit for the Ballsy Boys."

"His video was good," I say. "He's clearly not talented at filming, but he had a spark and energy. I could see him working for us."

Rebel nods. "Same here. And I know that meeting someone once isn't enough to go on, but he really was a sweet, cute guy. I don't know what kind of trouble he got into, but I can't imagine it's anything bad."

I pick up the pictures he sent in before I requested his video. Those were definitely not shot by himself, which was smart. He arranged for a somewhat professional photographer to take some nice-looking nudes of him that show off his body. That cheeky, flirty smile he has will do well on camera.

"He reminds me a bit of Pixie," I say, my face going soft as I remember our lovemaking from that morning.

Pixie rimmed me until I not only saw stars, but the entire universe, before riding me into an explosive orgasm. It's still our favorite position, him riding me. There's nothing I love more than to see him lose himself in pleasure on my cock. His face when he comes, it's pure bliss. And the sounds he makes when it's just him and me... They're sweeter than any music I've ever heard.

Rebel snaps his fingers in front of my eyes. "Boss man, you still with me?"

I shrug, not even embarrassed about my little daydreaming. That's what being in love will do to you. "Just lost in memories for a second."

Rebel chuckles. "Yeah, no shit. Your face went all lovey-dovey, man. You got it bad."

Through the window, I see a car pull up outside, so Byron must be here. I rise and give Rebel a hardy slap on his shoulder. "Nothing bad about it. I'm loving it."

"Yeah, the video you two shot made that crystal clear," Rebel says.

He's not wrong. I've watched the fully edited version a few times now—with Pixie of course, though the two of us haven't been able to watch the whole thing without getting distracted in between so far—and I have to admit, it's a powerful video. The sex is hot, yes, but it's easy to spot the trust and love between us. I've never realized how obvious that would be in just one scene, but it is.

Hunter was ecstatic when he watched it. He predicted it would go viral right away. He and Rebel are already planning a marketing campaign around *Pixie and Bear Break the Internet,* or something along those lines.

Usually, I take those predictions with a grain of salt, but in this case, they may be right. Hunter's got gold there, and I couldn't be happier for him. That hefty paycheck Pixie and I cashed for that video doesn't hurt either, of course. That will be a nice contribution toward Pixie's college fund.

Byron is as cute as he looked in the pictures, dressed in a pair of jeans that would make Pixie approve of him instantly and a purple T-shirt with a unicorn. I let him into my office, and after we've gotten the introductions out of the way, I gesture toward a chair.

"So, tell me why you think you'd be a good fit for our studio," I say.

"Look, I'm going to be really honest with you," Byron starts.

I nod in approval. "That's much appreciated."

"I got fired from my job for bullshit reasons, so now I'm super short on cash, like one bill away from bankruptcy. I remembered meeting Rebel, and since I enjoy having sex, I thought this might be a good fit. Not for the long term, probably, but at least until I'm back on my feet financially."

"There is nothing wrong with a financial motivation," Rebel assures him. "Most of us do it for the money, let's be honest. Sure, liking sex is a big prerequisite, but it's not like this is a hobby."

Relief fills Byron's face. "I'm glad to hear that. I just wanted to be upfront about my ambitions and not deceive you guys into thinking this is something I would want to do as a career."

"That's fine," I tell him. "We need both: career stars and temporary fresh meats, pardon my expression. Can you tell me a little about any experience you have with any kind of porn or sex in public?"

Byron's eyes harden and his mouth grows tight. "The only experience I have with porn was something that was made without my permission," he says, and it's clear he's still upset about that.

"Officially going into porn isn't gonna wipe that away," I tell him gently.

"I know. But it does feel like at least I'm doing this on my terms and getting paid for it. I do really like sex, and I've always been very open to experimenting."

I shuffle the printouts from his online application and check the list of sexual practices he's checked off as having experience in. It's quite the list, which confirms what he's telling me. "It also says here you're interested in exploring more," I say. "Care to elaborate?"

Byron shrugs. "I've always wanted to do a DP, but that's not something I feel comfortable doing with random hookups. You guys have a lot of experience shooting those, so that seemed like a good fit. Plus, you know, any kind of kink is always fun to try. Nothing hard-core, but I could definitely be persuaded to try new toys, accessories, or whatever you have in mind."

Rebel turns his head toward me at the same time as I look at him. I think we're on the same wavelength here. As much as I would love to keep Byron for Ballsy Boys, it almost sounds like Hunter's new studio would be a much better fit for him. Rebel nods at me.

"Byron, there's a guy I would love for you to meet. His name is Daddy."

26

PIXIE

"Wake up, baby boy," Bear says, kissing my forehead gently.

"Sleepy," I complain, grabbing the covers and trying to pull them over my head but finding my movement stopped. The past week was my first week at school, and it was *way* more exhausting than I expected.

"Campy and Jackson's wedding is in a few hours, and I know you well enough to know you're going to want the extra time to get ready."

"Ugh," I groan. "Don't wanna get up, Daddy," I complain with a yawn.

To my surprise, he gets out of bed without another word, going into the bathroom and closing the door behind him. I snuggle back into my pillow and drift back to sleep for a few more minutes until Daddy Bear returns.

"Get up without any more complaints and you can have something special."

"Sexy special?" I ask, peeking one eye open with interest. He's towering over the bed in all his naked glory, his strong arms crossed over his broad, furry chest, his cock half-hard, the foreskin still covering the head. My cock stirs under the blankets as I consider climbing him like a tree.

"Come on," he says, neither confirming or denying whether my treat will be sexy special or regular special.

Not daring to grumble again, just in case, I throw back the blankets and climb out of bed, my erection bobbing in front of me. Daddy Bear gives my ass a quick slap, and I squeal in surprise, eliciting a gruff laugh from him.

"Into the bathroom," he instructs.

I shuffle across the room with Daddy Bear right behind me and step into the bathroom. The relaxing scent of my favorite lavender bath bomb tickles my nose, the air inside warm and humid.

"You drew me a bath?" Not that I should be surprised. Daddy Bear is always finding new ways to take care of me and make me feel loved.

"That's right."

"Are you getting in with me?" I ask, fully awake now as I wrap my arms around his waist and press my body against his enticingly. "I might need help washing my back...and other places."

"Such a naughty boy, always thinking about sex," Daddy Bear tsks with a twinkle in his eyes, fighting a smile.

"I think you like me like this, Daddy," I counter, humping my little cock against his thick thigh. "Always horny for your cock to fill me up."

He bends his head down so his breath tickles my ear, his hands coming to rest on the globes of my ass, giving each one a little squeeze. "Get in the bath."

"Yes, Daddy," I say breathlessly.

I get into the warm water, scooting as far forward as possible and shooting Daddy Bear one of my patented wide-eyed looks over my shoulder.

He chuckles and shakes his head at me before climbing in and settling himself behind me. He reaches for me, and I happily slide backward until his arms are around me and my back is resting against his chest. I can feel his cock against my lower back. I wiggle a little to tease him. His arms tighten around me to hold me still, and I giggle, tilting my head back to rest it against his shoulder.

"You don't want to play with me this morning, Daddy?"

"I want to get my boy squeaky clean, and then we'll see about the rest," he says firmly. Sometimes, I think he makes me wait for sex just for the fun of it... I mean, okay, waiting *does* make it even better. *Sigh.* Daddy always knows best.

I relax into him as he reaches for the bar of soap in the little dish on the ledge of the large tub, dipping it into the water and then rubbing it between his hands to make it nice and sudsy.

I sigh happily as he uses his hands to wash my shoulders, chest, down my stomach—avoiding my cock, hard between my legs—and then along my thighs. He makes me sit forward and washes my back, every touch of his hands making me needier and more impatient. I can feel his cock getting harder against me as well as he washes me, but unlike me, Daddy Bear never shows any urgency, washing me with careful patience that doesn't waiver.

"Daddy," I whine as he eases me even farther forward, using his soapy hands to massage my butt cheeks, getting the suds between them but avoiding my hole like he did with my erection.

"Shh." He puts me onto my knees, and I put my hands on the edge of the tub to brace myself, quivering with anticipation. He puts his hands between my thighs, spreading them and running his hands all over them.

My cock aches, and I bite my lip against begging for him

to hurry up or give me more. Daddy Bear does things on his own time.

He parts my cheeks and drags his index finger over my pucker, and my moan echoes against the bathroom walls. I twitch my hips, my cock jerking at even the slight contact where Daddy always knows how to make me feel good. He teases my rim with the pad of his finger, all slick with soap, until I can't hold back from begging anymore.

"Please, Daddy. Please, please," I pant, digging my fingers into the edge of the tub harder to keep from touching myself.

When he finally pushes his finger inside, I sigh with relief, squeezing my channel around his digit so it feels bigger as he eases it inside. He takes his time working it in and out, occasionally crooking it to hit my prostate, but not establishing any sort of rhythm that I can anticipate.

I hear him reach for something else, and I turn my head to see him grab a bottle of lube that's resting on the side of the tub. Daddy's always prepared. What I don't notice is a condom. Now that I'm not filming with any regularity, we both got tested again and have had *many* long talks about going without condoms. He told me he's never gone bare with anyone, and I can understand his hesitance, with his history and all, but I'm also dying to feel him bare inside me.

I jump as a trickle of cold lube is drizzled over my hole, his finger still buried inside me. He pulls it out slowly, and adds a second finger, fucking me with them until I think I might go insane.

"Getting impatient, baby boy?" he asks with amusement when I start to squirm on his fingers.

"Want your cock, Daddy."

He pulls his fingers out, and I whimper.

"Come here."

Daddy Bear grabs my hips and pulls me backward until I can feel his bare cock pressing into the crease of my ass.

"Oh, yes, Daddy," I whimper. "I want it so bad."

"I know you do." He kisses the side of my neck while he lines up with my hole and guides me down. A loud moan falls from my lips as I take him inside. Without the condom between us, he feels so hot as each inch pushes inside, filling me up and splitting me open.

When he's fully seated, his hands tighten on my hips, holding me still for a few seconds that feel like they go on for an eternity. His lips trail along the back of my neck and over my shoulder as his cock seems to grow even bigger inside me with each passing second.

"Please, Daddy," I beg again.

"Ride me, baby."

I bring my hands back to loop around his neck, lifting myself up and then quickly slamming myself back down, water sloshing all around us as I do. I swivel my hips and fuck myself with his cock, drawing deep, growly moans from his chest. His cock drags against my prostate with every thrust, my whole body lighting up at the feeling of being full of him, and surrounded by him—his arms around my waist, his lips on my neck, his words of praise lighting me up from the inside.

His hand wraps around my cock, completely engulfing it, and I let out another cry.

"Yes, Daddy, yes, yes," I chant, fucking myself faster on his cock, feeling my already tight channel start to tighten around him as my balls ache and heat fills the pit of my stomach. "So close, please, can I come?"

"Such a beautiful, perfect boy," Daddy purrs near my ear. "Come for me, baby."

My orgasm tears from me, my release making Daddy Bear's fingers sticky, my hole pulsing around his thick cock as wave after wave of pleasure rolls over me.

I can feel it when his pleasure joins mine, his cock stiffening before it starts to pump his hot seed deep inside me, with nothing in the way to block it. I squeeze my hole tighter as he starts to pull out, not wanting any of it to drip out. I want to feel Daddy's cum inside me all day. Then a thought occurs to me.

"Daddy, can you plug me to keep it inside me?"

He groans in approval. "Such a perfect boy," he says again. "Come on, let's go get one of your plugs."

I get out of the tub on shaky legs, and he follows behind, grabbing a towel for me.

"Wait here, I'll be right back."

He wraps a towel around his waist and disappears back into the bedroom while I wait, my ass clenched tight, giggling a little to myself as I dry myself off. He returns with one of my smaller plugs.

"Turn around and bend over the sink for me."

"Yes, Daddy." I do as he says, putting my hands on the sink and bending forward. He works the plug inside me with ease and I let out a happy sigh. "Thank you, Daddy."

"Anything for my boy," he says. "Now, we'd better get dressed so we have time for breakfast before we leave."

Once we're dried off, I take my time styling my hair and getting dressed in the outfit I picked ahead of time for Campy and Jackson's wedding.

"Can you help me with this?" I ask, holding up the strip of silky fabric in my hand that's meant to be a bowtie. "I've never tied one before."

"Of course. Come here, baby boy." Daddy Bear beckons me over, taking the bowtie from my hand, flipping up my collar, and putting it on with ease. I watch his face, his brow furrowed with so much concentration as he ties it perfectly for me, and my heart flutters with the love I have for him that seems to get bigger every single day.

"There you go," he says once he's finished.

"Thank you, Daddy." I put my hand on his chest, pushing up onto my tiptoes to reach him. "I love you." I press a kiss to his lips, his arms coming around me to hold me close as he kisses me back.

"I love you too, baby boy, more than anything."

"You look really handsome today," I tell him once we part from the kiss. I smooth my hands over the soft, expensive fabric of his dress shirt he let me pick out for him. "Ready to go?"

"I'm ready," he says, putting a hand on my lower back and leading me out to his car so we can head to the wedding.

∾

BEAR

THE SKIES ARE CRISP BLUE, the air still fresh this early in the morning as we gather in a meadow behind Ethan's sprawling ranch. Jackson's costar was generous enough to offer him the use of his home for the wedding. It was already gorgeous when we visited it the first time, but it's been transformed into a little piece of heaven.

Look, I am about the least sentimental person there is, and usually, I don't give a flying crap about decor, but I can't deny how pretty this looks. White, comfortable chairs have been set up in the grass for us guests, and there's an elegant-looking gazebo in the front where I assume Jackson and Campy will stand during the ceremony. There are flowers everywhere, all in bold, vibrant colors. This has got to be all Jackson, because I can't see Campy giving two shits about this.

They've hired a security detail, a whole bunch of men dressed in somewhat ill-fitting suits, looking all professional and detached from the rest of the guests. It's a sobering thought they even need this, but it's to make sure no unauthorized guests are entering. There's one extra photographer from a well-known magazine, but he's been instructed to take pictures of the couple only, and the guests only with their permission.

It's a small group of guests, and the funny thing is that it's about a fifty-fifty split between Hollywood stars and porn stars. Jackson's costars have all showed up, and even I am somewhat in awe of this much celebrity power in one place. We've kind of gotten used to Jackson hanging out with us, but this is a whole new level.

But they're all super friendly, and they don't treat us like pariahs, which, let's face it, wouldn't have been out of the question. Then again, Jackson is a decent guy, so I should have known he'd have equally decent friends.

Campy's mom is a wonderful, warm-hearted woman. I talk to her for a little bit, and she's nothing but proud of her son. She reminds me of my own mama, and I know Rebel has been lucky in that sense as well, but we're the exceptions, sadly.

"Dear guests, we're about to start, so if you could all please take your seats?" a petite, professionally dressed woman calls out.

She's the wedding planner, Pixie informs me, and apparently, she's well known for pulling off secret weddings for

Hollywood stars. Good for her, as these people have as much right to a private ceremony as anyone else. She also advised them to do the wedding this early, not even ten-thirty in the morning, as apparently that's not a time when most paparazzi are up and at 'em yet. The fact that it's not yet blazing hot outside is a nice bonus.

I take my seat, Pixie immediately scooching his chair closer to me. He can't stand to not be touching me when he's sitting next to me. It's the sweetest thing, and I've totally become addicted to feeling him close to me.

We all rise when the two grooms arrive. They've chosen to walk down the aisle together. Campy is wearing a gorgeous suit that looks like it cost a couple of grand, and Jackson is decked out in a similar style, though he's still wearing his cowboy hat and a pair of shiny, new boots. I love that he has managed to hold on to who he is, even in this city.

The ceremony is mercifully short, both men beaming like beacons when they exchange their vows. My heart is so full, it feels like it's gonna burst. And when they are pronounced husband and husband, and Jackson takes Campy's mouth in a passionate kiss, my eyes grow suspiciously moist. Next to me, Pixie sniffles, discreetly wiping his eyes as well.

"They're so beautiful together," he says wistfully, and the look of longing on his face is hard to deny.

After we've all congratulated them, there's an extensive brunch buffet set up in a large barn, and I load up my and Pixie's plate with all kinds of yummy goodies.

"I'm not going to eat all that, Daddy," Pixie protests when I put his plate in front of him. He chose a table with Tank and Brewer, and I already spot the other boys coming our way as well.

"Don't think I didn't notice you skipped a meal yesterday evening," I tell Pixie, looking stern. "Eat up, baby boy. You've lost some weight recently, so I'm just taking care of you."

Brewer rolls his eyes at me. "You sound an awful lot like Tank over here, who forever shoves food into my mouth."

"That's not the only thing he shoves in your mouth," Heart quips as he plops down on a chair, his two men flanking him.

"Har, har," Brewer says, then sticks out his tongue at Heart. I see we've already reached the expected maximum maturity level, but I can't help but smile.

"That was beautiful," Rebel says as he, too, grabs a seat, Troy on his heels. "It's wonderful to see Campy this settled and happy."

"The same is true for you," I tell him. "I'm so proud just looking at you two."

Rebel's cheeks heat up a little as he shoots a glance in Troy's direction. Troy nods at him, some kind of signal, and Rebel says, "We got engaged yesterday."

The loud explosion of cheers at our table makes everyone look in our direction. "Oh my god," Pixie says, "That is so freaking awesome. Who asked who?"

Rebel shares another look with Troy, and I love that he's so understanding to Troy's sensitivities in this.

"I asked Rebel," Troy says, surprising not just me. "I knew he wanted this for a while now, but I also knew he would never ask me, too scared of pushing me beyond what I was comfortable with." He shrugs. "So I asked him, because I know it matters to him."

After a new round of congratulations has died down, it's Pixie who looks at Tank and Brewer, merely lifting his eyebrows.

"We didn't want to say anything when Campy and

Jackson announced their engagement, because we didn't want to upstage them," Tank says in his usual low grumble. "But Brewer and I got married in Vegas a few days before that. We just didn't want to tell anyone, because to us, it was a private matter. But it's not like it's a secret, so..."

I lean back in my chair, too overwhelmed with emotions to even speak. Those two sneaky bastards. And yet, it's perfect for them. Tank hates being the center of attention, which is a weird thing to say about a porn star, but it's the truth. He would've hated a ceremony like today, and sneaking away with the two of them, that's totally them.

"Trust me, as soon as it's legal, I would marry these two in a heartbeat," Lucky says, kissing first Heart's hand, then Mason's, whose hand accidentally catches the pretty tablecloth and almost brings the whole thing down. Lucky's reflexes must've improved significantly since dating Mason, because he calmly prevents the disaster with a lightning-fast grab and holds Mason's hands afterward, as if it's the most normal thing in the world. Well, it probably is to him by now, accident-prone as Mason is. He's a cute kid, a total sweetheart, but a walking liability.

"That leaves you two, Bear," Brewer says with a wink.

Pixie laughs uncomfortably, avoiding my eyes. My thoughts briefly go to the elaborate thing I was already planning to ask him, a proposal that I felt would be worthy of him, and I decide on the spot to toss it all out the window. I gently grab his chin with my hand, turning his head in my direction.

"Are you ready for this, baby boy?" I ask, and his eyes go big as saucers.

I sink to my knee, determined to get this right, and reach for the blue velvet box that I've been carrying with me for weeks now, just in case there would be an opportunity even more perfect than what I was planning. But there is no moment better than right now, surrounded by these men, by this much love and happiness. So I open the little box and present the outrageously expensive diamond ring to my sweet Pixie.

"You know I love you more than anything. I want to spend the rest of my life taking care of you, my precious boy. Eli, will you please marry me?"

The last syllable hasn't even left my lips when Pixie lets out a loud and enthusiastic, "Yes, please!"

His hand is shaking as he holds it out to me, and I gently put the ring on his finger, where it blings like it's supposed to. "Daddy, I love you so much," Pixie says, his voice choked up with emotions.

I look at his radiant face for a few seconds more, wanting to soak in all his happiness, but then I can't resist my need to kiss him. Our kiss is long and passionate, and neither of us lets the loud whoops and cheers around us interrupt us.

When we finally have enough of each other—at least for now—I make my way back onto my chair, pulling Pixie on my lap. He can't stop looking at his ring, and the sheer joy and pride on the faces of everyone at the table make me realize this is the happiest I have ever been in my life.

My journey with Pixie is just beginning, and I can't wait to see what the future holds for us. I don't know what it will be, but I do know it will be sparkly and full of joy.

Just like him.

COMING SOON: KINKY BOYS

If you loved the Ballsy Boys, keep an eye out for the spin off series called Kinky Boys. You *may* see some familiar names and secondary characters pop up!

Coming soon...

MORE ABOUT K.M. NEUHOLD

Author K.M.Neuhold is a complete romance junkie, a total sap in every way. She started her journey as an author in new adult, MF romance, but after a chance reading of an MM book she was completely hooked on everything about lovely- and sometimes damaged- men finding their Happily Ever After together.

She has a strong passion for writing characters with a lot of heart and soul, and a bit of humor as well. And she fully admits that her OCD tendencies of making sure every side character has a full backstory will likely always lead to every book having a spin-off or series.

When she's not writing she's a lion tamer, an astronaut, and a superhero...just kidding, she's likely watching Netflix and snuggling with her husky while her amazing husband brings her coffee.

Stalk Me
Website: www.authorkmneuhold.com
Email: kmneuhold@gmail.com
Instagram: @KMNeuhold

Twitter: @KMNeuhold

Bookbub: https://goo.gl/MV6UXp

Join my mailing list for special bonus scenes and teasers: https://landing.mailerlite.com/webforms/landing/m4p6v2

Facebook Reader Group Neuhold's Nerds: You want to be here, we have crazy amounts of fun: http://facebook.com/groups/kmneuhold

MORE ABOUT NORA PHOENIX

Would you like the long or the short version of my bio? The short? You got it.

I write steamy gay romance books and I love it. I also love reading books. Books are everything.

How was that? A little more detail? Gotcha.

I started writing my first stories when I was a teen...on a freaking typewriter. I still have these, and they're adorably romantic. And bad, haha. Fear of failing kept me from following my dream to become a romance author, so you can imagine how proud and ecstatic I am that I finally overcame my fears and self doubt and did it. I adore my genre because I love writing and reading about flawed, strong men who are just a tad broken..but find their happy ever after anyway.

My favorite books to read are pretty much all MM/gay romances as long as it has a happy end. Kink is a plus... Aside from that, I also read a lot of nonfiction and not just books on writing. Popular psychology is a favorite topic of mine and so are self help and sociology.

Hobbies? Ain't nobody got time for that. Just kidding. I

love traveling, spending time near the ocean, and hiking. But I love books more.

Come hang out with me in my Facebook Group Nora's Nook where I share previews, sneak peeks, freebies, fun stuff, and much more:
https://www.facebook.com/groups/norasnook/

Wanna get first dibs on freebies, updates, sales, and more? Sign up for my newsletter (no spamming your inbox full… promise!) here:
http://www.noraphoenix.com/newsletter/

You can also stalk me on Twitter:
https://twitter.com/NoraFromBHR
On Instagram:
https://www.instagram.com/nora.phoenix/
On Bookbub:
https://www.bookbub.com/profile/nora-phoenix

BOOKS BY K.M. NEUHOLD

Stand Alones
Change of Heart

Heathens Ink
Rescue Me
Going Commando
From Ashes
Shattered Pieces
Inked in Vegas
Flash Me

Inked (AKA Heathens Ink Spin-off stories)
Unraveled
Uncomplicated

Replay
Face the Music
Play it by Ear
Beat of Their Own Drum
Strike a Chord

Ballsy Boys
- Rebel
- Tank
- Heart
- Campy
- Pixie
- ***Don't Miss The Kinky Boys Coming Soon***

Working Out The Kinks
- Stay
- Heel

Short Stand Alones
- That One Summer (YA)
- Always You
- Kiss and Run (Valentine's Inc Book 4)

BOOKS BY NORA PHOENIX

Perfect Hands Series

Raw, emotional, both sweet and sexy, with a solid dash of kink, that's the Perfect Hands series. All books can be read as standalones.

- **Firm Hand** (daddy care with a younger daddy and an older boy)
- **Gentle Hand** (sweet daddy care with age play)

No Shame Series

If you love steamy MM romance with a little twist, you'll love the No Shame series. Sexy, emotional, with a bit of suspense and all the feels. Make sure to read in order, as this is a series with a continuing storyline.

- **No Filter**
- **No Limits**
- **No Fear**
- **No Shame**

- **No Angel**

And for all the fun, grab the **No Shame box set** which includes all five books plus exclusive bonus chapters and deleted scenes.

Irresistible Omegas Series

An mpreg series with all the heat, epic world building, poly romances (the first two books are MMMM and the rest of the series is MMM), a bit of suspense, and characters that will stay with you for a long time. This is a continuing series, so read in order.

- **Alpha's Sacrifice**
- **Alpha's Submission**
- **Beta's Surrender**
- **Alpha's Pride**
- **Beta's Strength**
- **Omega's Protector**

Ballsy Boys Series

Sexy porn stars looking for real love! Expect plenty of steam, but all the feels as well. They can be read as standalones, but are more fun when read in order.

- **Ballsy** (free prequel available through my website)
- **Rebel**
- **Tank**
- **Heart**
- **Campy**

- **Pixie**

Ignite Series

An epic dystopian sci-fi trilogy (one book out, two more to follow) where three men have to not only escape a government that wants to jail them for being gay but aliens as well. Slow burn MMM romance.

- **Ignite**

Stand Alones

I also have a few stand alone, so check these out!

- **Kissing the Teacher** (sexy daddy kink)
- **The Time of My Life** (two men meet at a TV singing contest)
- **Shipping the Captain** (falling for the boss on a cruise ship)

Printed in Great Britain
by Amazon